A
Somniator's Dream

The Tale of the Devil's Kettle

Book 1

By
For His Glory

Available as ebook

ISBN   979-8-9912031-3-5 (paperback)

ISBN   979-8-3388208-3-4 (hardcover)

Copyright © 2024 by For His Glory

All Rights Reserved. No part of this publication may be reproduced, distributed, or transmitted in any form or by any means, including photocopying, recording, or other electronic or mechanical methods without the prior written permission of the publisher. For permission requests, solicit the publisher via the address below.

Publify Publishing

publifypublishing@gmail.com

Dedication

I would like to dedicate this book to my wife. She has been nothing but supportive as I have tackled this project. Not only with this book, but with everything in life. She has never once doubted me in this process and her love and support is a beautiful reflection of Christ's love that I wish the whole world could see.

Table of Contents

Chapter 1

You Wanted an Adventure, Didn't You?

"Quick! Get down here," Andy forcefully whispered. Eva crouched down to her hands and knees and scuffled forward to meet Andy, who was using a fallen log covered in thick green moss to hide his body from sight.

"Andrew! I really don't think we should be here; you know what the legend says," Eva whispered with a quiver in her breath.

"You said you wanted to go on an adventure, didn't you? Besides, the legend says that anyone who falls in never returns. It doesn't say anything about those who just go to take a peak!" Before Eva could respond, Andy's attention turned to the road on their left.

From where they lay, the fallen log and the thick brush that surrounded them gave them perfect cover. From there the two teenagers could see both the road and the clearing it led to. As they peered over the fallen log, they could see a great white Pegasus standing in the clearing.

You could tell he was young by the way he looked. His white mane was short and stubby, as if someone had taken a hedge clipper and squared it up perfectly. His wings, fixed to his strong fore shoulders, were folded tightly against his body. They came forward over his chest, and then at the elbow his wings folded back to cover most of his torso. Although they were large compared to the size of either Andy or Eva, the wings were very small compared to many of the other Pegasi in the King's royal cavalry.

"Ah, with a young guard like this one we will be able to trick him easily," whispered Andy. "Look, he only has a few black hairs developed just above his hooves. Most Pegasi are born with those markings." A grin smeared across Andy's face.

He was, of course, referring to the fact that the white Pegasus had very little black hair on his hide at all. Although all of these beautiful beasts are born with some black hair, the more black markings the Pegasus developed, the greater the Pegasus was valued for its great courage and valor in the presence of the king. If a Pegasus saw battle or upheld their royal duties, bringing peace and order to the land in the name of the king, their hide would begin to change. Only one Pegasus has ever matured to such a majestic steed and his name is Malus. But of course, you would have heard of Malus at the village gatherings each week, for he was a major topic of conversation among the elders of the village.

Suddenly, the sound of gravel being stirred up by the pitter patter of feet came from the road to Andy's left. The road was full of windy bends and the forest was so thick that, although the kids could clearly see who it was from their vantage point, the Pegasus could only hear the sound of someone coming. The Pegasus straightened out and stood even taller than before, the elbows of his wings now lifted slightly from his chest to help portray a larger frame to a foe. Both of his ears cocked forward, listening intently for the potential threat headed his way.

Of course, Andy and Eva knew who it was because it was all a part of their plan. It was Richard and Jessie, new friends of Andy's. All three boys belonged to an orphanage back in the slums of Regnum.

The brothers made their way around the bend in the road towards the winged beast. "Here we go! Wait for the signal," Andy whispered.

"Stop right there!" shouted the Pegasus. The assertive voice of the beast must have startled the two brothers more than they had planned because they both stopped in their tracks, looked at each other with big eyes, slouched and then awkwardly giggled one of those 'uh-oh, we are in for it now' giggles. The Pegasus slowly walked toward the boys. As he approached them, he seemed to grow larger with every step. "State your business!" the beast shouted.

"Uummm-mm we are umm," mumbled Richard, the younger brother.

"Visiting!" exclaimed Jessie, as if his answer was to save the day.

"Visiting? It is by order of King Fraust, that no one proceeds past this point! You wouldn't be planning to try and sneak past me would you?" questioned the Pegasus. At this point the winged beast stood proudly looking down his nose, as if he had his snout lifted as high as he could without losing sight of the cowardly looking pair below him.

"Over there?" Richard cautiously asked while extending his arm to point to the thick forest resting behind the Pegasus.

"Of course not!" blurted Jessie. "Have you not heard the dreadful legends?"

The boys glanced at each other briefly. Their plan to get past the Royal guard was coming together. This master plan was a beautiful plan, but just before it could be executed, something was about to go wrong.

Eva had been trying to scooch closer and closer to hear everything the boys had been saying to the winged beast. Doing her best to remain out of sight. She scooched so close to the log that her nose had burrowed right into the moss growing from the log. The rough, spongy, hair-like moss tickled the end of her nose and the dust that had settled into the moss was now disturbed. The gentle breeze carried the disturbed dust into Eva's nostrils. Her eyes grew wide because she knew what was coming next. Doing all she could to ignore the tickling sensation in her nose; She began taking large breaths trying to overcome the sneeze.

"Ah..ahh..AHH-CHOO!" It was no use; Eva couldn't hold it back any longer. Although she did her best to depress the volume of the sneeze, the soft, yet high pitched blurt pierced the air.

The Pegasus' left ear swiveled sharply in Andy and Eva's direction, but his eyes remained fixed on the boys. "What was that?" calmly asked the beast.

"Our cover has been blown," Andy angrily announced. His loss of hope in the plan made him unaware that his head was now exposed above the log. The winged beast caught sight of him out of the corner of his eye. Adjusting his body to face this new threat head on, the Pegasus let out a forceful breath from his nostrils. The way a bull would when he's ready to charge.

Eva let out a fearful shriek that led to major disruption in the tense stillness of the clearing. Her cry startled the Pegasus and caused him to rear up on his two hind legs, his wings unhinged into a full span that must have been twenty feet wide. A gust of wind generated from the massive wings and sent Jessie and Richard back on to their butts. The majestic beast was now standing tall on its hindlegs allowing his two front legs to paw at the air.

"Ruuuunnnn!" Andy shouted from behind the log.

Andy and Eva turned to high tail it out of there, but Jessie looked at Richard and smiled with one eyebrow raised. Somehow Richard knew exactly what his brother was thinking. You could say it was some sort of sibling tele-communication.

Jessie jumped to his feet just as the Pegasus' front hooves pounded the ground. Then he ran around the left side of the Pegasus causing the creature to begin rotating with him.

With his brother's distraction, Richard scrambled to his feet and darted around the right side of the beast. This confused the beast into switching his direction so he began rotating back towards Richard. Both of the boys made it around behind the Pegasus and dashed off into the thick brush.

The Pegasus ended up making a full circle in place because he couldn't decide which one of the teenagers he should pursue. The boys that snuck into the forbidden circle or the other two, who were crouched behind the log.

"We are in!" shouted Richard.

Andy heard the faint shout of victory and grabbed Eva by the hand, pulling her sharply to their left. They ducked under low hanging branches, weaved in and out around tree trunks, and scrambled over rocks and vines that were interlaced with the brush and foliage of the forest floor. Eva was shocked at how well Andy had led the way up and over, around and under the forest and its obstacles. She could only assume that being from the orphanage with very little supervision and the apparent trouble she had found herself in now, that this wasn't the first time he had to make a break for it in the forest.

The Pegasus knew that his great size was no match for the nimbleness of mankind. Going through the forest was not an option. His great wings lifted high into the air and thrusted down, causing all four hooves to lift from the ground. At the pace of five more flaps the Pegasus was hovering above the treetops. To his dismay the leafy canvas concealed the whereabouts of all four treasonous villains. He knew his only way of spotting them from above was to fly straight south towards the Devil's Kettle. After all, that's where the humans were headed. The Pegasus had to find them; he couldn't let them get to the mysterious Kettle. Malus would be furious with him if he had let them slip away. No one is allowed in the Forbidden Circle; by sneaking past the Pegasus guard the four teenagers had already broken one of the most enforced laws of the land.

Imagine the disorder that would cause, the Royal Pegasus thought to himself. Many creatures believed that the Devil's Kettle was a mysteriously dangerous place full of secrets, but not the Pegasi. That was because Malus, the leader of the Pegasi, had assured all the Pegasi that this cavern was just a fairy tale made up by followers of the Great White Eagle. As far as the Pegasi believed, there were no secrets to be discovered, only dangers that could bring harm to anyone who dared travel within the Forbidden Circle. Harsh weather conditions, wild beasts, and many other dangerous things they were told, but no secrets like the followers of the Great White Eagle liked to believe.

That's why he was there in the first place to maintain peace and order among all the creatures of Regnum. It was his job to keep all creatures of Regnum safe. By guarding the edge of the forbidden circle and upholding the law of the land. Besides that, this Pegasus was a kindhearted steed, he wished no harm to be brought upon these four teens.

As the Pegasus soared above the trees, flying further and further south towards the cavern, the four kids frantically wandered the forest trying to find one another in the unfamiliar dense place. Andy began to feel nervous; he was a dare devil but never really expected this to work. Here he was, lost in a forest, separated from his friends with one of the royal guards hunting him down. However, he remained calm. He knew if he showed his true emotions that Eva would begin to panic if she hadn't started already.

"We will meet up with them soon, my plans always work out!" explained Andy to Eva who seemed rather tired. The forest was becoming difficult to navigate for the sun was beginning to fall below the horizon.

"My parents are gonna be worried sick," cried Eva.

Andy stopped and felt a rush of cold flood from his forehead to the back of his head, then a shiver shot down his spine. All of this was followed by an overwhelming flash of heat. Andy swallowed hard. He never thought about her parents. As a young boy, Andy's parents had died or left. He never really knew which. So being concerned with what someone's parents might think never occurred to him.

"They shouldn't worry too much," he said, trying to comfort Eva. "Besides it's getting much too dark to make our way back now, we'd better find a safe place to stay for the night." Eva knew that staying the night would worry her parents sick, but she also knew that Andy was right, it was getting dark fast.

The two teenagers crawled on top of a larger boulder, the jagged edges and sharp crevices made it easy for them to scale it. The height of the boulder allowed Andy to spot an opening. It was about half a mile south, down a gradual slope.

The last few rays of red and orange painted the sky as the sun slipped away; the shadows grew longer and the forest felt colder. Andy thought to himself that the clearing would feel much safer and much more comfortable for Eva, if being comfortable was an option in this grim forest. They crawled down from the boulder and headed to the opening, each step getting more difficult for the roots of the trees were left exposed above the soil and no apparent trail had been paved to follow. As the darkness crept its way through the forest the two stumbled and tripped time and time again. What seemed so easy in the daylight, was now a challenge. Sooner than they hoped the last rays of sun vanished and all that was left was darkness and silence. The only sound was the thumping of their heavy feet and their laborious breathing.

Suddenly, the silence of the night was shattered by a twig being snapped under pressure. The loud crack echoed through the forest and scared Andy and Eva. They both froze in their tracks. The two stopped breathing for what felt to them like an eternity, and they both turned so pale you would have thought they glowed in the dark. Then, out of the darkness Andy and Eva felt something like large spiders beginning to crawl around their body. One over their shoulder and one crawling around their waist. The spiders, with surprising strength, forced both Andy and Eva backwards, sweeping them off their feet. The two could now feel themselves being pulled into a hole. This all happened so fast that neither one could react to the sudden jolt, nor could they find the strength to scream for help. They finally realized that what they felt before were not spiders at all but the fingers of someone trying to grab them.

They began to kick and scream, trying to fight their way out of the hold that they found themselves in. Surprisingly their adversary stopped dragging them and all was still.

"It's okay, shh!" a familiar voice whispered.

Finally, Eva found her voice. At first all she could do was let out little noises, but those single syllables eventually formed into words.

"Je…Je.. Jessie?" Eva babbled.

"Shh-shh-shh, It's just us," the two brothers harmonized.

"Phew," Andy said. "I almost wet myself!" All three boys giggled at his words. Eva just rolled her eyes in the darkness.

"What an adventure that was! I feel so alive!" Richard exclaimed. The boys giggled. Not Eva, she was quite nervous about the whole situation but was comforted knowing that the boys didn't seem to be worried.

"How did you find us?" whispered Andy.

"Just lucky, I guess," Richard said as he shrugged his shoulders.

"We actually stumbled upon this old mine shaft long before the sun went down, the entrance was covered by vines and sod. We thought it would be a great place to hide from the Pegasus," Jessie explained, as he grabbed a handful of dirt from the mine's floor and threw it in the direction of Richard's voice.

"Hey!" Richard said as he began to wipe the dirt out of his hair. Jessie had a lucky shot and smoked the ceiling above Richard so that the handful of dirt rained down on him. Richard flailed his arms trying to hit his brother, but the darkness protected Jessie from the counterattack.

"Plus, it's a rather spooky mine, with all those vines and tree roots dangling over the mine's opening. We just had to investigate," said Richard.

"That's why it must have felt like we were being pulled through a small hole when you grabbed us. The overgrowth had basically closed up the mine's mouth," mumbled Andy. He was growing very tired from their adventure, as a matter of fact all three boys had begun taking turns yawning.

Thinking about the mine shaft Andy remembered the stories he had heard during the village gatherings each week. They taught him about how all four kingdoms of their land used to live in harmony and a Great White Eagle ruled the land. At that time everyone loved him. The Great White Eagle had discovered this lost land before anyone else had, he brought forth seeds of all kinds in his talons and sprinkled them throughout the land. Trees, flowers, fruits, and grasses began to sprout, bringing extraordinary color and life to the empty land. His great talons forged the heights of the mountain peaks of each region and his beak carved out the four great rivers that begin high in the mountains and weaved their own way down to feed into the mouth of the Devil's Kettle itself. No one really knows where the Great White Eagle came from, but all creation of their land was credited to him.

Andy didn't really pay much attention to the lessons, but knew that all the creatures and beasts of the land eventually came to be because of some great power the Great White Eagle had. However, by that time Andy's thoughts became sluggish, he could feel himself fighting to stay awake. He did all he could to ponder on the lessons he had once heard but only could picture the Great White Eagle spreading his gigantic wings. Before too long, he and the others found themselves in a deep sleep.

Chapter 2
The Lie That Started it All

Meanwhile, the Royal Pegasus guard, Gillian, had to make sure he returned to his post in time for the next Royal guard to change places with him for the evening. Although he hadn't been able to find the treasonous scoundrels he knew if the next guard had found out about them, he would be in big trouble. *I will find them tomorrow, bright and early,* Gillian thought to himself, trying to stay positive.

He swooped back to his post just in time as the sun slipped away. As his wings brushed the floor of the clearing, his hooves landed firmly on the ground. He folded up his wings tightly to his body.

As sweat glistened on his neck, the Pegasus took deep breaths trying to recover to his normal breathing before the next guard arrived.

"What am I going to do?" cried Gillian to himself, not realizing that his words were mumbled out loud. "If I tell the truth then Malus will have my head! But lying about it makes me feel sick." Gillian's stomach was tumbling and turning faster and faster for he tried not to lie, but knew that if King Fraust or Malus had discovered his failure he would be punished.

Gillian thought deeply about this punishment. *Being a Pegasus of the Royal Cavalry, the punishment is far worse than any kind of punishment known to man, beast, or any other creature of their land - it's worse than death itself!*

You see, when a Pegasus fails the king, or disobeys Malus they receive what's called the Alatum punishment. The Alatum punishment is specific to Pegasi.

Young Gillian swallowed hard as he remembered the day he witnessed an Alatum punishment firsthand.

It was a cool fall day. He had been warned only a few days before; there had been an announcement of a Pegasus that had committed treason against Malus, and that there would be an Alatum punishment carried out. Gillian had only been training to become a guard at that time, but had received notice that he would be required to attend the ceremony.

As the wind blew colored leaves across the castle's courtyard, Gillian watched as the Titan's (Regnum's army of mankind) tied down a mighty Pegasus for the whole kingdom to see. They forced the beast's wings straight out to his sides at full span. Then the royal executioner came forward, yielding a two-handed, double-sided battle ax and the King announced the crimes that the old Pegasus committed against the Kingdom.

Gillian remembered the words that the crowd chanted.

"Long live King Fraust!" they roared. It grew louder and louder as the executioner, dressed in all black, drug the blades of the battle ax through a garden of burning coals. (This garden was not normally there but specifically placed for all to see when an Alatum punishment was to be delivered.)

Gillian watched as the sharp blades slowly began to glow orange from the heat. He remembered how terrible he felt. How sick he felt. But he knew this was a requirement, a warning from the King to never disobey him or Malus.

As the executioner took his stance over the tied down Pegasus, the King raised his hand high into the air making a fist, and quietness fell upon the crowd. Gillian remembered how the executioner's ax followed suit and raised high into the air dangling above the Pegasus. The King's words boomed in Gillian's head as he recalled the horrifying experience.

"Let this be a lesson to all in Regnum who do not obey me!"

Then, as if the King controlled the ax itself, the King's hand dropped, and the ax fell too. The burning hot blade fell and stripped the Pegasus' left wing and then the blade swung into a full circle bringing the ax high above the executioner's head and fell once again stripping the Pegasus of its other wing.

The look of agony on the Pegasus' face was unbearable for Gillian to look at. Gillian shivered at the thought of what the king would do or say about his failure in protecting the forbidden circle.

My wings, the one thing that brings pride and dignity to me. He thought, as he pondered the idea of himself receiving the punishment.

Not only would the King strip him of his wings, but after that, a treasonous Pegasus is sold to the Dwarves as a slave. If the King found out, Gillian himself could be forced to work in the mines high up in the Nani mountains of Borrian (the East region).

Dirty, greedy, filthy dwarves thought Gillian.

Just then the next guard swooped in from the air into the clearing. Vincent was his name. He was a noble steed of the King's cavalry. Over half of his hide was covered in shiny black hair. His mane flowed half ways down his strong sturdy neck and the tips of his wings covered all the way back to his rump.

"How was your day shift, Gillian?" asked Vincent.

"It was... was…" he couldn't decide, should he lie or should he face the consequences? "...It was good," he finally blurted out. He had chosen to lie, but his guilt weighed heavily.

"Wonderful, be on your way young steed," ordered Vincent. Gillian lowered his head and drooped his ears as he walked away, but began to correct his posture in fear that Vincent would notice something was off. He picked up his pace into a light trot and headed north up the windy road that would bring him back to Regnum.

"Hold it!" ordered Vincent. Gillian felt his heart sink.

Vincent is a noble steed of King Fraust's cavalry. Of course, he noticed something's off, thought Gillian to himself.

"You're not telling me something, what is it!" Gillian's ears drooped, "Out with it!" ordered Vincent.

Think, think, think! Gillian thought.

"Well, it wasn't *exactly* good," explained Gillian. Vincent stomped his foot, pinned his ears back and cocked his snout slightly higher in the air anxiously waiting to hear what Gillian had to say for himself. "Well… during my shift. This morning actually, I was standing right where you are now," explained Gillian using the elbow of his right wing to point to Vincent's position. "When suddenly I heard something barreling my way! Right there, out of the brush," again, using his wing to point to the log that traitors had been using to hide themselves from sight. "A pack of wild boar burst out into the clearing and charged right at me!"

"Ha-ha-haah," laughed Vincent. "Scared by a couple of piglets!"

"By no means were they piglets! They had tusks like daggers and tall, sharp looking spiked hair running down the center of their backs!" described Gillian. By this point Gillian had run over to the edge of the clearing where he said the pack of boars came from and began acting out the scene. "They came out right here, and then," - he spread his wings out so the tips of his wings scraped the ground as he trotted through the clearing towards Vincent - "they ran right at me!" Gillian whinnied. He was surprisingly enjoying this tall tale of his and he became more comfortable with his lie.

Vincent reared up, laughing at Gillian and the story he was telling. "Ahh, I remember my first run in with wild beasts such as those. I was just a young pony, not much older than you. I had been stationed at one of the clearings in the East Region. As you know the Midland of the East Region belongs to the Centaurs. Those filthy half breeds. It's quite sad how much pride they have in their way of life. Growing their own foods like peasants and chasing down wild animals for sport," he scoffed.

"Well anyways, I had been standing guard and found myself being ambushed by a herd of elk! The elk pounded into my clearing; Zig zagging this way, leaping that way, and one with such mighty legs completely cleared my entire being. I froze with fear when the sudden rush of spiky antlers fell upon me. I must have thought at that moment it was going to be the end of me, because I... Well, I relieved myself... if you know what I mean," chuckled Vincent. "Soon the antlers dashed and dodged around me through the clearing and into the forbidden forest behind me. As their fuzzy tails flickered away into the thick brush four large Centaurs emerged from the East. The half horse and half men halted as soon as they saw me. All four had been carrying with them bows with strings made from Pegasi mane that they had traded with the Dwarves of the Eastern mountain ranges," Vincent snarled with hate for those half breeds.

"I hate those half breed creatures too," Gillian chirped in.

"Of course," Vincent laughed. "Half man, half horse? Choose one, am I right?"

"Right! Not to mention those silly beasts believe in the Great White Eagle. What good has their great founder done for us?"

"They are lucky so many other creatures believe in a Great White Eagle, for if there were fewer we could abolish such a belief and only hail Malus and the King," explained Vincent. Gillian brayed and shook his head in agreement. "Anyways, the point of my story is that it's okay to be startled now and then, it can even happen to a Pegasus like me!"

"Thank you for that story," Gillian responded. He would have felt better, but he remembered that he had bigger problems than those blasted centaurs. "I must be on my way now," he said as he abruptly and rather rudely shot into the air and hurried off home. *I must rest to regain my energy! First thing in the morning I will go back and find the four humans*, he thought to himself.

"See you next week!" Vincent shouted as Gillian disappeared over the tree line.

Gillian quickly swooped back to Regnum and landed firmly in the Pegasi stables of the castle. He kept his head down and scurried into his three-sided barn. The servant boys had left him fresh hay and oats but he felt too sick and worried to eat.

Instead, he knew he would have to leave bright and early so he laid down to rest. It took him longer than usual to drift off to sleep because thoughts danced in his head about how he failed, but he hadn't lost hope in fixing his mistake before anyone else could find out. *I'll fix this! I know I can. Tomorrow I'll sneak into the forbidden circle myself. I'll catch them before they can get too far and all will be right again.* He repeated in his head until his eyes grew heavy and he was fast asleep.

The morning came quickly. At the rooster's first crow Gillian had already headed out. The sun had just begun to peak above the Eastern horizon to bring on the new day.

Before long Gillian had made it to Regnum's forest; Beyond the village, the slums, and out skirting farms of Regnum. Soaring low, his hooves brushed the treetops, in an effort to remain out of sight from any and all creatures as he made his way towards the clearing that he had left Vincent at last night. Gillian knew he could not go around Vincent, for Malus the great black Pegasus had strategically arranged twelve clearings in the thick forest for twelve guard posts. Each one was positioned in a perfect circle which surrounded the forbidden land. Each region has three guards to prevent anyone from entering the forbidden land. The land and sky that one guard couldn't see, the next one could. It was a full proof design if it hadn't been for Gillian's own error.

The only section unguarded was the South region, Terribbia. No one dared venture there, not even the royal cavalry. The wild beasts of that land were vicious and ferocious. All the jokes say that Terribbia had such horrific beasts and monsters that the name Terribbia came from the word Terrible. So, Gillian had to figure out a plan to get Vincent to leave his post so he could get into the forbidden circle and find those traitors. *But how?* He thought to himself.

To Gillian's dismay, as he breached the last few treetops and the clearing came into view. Sulking, he had failed to find a solid plan.

Gracefully his hooves hit the ground but his body continued forward which allowed Gillian to transition from flying to a smooth trot. His trot quickly slowed to a stop as he came before Vincent.

"Breeeehhh! What a landing," Vincent whinnied. "I did not expect to see you back so soon. Not to mention my shift doesn't end until this evening. To what do I owe this unexpected pleasure?" Still trying to figure out what to say, Gillian's thoughts were interrupted. Without hesitation Vincent asked Gillian an unexpected question. "Hey, what a beauty mark that is! What good deed did you have to do to earn that one?"

Unaware of any new marking, Gillian lifted his wings and frantically began looking for any new markings. This question from Vincent was shocking to say the least.

"What mark?" Gillian questioned.

"Why the one that has formed across you face good sir!"

Gillian twirled around and anxiously trotted over to the water trough across the clearing that was there for the guards to drink from. The wooden trough's corners were packed with mud and laced with pongo leaves. These leaves were about the size of a typical Pegasus hoof, and came from the Pongo forest, which planted its roots in the west region. Once the leaves were pressed into the mud and given a few hours of cure time, the mud hardened and gripped the leaves tightly allowing the wooden trough to hold water. As Gillian peered into the water the smooth surface exposed his reflection. Gillian's eyes grew wide because in his reflection he could see a new marking on his long face. From his left ear, across his left eye, and down and over his snout there was a black gash-like marking across his face.

"Neighhh-whoo!" snorted Gillian. "My first real Nobel Marking!"

As a young pony, Gillian and his friends would play in the mud, making their own 'markings' and dreaming of the day that they would each earn a true Noble Marking. Now, the day has finally come. Gillian was so excited that he pranced around the clearing, bucking, and kicking with excitement just as he had done with his friends years before.

"What noble deed did you do?" asked Vincent again, laughing at Gillian's ridiculous actions. Gillian paused for a moment; this question bothered him. *What have I done?* He asked himself. The only memory he had from the day before was that he let the children slip through into the forbidden circle. He failed the King, he failed Malus, and even worse he lied to one of his comrades. The joy he felt moments ago, now felt dirty and lingered over his conscience. *If Noble Markings come from being noble in the eyes of the King or Malus, and all I have done has been the opposite, why have I earned this mark?*

"I... I guess I really don't know what I did to earn this mark," Gillian admitted.

"Must have been something mighty."

"I'm really not sure if I even deserve it," mumbled Gillian.

"Nonsense, remember, a deed that keeps order in the land is noble in any sense," said Vincent proudly as he gazed upon his own hide. "I got this marking here..." he lifted up his right wing to show a large smudge painted on his side, "when a commoner was trying to sell produce outside the castle's front gates. Everyone knows that those dirty common folk are not allowed anywhere near the front gate... Unless requested by the king of course. Haha! I used my wings to create a gust of wind that blew their vegetable stand right onto its side. They quickly gathered up their things and went on their way! Could you imagine if those filthy creatures just roamed where they pleased? There would be no peace or order in the Kingdom!"

Gillian was puzzled, for nothing seemed noble about that. Something wasn't quite right. However, before he could think about it too much Vincent interrupted. "Now, what was it you came to see me for?" he asked. Gillian's focus had been completely shifted away from his mission. Thinking quickly, he blurted out the most obscene lie.

"You remember Miss Polly, don't you?" he spoke quickly, not even letting Vincent respond. "Well, I told Miss Polly that it would be mighty nice of her if she gave you the whole hoof treatment special down at the Mangled Mane Salon, and she agreed! I told her I'd take your shift today so you could relax!" blurted Gillian. Obviously he had never actually talked to the little green goblin, but he had to stick with the lie now, for he was in too deep. Oh, how he felt just downright dirty about it, but he could think of no other way.

"Wow, what have I done to deserve such treatment from you?" Vincent asked hesitantly, wondering what kind of a trick Gillian was trying to pull.

"Well, to be honest, I felt bad for not telling you the truth right away yesterday. I want to make it up to you."

"Well!" snorted Vincent. "That's not at all necessary." Gillian's thoughts panicked. The plan wasn't going to work; His heart began racing. "But I could never turn down a hoof treatment," Vincent finished.

A sense of relief flooded Gillian as he whinnied, "Wonderful, I will take it from here!"

"Thanks, a Warcrox," spouted Vincent as he trotted off down the road back towards Regnum. Vincent was the type of Pegasus that always tried to get the most out of his shekel coins. Vincent's intention was to trot all the way to Sod-Omen, (the village where the goblins dwelled) to make sure his hooves were good and dirty. That way there was more to clean. Seeing a Pegasus trot when he was perfectly capable of flying, truly was a silly sight. However, this worked out great for Gillian for it would take Vincent most of the day to return to the kingdom instead of just a couple hour flight.

As soon as Vincent disappeared around the first bend of the road, Gillian was off the ground and rushing south into the forbidden circle. He couldn't find the children the evening before and knew that he needed a new plan to find them. Gillian flew straight south until he came upon a meadow. *I'll land here and hide myself along the edge of the meadow. Hopefully I can catch them here, before they make it to the Devil's Kettle!* As Gillian landed in the meadow, the tall waving grasses of the earth's floor brushed against his legs.

The fresh air filled his nostrils and he could smell some of the most amazing grasses he had ever had the pleasure of smelling. Gillian lowered his head and buried it into the sea of grass. He ripped up a tuft of grass and chewed it as he scanned the meadow. His mouth began to water as he realized that this grass was the best grass he had ever tasted in all of his days.

The dew, produced from the chill of the night, rested on the coarse stocks of grass, adding a refreshing feeling to the sweet, tangy taste of the meadow. He wasn't sure if the meadow was magical, or if he was just so hungry that anything would have tasted this good. It was so delicious he almost forgot what he was doing. Slowly nibbling at the grass as he walked along, he found a place along the edge of the meadow to spy on the ocean of green.

There was a large oak tree Gillian used to conceal himself from the meadow. He laid down and the tall grass that surrounded the tree's base hid him from sight even more.

Confident that he would be able to see the four traitors if they stepped into the meadow, Gillian settled in, finding that his outlook was very comfortable. The mighty oaks provided shelter from the sun and the breeze from the wind filled his nostrils with the smell of spring. As the grass danced and sang songs that sounded like waves crashing into a shoreline, Gillian could see the blooming flowers, he could hear the babble of the Northern river flowing. The waving grass hypnotized him and if you asked Gillian yourself, he would tell you it was almost as if the grass whispered, "Eat us!" It didn't really, however, he only claims this because he couldn't help himself from indulging in the sweet, sweet grass.

Despite the obvious mess he was in, he found himself at great peace. It was the kind of peace you didn't know existed until you had actually found it. For the first time in his life all the problems he had seemed to melt away. Which is saying a lot, considering he was in the most trouble he had ever been in before.

Chapter 3
Time to Go Home

Back in the forest, stuffed into the mine, all four of the kids were now fast asleep. The sun had not yet risen to bring a new day upon the forest. Outside the mine, it had grown colder. It was still as a statue, not even the wind blew. The shadows of the trees produced by the faint and falling moonlight stood guard. The quietness of that morning would have brought an overwhelming sense of fear to even the greatest of warriors in all the land.

Suddenly, a flash of the whitest light lit up the entire inside of the mine. All four children shot up to their feet in terror, blinded at first, their eyes began adjusting. They couldn't make out where the light was coming from since it seemed to be engulfing them from all sides.

"FEAR NOT!" A voice shook the entire mine, so much so that dust and small amounts of dirt broke loose from the ceiling of the mine shaft and sprinkled on top of their heads. They trembled with fear.

"Fear not, for I am the Great White Eagle, founder of this land!" spoke the Eagle. They could now see the darkness of the night was still present from behind the creature, interlacing with the tips of the Eagle's white feathers. Finally, they could now see that the light was coming from the underside of the creature's wings, possibly his feathers. The light seemed to shine from the heart of his wings near his body. As the light seemed to dim, they could see golden plates beautifully interlaced with his feathers. Each feather was so crisply white that the light that had seemed to blind the four, was somehow being generated from them. The shimmering streaks of light bounced off the gold plates and reflected the beams in every direction.

"It is time! IT IS TIME!" boomed the Eagle, and then His wings clapped ferociously together consuming all the light. The wind gust from the wings knocked the four children back into a deep sleep. Bringing once again darkness into the still and silent forest. There were no other disruptions that morning, and soon the sun began to peak through the forest.

Eva was the last to wake up and found herself alone inside the mine. As she looked around, the sun peeked through the thick grasses that engulfed the mouth of the mine enough for Eva to see that the mine was very shallow. It seemed to be more of a cave now, rather than a mine. At some point in time the mine must have caved in, cutting off the rest of the tunnel from the outside. Normally she would have been nervous waking up alone in a strange place, but fortunately Eva could hear familiar voices from outside the mine's entrance.

"What a crazy adventure that was," one of the voices said.

"Yeah it was! I didn't think that we would actually make it past that guard."

"Right?! I'm honestly shocked… But I really think we should head back now." Eva recognized this voice as Andrew's. She agreed, she missed her parents and her warm bed. The thought of being wrapped in a blanket curled up by the fireplace brought a soft smile to her face.

"No way! We have already made it this far. To go back would be a shame!" Eva's slight smile now vanished.

"I know, and it's been great! I mean, just think about the mine!" Andy exclaimed, as he pointed towards Eva, who flinched and hid herself from sight not wanting them to know she was listening.

"I'll bet the Dwarves of Borrian dug these mines! Way back, hundreds of years ago, when the Great White Eagle ruled the sky!" Andy's excitement carried on with the boys. He found himself feeling just as disappointed to turn back as they were.

"Just think about all there is to discover." Eva finally recognized Jessie's voice from his brothers.

"I know, I know… But Eva's parents will be worried sick. We should do our best to get her home," Andy said, causing Eva to blush at his sweet consideration of her.

"At least she has parents!" Richard scoffed.

"Yeah! She should be happy about that. Why does our adventure need to be ruined just because she has parents and we don't?" The other brother cried.

Eva felt horrible. She knew that just over a month ago Jessie and Richard's mother had passed away. That's how the brothers had met Andy. After their mother died they were placed into the orphanage.

Although Jessie was almost eighteen and would soon be able to move away from the orphanage, all three boys didn't have anywhere to go and felt as if the world was against them. *How could I ruin this for them? What if Jessie is forced to join the King's army?* she thought.

Knowing that most orphan kids ended up being forced to serve the kingdom in one way or another, she decided that she only had one real option. *I will let them continue on their own and find my own way home,* she thought confidently to herself.

Eva put on a smile, pretending she had not overheard anything the boys were talking about and poked her head out of the mess of vines and roots until her head was exposed to the forest outside. Sitting there were all three boys with their backs turned to the mine's entrance.

Andy was sitting on the left. His thick brown hair was ruffled with volume. Eva had known him for a few years now and knew his hair was getting too long for his own liking. She noticed that he was leaning backwards putting all his weight on to his arms which were fully extended behind him. He was wearing a brown, long sleeve shirt that had holes worn through near the hems of his shirt. His blue jeans had been muddied from the forest floor, and his shoes used to be white but now you couldn't tell.

Next to Andy, Richard was perched on a rock, his dark skin glistening in the morning rays of the sun. His jet-black hair was very short, as if he had just received a buzz cut. He was wearing a white t-shirt stained with mud and had a green and blue plaid button up shirt tied around his waist. He and his brother both had tan pants with large pockets on the side, just above their knees. In comparison to Andy, they wore nice clothing since they were able to keep most of their things before being taken in by the orphanage.

Lastly, Jessie was sitting on the far right leaning back against the trunk of a tree. He looked very similar to Richard, yet his hair was slightly longer, poised with lots of tight curls springing in every direction. He was wearing a navy-blue t-shirt with a left lapel pocket. All three boys looked to be enjoying the warmth of the morning. Wiggling their toes back and forth as they soaked up the quiet moment. Andy's left big toe poked out through a hole in his shoe, and the two brothers both wore sandals.

"Good morning boys," she said.

"Good morning," the boys mumbled, in a way that made it obvious that they were embarrassed about their conversation they had about her moments ago.

"I was thinking… I'm gonna find my own way home today. Why don't you guys keep going, and tell me about the Devil's Kettle when you get home," she suggested. The boys remained silent for a second. Embarrassed that any of them had suggested that she was ruining their trip.

"I'll head home with you, Eva… Richard and Jessie, you guys continue on," Andy said. He didn't want her to feel left out. They had been friends much longer, so to exclude her and continue on himself felt wrong.

"No Andy, that's not necessary! Besides, this was all your plan, you have to keep going," she pleaded. Her hazel green eyes began to flutter because she was so moved by Andy's gracious offer to bring her home.

"That is true! Plus, she just has to head that way." Richard pointed north into the thick forest. "I know she could find her way."

"I don't mean to be rude, but if she thinks she can get back, we should let her go! Andy we can't go on without you!" Jessie exclaimed. Andy was torn.

I want to see the Devil's Kettle, but I do not want to leave Eva wandering aimlessly in the forest. He pondered his options, but he felt like it was his job to protect her.

"I will be fine!" she insisted. Even though Eva was nervous she didn't want to guilt Andy into joining her.

"Okay…," Andy sighed. "I'll continue with you," he said looking at the boys. "But Eva, won't you please stay with us until we can find something to eat?"

Realizing that she hadn't eaten since yesterday afternoon, she felt her stomach grumble.

"Oh yeah! I can do that," she said. Realizing now just how hungry she really was, she cared more about finding some food than she did about returning home. "What is there for us to eat out here?"

"I'm sure that there has to be some fruit or nuts out here if we look hard enough," said Richard.

"Let's go down to the clearing we saw last night before Jessie and Richard snatched us into the mine," Andy said while looking in Eva's direction. "I'll see if I can find anything edible." Andy was kind of a survivalist. He spent lots of time in the forest and had learned of many wild plants that they could use for food. Now he just had to find some.

"Good idea!" shouted Eva.

The crew of four began down the gradual slope to the clearing. Now that the sun had illuminated the forest, they found themselves on the remains of what looked like an old walking path. The ground was rutted, which must have been carved years ago by the dwarves. Matted grass had overgrown the pathway which made it hard for them to gauge the depth of each step.

The path led the four right into the clearing which was on the brim of a much larger open plane. The forest that they came from halted almost instantly as if the forest and thick brush had been commanded to grow no further. This large meadow extended in both directions for what seemed like miles. The rolling hills of the meadow looked like an ocean of green as the grasses waved in the breeze. The sun kissed the tops of the gentle hills and painted them a golden yellow. Although to the East and West the Meadow extended greatly, to the south, the meadow was rather shallow, maybe only one hundred yards across. The southern border of the meadow was lined by a forest of gigantic

Blackwood trees. These trees were so large in size that even if the four of them linked arms they could not reach around the massive black stained trunks.

Eva brushed her hands over the tops of the meadow grass and Andy plucked a stem from the ground and stuck it into his mouth.

As they began to wade into the sea of grass, the Northern river whispered to them in the distance. Its babble told the story of a land that had been untouched by man for years, and it left the four of them in awe. As if controlled by its story, they were drawn to its shore. Through the meadow they made their way up and over a small rolling hill. Just as the hill crested, the ground on the other side angled steeply down to the great Northern river.

The brothers began running down the hill and found themselves sliding onto their knees skidding to the water's edge. As the water raced by, the two boys reached in with their hands and felt the cold-water flow around their fingers. Desperate for a drink, the brothers leaned down like dogs and lapped up the water with their tongues.

Andy followed suit, running to the edge of the roaring river. He crouched down, using his hands to cup the water, he splashed his face. The burst of water shocked Andy's senses but in a good way. He rubbed his face and ran his fingers through his hair causing the wavy brown locks to stray in different directions.

Lastly, Eva made her way to the water's edge. She plopped to her knees and proceeded to cup her hands. Capturing the water, she brought small pools to her lips. The fresh water tasted crisp, bringing her a refreshing new feeling she didn't know she needed. After a few moments their thirst had been quenched and the four sat in silence enjoying the beautiful landscape they gazed upon.

Eva laid back on the steeply angled bank and stared up into the fluffy white clouds, looking for any familiar shapes she could pick out. However, her mind began to wander back to last night. The bright light consumed her mind and the words of the Great White Eagle echoed in her head.

"Hey, what do you think the Eagle meant last night?" Eva asked as she pondered the question herself.

"The Eagle?" Andy asked. The boys, puzzled, looked at Eva.

"The Great White Eagle? Don't you remember the blinding light?" she gasped.

"Oh right! The light that came right after we had some of Mama's homemade ice cream!" Richard said sarcastically. He had no clue what she was talking about so he began to poke fun at her. In fact, none of the boys had any idea what she was talking about.

"I'm serious! The Great White Eagle came to us in the mine. There was a bright light and gold in his feathers! Don't you remember?" Eva cried.

"I'm pretty sure if there had been gold in that mine shaft, the Dwarves would have found it and taken it long ago," Jessie spouted.

"You must have been dreaming. I'm pretty sure you passed out as soon as we pulled you into the mine. It was really quite impressive," Richard said.

"I'm sorry Eva but it was dark, cold, and quiet all night," Andy said softly. Eva's face looked as if she had seen a ghost.

But it felt so real..., she thought to herself. "So...You don't remember anything?"

"I'm sorry, but I don't know what you're talking about," Andy admitted.

"Last night the Great White Eagle came to us in that mine! And you guys don't remember?" Eva shrieked as she pointed at the direction they came from. She was almost growing angry. She was convinced that the Great White Eagle truly had come to them last night. Yet for some reason no one else could remember.

"Umm… no he didn't!" Richard argued.

"Yes he did! He yelled 'It is time' and then disappeared!" Eva exclaimed.

"It is time?" questioned Jessie.

"What does that mean?" asked Richard.

"I don't know," exclaimed Eva "but you guys seriously don't remember anything? The light was so blinding! His voice was so loud! All of you jumped up when he first came!" she cried.

"Maybe it was a dream," said Andy. However, something strange began to happen as he spoke those words. Somehow what Eva was describing felt familiar. Call it deja vu, but something about what she said stuck with him. Yet, he couldn't quite understand what it was that felt so familiar. He truly did not remember anything happening the night before, yet as she spoke of her possible dream, he could close his eyes and see what she described as if it was a painting on a canvas set before him. Then the words of the Eagle began to ring in his ear.

"It is time," Andy repeated out loud, pondering the phrase. Yet again, something was familiar about it. It's as if he had heard it before but wasn't sure of where it came from.

"Maybe it means it's time to go home?" Eva cautiously asked, trying to be subtle about her desire to end the adventure. Andy remained silent. He wasn't quite sure what the Great White Eagle from Eva's dream had really meant, but he was certain it didn't mean it was time to go home.

Eva felt embarrassed because the entire group seemed to ignore her hint. Andy remained quiet and both the brothers were now making their way downstream.

Taking off their sandals, they waded into the water. They splashed and giggled on the outer edge of the river dashing in and out of the water, heading further and further south letting the river guide their way.

Eva decided it was time to go home. She wasn't sure that her dream, or whatever it was, was actually telling her to go home, but she was going to take it that way. She had hoped that the boys would return with her, but that hope was lost once Andy joined in, splashing the brothers with the water of the river.

As she accepted her lonely reality she mustered up the courage, "Andy, I'm going to head home now."

"Oh, well… I really… I'm sorry," Andy said as he hung his head low. He really didn't want to leave her alone but he had told Richard and Jessie that he would continue on with them. As he approached Eva to say goodbye, Jessie and Richard ventured further down the river.

"We won't be too long. And I promise to tell you all about it when we find it," Andy assured her.

Eva just rubbed her opposite arm and looked at the ground. She felt like she wanted to cry but held back the tears.

Just then they heard a faint shout in the distance. Startled by the noise, Andy and Eva rushed down the river side towards the shouting. As the river darted off to the left, the sound echoed from straight south of them. Up the river's bank the two crawled until they could see over the grassy hill. On the other side, they could see Richard and Jessie's feet scrambling around in some thick bushes that were resting under the shade of the large Blackwood trees.

"Mmmm theth are delithouth," Andy and Eva could hear the sound of mumbling from the two boys who seemed to have their mouths full. Out of the bushes came Jessie. His face was covered in a purplish-blue substance and his cheeks were stuffed. He looked like an overgrown chipmunk.

"Guyth!" mumbled Jessie as blueberry guts splattered out of his mouth. He managed to swallow what was left in his chipmunk cheeks. "These are some of the biggest, ripest, and juiciest blueberries I have ever seen!"

From the heart of the bushes, they could hear Richard making the most absurd noises concerning the delicious berries.

"That good?" Andy hollered to Richard.

"Yes sir!" Richard shouted back.

Andy and Eva gravitated towards the bushes, as if the berries had some sort of magnetic pull. Soon, they too found themselves buried deep into the thicket looking for berries to munch on. Richard strategically laid under the lower branches of a bush and reached up plucking berry after berry. He simply let gravity do the work for him. As he plucked them, he let go of them and they fell right into his mouth.

Eva found herself sitting criss-cross in a small grassy clearing just big enough for her to be comfortable in, picking berries from the branches. She felt overwhelmed by the dream she had. *What does it mean? Why did I have the dream and not someone else? Maybe it was just a dream with no meaning at all.* She tried to commit to that thought, but her stomach fluttered with butterflies. She knew something was off about the whole thing.

Andy and Jessie had their fill and the two sat on the outskirts of the berry bushes looking back to the North. From where they sat they could see the Great Northern river appear from within the Forbidden Forest of Regnum and carve its way through the meadow and then sharply yield to the East in front of them, as if the berry bushes forced the river to wind around them.

At this point, Richard now regretted devouring such quantities so fast for his stomach felt bloated from all the fruit. He still laid under the bush but now his hands lay covering his stomach trying to relax.

Eva sat alone and although she tried to accept whatever had happened to her last night as a dream, she couldn't help but wonder if it truly did mean something. Ever since she was a little girl she had believed in the Great White Eagle. Going to all the village gatherings with her parents she had memorized all of the stories from the scrolls. She had been very fond of the Eagle and found herself talking to him as if he could hear her from wherever he was. None of the scrolls say what really happened to the Great White Eagle all those years ago but they do mention that one day he would return.

As a little girl, she remembered King Kieser reassuring all the people of Regnum that the Great White Eagle only had business elsewhere, which is why he left, but that he would be back soon. The scrolls seemed to be quite vague about his return so the people of Regnum took his word for it.

However, since King Kieser's death, his replacement, King Fraust never said much about the Great White Eagle at all.

Eva liked to think that the Great White Eagle was off in some other distant land bringing life to it as he had done here. Yet, in all the years that Eva had believed in the Great White Eagle, never had she ever seen him, nor had he ever spoken to her. Despite all the conversations she had had with him… by herself.

So, if it was really the Great White Eagle in my dream, why would he have come to me for anything? I'm just a sixteen-year-old girl. What do I know? Eva wrestled with these thoughts, until she heard something coming her way.

The rustling of the grass grew more aggressive, she knew it wasn't just the wind. As the sound traveled closer to her the bushes she was consumed by began to shake. Before she knew it three small balls of fur crashed through the thicket. Their sudden presence caused Eva to scream, which in turn frightened the three small bear cubs. The three fuzzy cubs bolted to the right, scrambling low under the thick brushy branches. They dashed right out of the brush and scampered right up the nearest Blackwood tree. The Blackwood trees are tall and straight, not until the very top of the tree do the branches drape out. The tops are very thick and the branches scatter massively creating a canopy for birds, squirrels, and other small critters to make their nests and homes.

The cubs scaled most of the tree before they stopped and peered down at the four intruders. They had never seen such strange creatures before, and in *their* berry patch? The teenagers stared in awe at the little cubs, for they too had never seen bears before. They were taught about ferocious beasts like these that thrived in Terribbia, but these cute, fuzzy little creatures didn't look scary at all. In fact, they looked just as scared of the teens as the teens were of them.

"Ahh, it's okay little guys," Eva said to the bear cubs. They cocked their heads slightly and their ears flickered at her voice as if they could understand what she was saying. The three cubs looked at each other and shimmied higher.

"Rawr be afraid," Eva mumbled as she took a few steps in their direction making her way out of the brush into the opening.

Richard in the mists of the excitement had made his way to the other two boys on the opposite side of the berry patch.

"Look at Eva," Jessie giggled. "Trying to speak to the bears," he continued as the three boys rolled back in laughter. "Rawr, Rawr, Rawr," they all mocked Eva. But to their dismay the three small bears seemed more comfortable with Eva, they had even begun to descend from the tree.

"Ha!" Eva shouted. "They like me!"

Chapter 4
Beware of the Bear

Two hours had flown by. Gillian almost couldn't believe it. By this time the sun had made its way higher into the sky, high enough that the full circle of light was visible just above the treetops off in the East. As he lay there he watched as the wildlife seemed to live in harmony. Creatures of all sorts filled the meadow. Elk grazed in the tall grass, birds soared above in the cloud speckled sky, and rodents scurried their way along the edge of the meadow occasionally passing Gillian; but none of which were the traitors he was looking for.

At first Gillian was puzzled. *How is it that these beasts are able to wander so freely in the forbidden circle?* Knowing that he was still in the Northern region of the Land, he recalled that Terribbia, the Southern region, was unguarded by the royal Pegasus cavalry. *They must be sneaking into the forbidden circle through Terribbia, then wandering around unbothered by the rest of us, since we are not allowed to be here.* He sat back and quietly continued to watch the unending abundance of life before him.

As the sun danced higher into the sky, he noticed something large making its way across the meadow. Although this large beast didn't bring any harm to the elk or other creatures roaming about, they all seemed to move strategically out of the beast's way. Occasionally it would pause and look back, but still Gillian could not make out what the beast was. As his curiosity grew, he decided he just had to know. Gillian arose from his grassy bed and began stalking the beast. Using the trees as cover, he made sure that he stayed within their shadows.

It doesn't have wings, so if it attacks me, I can fly to safety, Gillian told himself. He followed the beast as closely as he could without being spotted. Suddenly the beast stood on its hind legs and bellowed a nasty deep roar. It was one of the most terrifying things he had ever heard.

Gillian now knew what they meant by 'Terrible Terribbia.' Finally thrusting itself forward onto all fours it took off to the East. Gillian remained where he was for fear that the beast would change its course if it noticed him. He couldn't believe the massive power the creature had. It seemed as if it could run just as fast as he could fly! Baring its teeth, it plowed into a thicket of brush, causing twigs and branches to spring in every direction.

Soon he could see the beast was standing on its hind legs, because its head poked out above the bushes. It finally stopped long enough for Gillian to get a good look at it. He snorted with shock, finally recognizing that he had been stalking a great Gladiator bear. *Whoa! I can't believe it's an actual Gladiator Bear! I thought they went extinct,* he thought, in awe of the powerful creature.

The fearsome bear stood fifteen feet tall and could crush a Titan with one snap of its massive jaw. Its claws were like massive razor blades that could cut through the thickest armor known to any of the regions. Gillian trembled with fear. Never had he ever seen something so ferocious in all his days.

"Oh no," Gillian gasped. As he looked upon the gigantic bear, he realized that it was standing over one of the traitors. Over the girl. Then he noticed that the other three traitors had begun running back up the river away from the beast. The bear had torn apart the blueberry bushes and put itself between the girl and the others.

It's important to know that Gillian only witnessed this encounter from afar. Through the eyes of Eva, this encounter was much different. In fact, much scarier than Gillian could fathom.

Eva had still been trying to convince the three bear cubs to come down from the tree, when from far off she thought she heard someone yell

"Boys? Where are you? There is danger!" Then the earth began to shake.

Thumb, thu-thumb! Pounding the ground, a massive gladiator bear ambushed the bushes just behind her. The bear thrashed the bushes in search of her cubs. Before Eva knew it the horrifying bellow of the bear's roar overshadowed her.

The three boys frantically scrambled to their feet; Back up the river they bolted trying to escape to safety. It appeared to Eva that the bear was slicing straight through the branches with her claws.

Eva was so scared at that moment she couldn't even think of running. She just slowly backed away from it until, with a thud, she collided with the Blackwood tree standing firm behind her.

Having gained a little distance the boys realized that Eva was no longer with them. They spun around, panting like dogs and dropped down on their knees. It was clear the bear had no interest in them. They felt their bodies shake from the vibrations of the bear's vicious growl, even though they were so far away. They laid low to the ground but feared for Eva's life. But then the most peculiar thing occurred. Eva's head cocked sideways as if something changed.

"What did you say?" Eva spoke aloud. The boys looked at each other, wondering what she was talking about. "Grrrrawr rawrrr," Eva blurted out. The boy's jaws dropped, and Eva's grunt seemed to shock the bear, for the great beast looked to stumble two steps backwards.

"Grrruh?" the bear gently growled.

"Rwarr Grraw Grrrar," Eva responded to the beast. The bear swiveled its head in the boy's direction, causing them to duck lower to the ground.

"Grrraw, Rawr!" the bear huffed.

At this point Eva started running over to the boys, waving her hands in the air, and smiling uncontrollably.

"Rrrawwwwrrr Grrraw! Her Grrrr Grr is Maizey!" Eva shouted.

Her mysterious actions and apparent ability to speak bear scared the boys. So much so that as Eva ran towards them, all three jumped and tumbled backwards down the bank into the river.

The three boys cautiously crawled out of the river, soaked head to toe.

"You guys, the wild beasts of Terribbia, they can talk to us!" Eva shouted.

"Talk? Are you not hearing it? Are you not hearing yourself?" Jessie said in a panic.

"Why were you growling at the bear?" Andy asked

Eva looked shocked. "What do you mean? The bear was warning her cubs of danger. Then, when I realized she was speaking our language I told her we were of no harm to the cubs."

"Our language? Are you nuts! All she did, I mean all you did was growl," Richard said, shrugging his shoulders in disbelief.

"We thought that you were mocking the bear by pretending to speak to her. Honestly I thought that was idiotic and crazy! But apparently… you're just crazy," Jessie scoffed.

"You really think you can understand her?" Andy asked.

"Absolutely, she said her name is Maizey," Eva explained. Her excitement turned to concern. *Why can't anyone else understand Maizey? How can I understand a bear?*

The three boys stood at the base of the riverbank, dripping wet staring up at Eva who was standing at the top of the bank. The boys faces filled with fear as Maizey waddled up behind Eva and cast her shadow down upon the boys.

Maizey stood on her hind legs directly behind Eva and bellowed a grim rawr. Again, the boys tumbled backwards into the raging river.

"Gr Rawr?" Eva questioned. As she calmly turned around and looked up at the towering bear.

They must have had some sort of conversation because the two exchanged grrs and growls for five minutes.

The boys just sat in the river, baffled in amazement. Eva finally swiveled around and had a big smile painted across her face.

"Guys!" she shouted. She jumped down the riverbank and stopped at the edge of the water. "I'm a Somniator!" she exclaimed; the boys looked at each other.

"Huh?" they all harmonized.

"Maizey said that long ago, after the Great White Eagle disappeared many creatures developed a gift. They were able to speak to others, those who had different languages. Those creatures also received dreams," Eva explained.

"And you're one of those? A Somniator?" Andy asked.

"Yes! So, my dream was real and it meant something," she said excitedly.

"Wait, wait, wait! Why haven't I ever heard of them?" Jessie butted in.

"Well, we don't ever go to the village gatherings…," Richard said, elbowing his brother.

"I guess I've heard of them, the King requested anyone who was gifted with it to offer their services to him. I think?" Andy said, recalling an announcement he heard years ago.

"That's right! Maizey said that after the Great White Eagle disappeared, Malus gained control of the land. He divided the regions into four: Regnum, Gravis Terra, Terribbia, and Borrian. But over time the Somniators began to fade away," Eva said.

"Huh… Maybe that's why the king wants their help. Because it's rare?" Jessie thought out loud.

"Maybe? The Somniators were a key part in keeping peace amongst all creatures. Even to keep peace with the beasts of Terribbia. But as Somniators faded away, the beasts could no longer communicate!"

"I thought all creatures that could communicate intellectually could speak our language?" Richard asked, in a way that he thought made himself sound smart.

"Yeah, like the Dwarves and Elves, they can speak our language," Jessie chirped in.

"For some reason the beasts are unable to speak any language other than that of their own species. All the other creatures were able to learn a common language. Even the Centaurs and Pegasi learned to speak. But special animals, like Maizey, were never given that ability,"

Eva explained. Occasionally she would have to rawr towards Maizey to clarify because she was learning most of this as they went.

"So, can you talk to my steak? I mean like cows?" Richard asked.

"Maizey says farm animals are different. She doesn't know why. But it seems that those animals were only meant for food. So, they can't even talk to a Somniator," continued Eva.

"Don't the scrolls say something about that?" Andy said, trying to think back to a list of animals mentioned in the scrolls.

"Oh yeah, the scrolls say that cows, sheep, wild deer, and chickens are good for food. There are other service animals as well that are non-lingual. Horses and donkeys are among those. None of them are like Maizey," Eva remembered.

"So, they are dumb?" Jessie spouted off.

"Maybe just unable… dumb sounds cruel. But either way we are commanded by the scrolls to use those animals for food, clothing, and service," Eva explained.

"Okay but why would we need a Somniator in the first place?" Richard asked.

Eva began to explain with extreme excitement. "Before Malus took charge, all the creatures used to live in harmony. The Beasts, the Elves, Centaurs, Dwarves, Pegasi and Mankind all got along and lived amongst each other," Eva said.

"I don't buy it. The Elves think they are better than everyone, the Dwarves only care about gold, the Pegasi hate the Centaurs, and us humans… Well, we kind of suck," Jessie rambled.

"Maizey used to live with the Elves before Somniators disappeared. Shortly after most of the Somniators disappeared, wars began to break out. At that time there was no common language and without anyone to keep peace they began to attack one another. Mankind against Centaur, Dwarf against Elf. Like kinds began to group and build forces," she explained.

"Medieval!" Jessie shouted as he high fived his brother, thinking the history of their land was cool.

"The High Elf of that time was a Somniator. He was able to keep peace amongst the Elves and some of the beasts. Maizey's Father, Samson for example, made an alliance and served him. As battles began to break out, they fought alongside the Elves in battle!" Eva continued.

"Then what happened?" the boys asked, still sitting in the river mesmerized by the story. Eva spoke to Maizey who had plopped down behind her and was listening to their unfamiliar speech.

"Maizey said that during a bloody battle in the Ruth Valley, just at the base of the Pious Mountains, the High Elf Timmins was killed," Eva translated.

"Oh no!" Andy said.

"It gets worse. Samson, who was feared as a great warrior at the time, tried to speak to the newly appointed High Elf. But since the old High Elf was the last known translator left and he was killed in battle, no one could translate for the new High Elf. Which means the new High Elf could only hear as you boys did," Eva explained.

"That's not good. She's quite scary. Could you imagine her father?" Richard trembled.

"It wasn't good at all. The new High Elf, his name was Rundo by the way, feared the great Gladiator Bear. Concerned about his own safety he did not trust Samson. With his new power as High Elf, he ordered Samson to be killed! Maizey's father was put to death because no one could understand him. He was innocent, only trying to help win the battles and end the war. But it didn't stop there, Samson's death fueled outrage among the beasts in Gravis Terra. Instead of ending the war against all, it caused more. An uprising of beasts forced civil war to break out amongst the two parties. The beasts and Elves who had once been at peace were now at war. Just like the rest of the land," Eva continued.

"That is crazy! I mean to think that creatures and beasts used to live in harmony. I thought the way it is now; is just how it's always been. But you're saying all creatures used to get along?" Andy asked.

"That's what Maizey said. But she says the Babble Wars were just dreadful. The whole thing was awful. Because of the war, the beasts were forced into the South region. Thankfully the Eagle's Plateau created a ridged border between Terribbia and Borrian, which naturally gave them protection from the dwarves and the vast untamed wilderness of Terribbia helped keep the Elves from entering from the west. The beasts settled in and called Terribbia home. Unfortunately, they have been on defense ever since."

Maizey roared to Eva continuing the story and Eva translated to her friends.

"She said after that they were cut off from the rest of the world. Pegasi began to show up in Terribbia and would attack them. All they wanted was to know what was going on. But since no one could understand them, the Pegasi feared the beasts and killed them. Eventually they felt they had no choice but to strike first."

"You should tell her that those Pegasi are the guards. Protecting the forbidden circle," Andy said.

"Yeah! It's the rule of the land. No one shall enter the forbidden circle, to protect all creatures from the danger that lives within it," Richard said, puffing his chest mocking the King and his rules.

Eva spoke these things to Maizey and oddly enough the boys could tell by her facial expressions that she was shocked.

"She says the only dangerous thing they ever encountered were the Pegasi themselves. And to be fair, how would the beasts have even learned of the law?" Eva translated.

"That's a good point," Richard admitted.

"Wait! So, there's nothing scary or dangerous here at all?" Jessie asked.

"Rawee gree gggrr Rawr?" Eva asked Maizey, who grumbled in response. "She said that there are sometimes weird things that happen at night but no harm has ever been brought to her or her family."

"What sort of weird things?" Richard asked slightly concerned of things that may creep in the night.

"Apparently some nights it feels like they're not alone, like something is there but never have they ever seen anything," Eva translated.

"Huh weird. Maybe it's a… GHOST!" Jessie said, while suddenly grabbing his brother's shoulders to try and scare him.

"Rawr… Grah Gruff," Maizey snorted.

"She said as far as she knows there are no dangers up here. Just a bunch of misunderstood beasts," Eva translated."

"Well!" Jessie said as he finally crawled out of the water, stood up and walked up the bank to the big brown bear. "I'm Jessie," he said as he extended his arm for a proper handshake.

Maizey looked at Jessie, then at his hand. Cautiously, she leaned forwards and sniffed his hand. She had no clue what he was saying. After a few whiffs she licked his hand. Jessie jumped back because he worried she might try and eat his hand, but Richard and Andy began to laugh loudly at the occurrence.

The three cubs who were still perched in the blackwood had been watching the whole situation pan out. Once they saw their mother lick the strange looking creature's hand they must have thought it was acceptable for them to come and investigate themselves. Quickly they bolted down the tree and came running. They looked like three fur tumble weeds as they barreled towards Eva and plowed right into her playfully. Eva giggled and giggled as she wrestled with the cubs. One cub actually ventured to the edge of the water and looked at Richard and Andy who had made their way to the river's edge.

The cubs trusted Eva for she spoke their language, but of the others the cub remained cautious, slowly extending its paw into the water. It keeped both its eyes on Andy and Richard, but then began to gently splash water at the boys.

"I think… he wants us to play?" Andy questioned.

Andy tried his theory and gently splashed water back at the cub. Leaping backwards to get out of the way, the cub then pounced back to the water and splashed the boys again.

Richard cupped some water and tossed it at the cub. Which made the cub dart into the water and circle around Andy and Richard. Wading further in the river the cub stood on its little back legs and used both front paws to splash water at the boys.

The next thing anyone knew, it had turned into a full-blown water fight. The two remaining cubs who had been wrestling with Eva and Jessie, evaded their match and joined the water brawl. Darting in and out of the water, they splashed the boys. Jessie ambushed one of the cubs from behind and tackled one of them bringing them both splashing down into the water.

It was quite the spectacle to see the four humans interacting with the gladiator bears in this way and Gillian had witnessed the whole thing from afar.

Gillian was astonished. He thought for sure that Eva would have been killed by the bear. Yet instead, before his very eyes, the whole situation had been defused by some sort of communication.

How is this possible? Gillian thought. At first Gillian stayed hidden as best he could. He heard horror stories of a Gladiator's great power and did not want to be harmed himself. He had none of his Royal armor, but even so, he had doubts that it would even have been enough protection for a fight against a Gladiator Bear.

As he laid low and watched their water fight, Gillian began to gain confidence that it was safe to try and get closer. Afterall, his mission was to capture the four traitors and he had them in his sights.

Gillian found himself moving closer more aggressively than before. Which allowed Maizey to catch sight of him.

She again stood tall in her hind legs, staring in his direction. He knew his cover was blown, Gillian's fight or flight instincts kicked in. The elbows of Gillian's wings raised out away from his body making himself look larger to a foe. His movement in turn frightened Maizey, who then plowed her way into the river growling, placing herself in between Gillian and those with her in the river.

"Get behind her," Eva whispered.

Maizey had warned her of the danger and the four teenagers and three cubs piled behind the mass of the bear. Richard peeked around the massive structure of the bear and recognized the threat. "A Royal Pegasus!" Richard gasped.

None of the teenagers were able to recognize the guard as Gillian. In just a night's time, Gillian looked different. Not only did Gillian have the noble marking on his face, but another new mark had formed under his left wing. Gillian had yet to discover it himself.

Gillian knew that a one-on-one match against the Gladiator Bear would not end well for him, so he launched himself in the air. *I can't let them get away again*, Gillian thought to himself. *I'll have to swoop in from the air and snatch the kids up before they get away.*

Hovering for only a moment, Gillian then charged the group. Swooping through the air at a sharp downward angle.

As he neared the ferocious bear he weaved right, dodging the massive paw that came swinging at him. His maneuver brought him around the group. The tips of his left wing stirred the water of the river as he sharply swiveled back around facing the group head on. This time he had a clear path to the traitors. Diving back through the air, he tried using his teeth to grab the back of Jessie's shirt, but Jessie ducked just in time. Gillian quickly lifted himself straight up to avoid another blow from Maizey. Her razor-sharp claws sliced below Gillian's hooves just missing him as he lifted himself out of her reach.

"RAWRR!" Maizey boomed. The boys assumed she commanded her cubs to run, for all three bolted out of the water and headed south into the Blackwood forest. Then her commands were aimed at them.

"Grrawwwrrr," Maizey commanded. Maizey dropped to all four paws again.

"Get on her back!" Eva shouted to the three boys. Eva used Maizey's thick fur to grab onto as she climbed up the massive bear's torso. Eva sat on the bear's back and reached out her hand to Andy, "Come on" she shouted, all the while Gillian was repositioning himself in the air for another attempt.

The boys frantically looked at each other, still wary of the gigantic beast. However, Gillian swooped in again. This time he was able to grab the back of Richard's white T-shirt. Forcing his wings downward, Gillian lifted Richard out of the water. Jessie thought quickly and jumped up, grabbing both of Richard's legs.

Jessie's extra weight caught Gillian off guard and Richard slipped loose from his grip. The close call gave the boys no other choice but to crawl onto the bear's back. Once all four of the teenagers had situated themselves on Maizey's back the bear thrusted forwards into the Blackwood forest.

Gillian looped in the sky and plunged towards the forest. A great chase had begun. The bear easily picked up speed through the forest. Her big paws and sturdy legs were made with power. The four bareback riders had to grip tightly. The magnificent power of the bear made for a bumpy ride.

Gillian weaved in and out, flapping his mighty wings as much as possible, trying to keep up with the bear's impressive speed. Unfortunately keeping up with the bear proved difficult. As the bear weaved left and right with ease, never did she have to slow down. Gillian on the other hand, naturally would have to flap his wings consistently to generate enough speed to catch up with Maizey. Alas, A forest always proved difficult for a large, winged creature to navigate and this Blackwood forest was no exception. Its trees were unevenly spaced. He could maintain enough speed to stay in flight, but had to time each flap perfectly, so he wouldn't hit any trees and come tumbling down. With limited ability to flap his wings correctly, Gillian soon fell behind and had lost sight of the bear.

He needed another plan. He noticed a small clearing ahead and made adjustments in his flight to land. Soon he safely folded his wings into his body and landed in a trot, bringing him to a stop.

Exhausted from the chase Gillian lowered his head while he tried to catch his breath. That was when he noticed something imprinted on the ground; A paw print was left behind from the Gladiator. The paw print could fit both Gillian's front hooves if he placed them inside the paw's outline. He looked ahead and noticed that he could see another print, and then another. Soon he found himself tracking the bear. Gillian thought to himself, *this must be how those lowlife Centaurs of the East hunt their prey. How far have I fallen?* He shivered at the thought of hunting down an animal, for he didn't much like meat and stuck to the leafy green good stuff. However, by tracking the bear's footprints, Gillian had not lost hope. Instead, he had to be patient and find them at a much slower pace.

Chapter 5
Farwell

Their hearts pounded, for the bear back ride was bumpy. There was a level of excitement and fear that seemed to balance each other out. Each wondered the same thought. *What would happen to them if the royal guard got a hold of them?*

At first, sneaking into the forbidden circle in search of the Devil's kettle seemed to be an innocent poke at the rules. Now it appears to have turned into a full-blown manhunt.

Maizey zig-zagged through the forest, racing towards safety. At this point, it was evident that Gillian had fallen behind. Eva had ridden horses a few times while visiting relatives on the countryside of Regnum, so she grew comfortable. Unfortunately, she became too comfortable. Maizey's large fluffy head blocked any view of what was ahead of them. Eva, unaware of a large log that stretched across the ground, loosened her grip. As Maizey abruptly leaped full speed over the log, Eva was caught off guard. The powerful leap jarred the four but Eva was the only one who had not held on tight enough.

The sudden jolt threw her from Maizey's back. Upon impact of the ground Eva blacked out, losing conscience. She was only unconscious for seconds, but during the incident she had short bursts of what seemed like another dream. In the wake of in and out conscience she saw the Great White Eagle soaring above her in the sky, and he said something about the harvest or a harvest to come. She was unable to comprehend much of the dream before she was woken up by the bear's slobbery tongue. Eva placed both hands on her head and squeezed her eyes shut for the pain of the fall caused her head to throb.

Maizey growled at Eva, and Eva responded in Gladiator bear, "Yes, I can keep going," they both wanted to get as far from the Royal Guard as possible. So, for now, Eva would have to deal with the pain.

Andy reached out his hand to help Eva back onto the bear's back. Once they had gotten Eva secured on Maizey's back, she lurched forwards and was off again.

Eva's head thumped with each step Maizey took. All she could do was squeeze her eyes shut and hope that they would arrive soon.

Finally, Maizey slowed down and came to a stop. She swirled her head around to see if the Pegasus had somehow kept up. With nothing but the tall Blackwood tree's insight, Maizey knelt down, so that the four teenagers could slide off.

"Oh, my head hurts," Eva said, with one hand plopped on top of her head. "Grrawrrah," she repeated to Maizey.

As the four teenagers looked around they noticed that Maizey had stopped in the heart of a small clearing. The canopy above had parted just enough that yellow rays of light shone through. It was peaceful and quiet. The ground was clear and grass had grown through. It was fine haired grass and had no strength to stand tall, instead it curled over in matts of grass. Only a few fallen leaves had been trapped under the matted leaves, otherwise the small clearing gave the wind enough room to blow loose leaves away.

This clearing was natural and calming, unlike the clearings that the guards of Regnum and the other Regions held post at. Those had been striped clean and the grass had been trampled into dirt over the years.

As the Blackwood forest loomed around them, Maizey led the four to a clump of large blackwood trees at the left side of the clearing. It was a set of four trees. Two large trunks shared the same base, but split up into a 'V' shape, then a third tree had been laid over in a storm. The great blackwood must have put up a definite fight because the roots, grasping the earth tightly, brought much of the sod and rich black soil with it as it crashed to the ground. This created a crater in the ground, leaving a void that had naturally filled with water.

The fourth tree of the clump was a regular single blackwood tree. It was the largest of the four, standing sturdy and tall, its canvas of leaves towered higher than the rest.

"Grraww," Maizey bellowed. Soon Maizey's three cubs, who had climbed the fourth tree as a way to hide from threats, came shimming down the single blackwood tree of the clump.

To the teenagers' surprise, each one carried large leaves in their mouth. Quickly they reached the bottom and scurried across the clearing grassy floor. The teenagers watched as the cubs pounced before Andy and Richard, laying the leaves down at their feet. Andy picked up the leaf and looked at Eva suggesting she asked the bears, *What are we to do with it?*

As he picked it up, he noticed that the leaves were all green except for sprinkles of black dots. He was surprised at its touch, for the leaves were not hardy and rough like a Pongo leaf or a great Oak, but instead it had a fuzzy feel to it. As he examined it closer he understood that the black dots were not actually dots of color, but were hundreds of tiny pores. When he realized that he quickly knelt down by the puddle of water and submerged the leaf. As he did he could feel the leaf begin to swell. The small pores allowed the leaf to absorb water.

Once it had soaked for a moment, Andy pulled the leaf out and gently squeezed it, until most of the water had drained from the pores. The fuzzy leaf now felt grippy and damp. He draped it across Eva's forehead to help with any swelling that might have been caused by the fall.

Eva closed her eyes to try and relax. Between the pain and adrenaline that she was feeling she had grown exhausted and quickly fell asleep. Maizey nodded her head, pointing her nose towards the head of the felled tree. Andy crouched down next to Eva and scooped her up off the ground. Cradling Eva in his arms, Andy and the others followed Maizey as she waddled alongside the trunk of the fallen tree towards its mangled branches.

Andy wondered where Maizey was bringing them, but had no way of asking so he just followed in silence.

The floor of this part of the forest seemed to be more uneven than others. Moss covered boulders protruded from the forest floor, and to their left a mound had risen and ran along for a good distance. Smaller blackwood trees had sunk their roots into the top of the mound and rocks popped up here and there around its base. Just beyond the shattered canopy of the fallen Blackwood, Richard spoke up.

"Where are you taking us?" he asked. Almost at the exact moment Maizey ducked into a hole in the mound. The way the trees and the rocks unevenly grew and were set about it made it hard for anyone to see it, until they were directly upon the opening themself. Soon, they realized that this opening was the mouth of a cave.

The cave's mouth was slim. Two large boulders crowded the entrance. The first boulder had been fused to the hill by the roots, sod, and dirt, but the other was tall and the top jagged and pointy. The pointy boulder looked like an immovable door. Its right side looked hinged to the mound, and the left side looked pried open leaving a fat sliver opening.

Following the bear inside, their eyes slowly adjusted to the darkness. The cave wasn't very large, but was just big enough for all four of the humans and Maizey to have some wiggle room. Unlike the mine shaft, the ceiling and walls of this cave had been formed by rocks and boulders piling together and then the spaces between each uneven rock had filled and been packed with the soil over hundreds of years. How a cave like that would form is anyone's guess, but the mighty Great White Eagle was definitely a crafty creator. The floor of the cave had been covered with a mixture of leaves, grasses, and twigs which made it quite fluffy and almost bouncy. Maizey motioned her head, in a way that hinted to Andy to put Eva down in the corner of the cave. Andy gently dropped to his knees and set Eva on the ground.

Eva hadn't been on the floor for a minute and started to flinch and jerk slightly. Andy could tell she was having a dream, perhaps another message from the Great White Eagle.

"Let's give her some space," Andy suggested. The three boys headed outside so they could talk about everything that was going on. They wandered back toward the clearing and began to discuss it all.

"Man, I really feel bad now," Richard said.

"Yeah, If we had gone back she never would have gotten hurt. We should have just headed back when we woke up this morning," Jessie exclaimed. Andy really felt bad at this point. After all, he was the one that convinced her to come along in the first place. Not to mention he chose to continue on with Richard and Jessie. *Now, out of nowhere she is having dreams and talking to animals! What have I gotten her into?* he thought to himself.

"I think when she wakes up we should head back," Andy said.

"I agree," Jessie spouted.

"Me too! But what about the Pegasus?" asked Richard. "Even if we make it back without him finding us, don't you think he will keep looking for us when he returns?"

"I really don't know what's going to happen. Maybe I can turn myself in, that way he will let you all go," said Andy trying to find a compromise.

"No way!" argued Richard "There is no way I can let you go alone!"

"Well, someone needs to get Eva home, and if turning myself in for her sake is the only way then so be it!" Andy said.

"I agree, we need to get her home. But that's not the way," Jessie assured Andy.

"How about Jessie and I go find the Pegasus, we turn ourselves in. That way you can get Eva to safety," Richard suggested.

"How is that any different?" Andy argued.

"Think about it, we might be able to convince him to let you go," Jessie said.

"But why should you face the punishments and not I?" Andy said.

"Frankly? What do we have left?" Richard said.

"Both Mama and Daddy are gone. We don't have any relatives, no jobs or money. If we don't end up in the dungeons now, we sure will be soon. It's either that or be forced to serve the king as servants or a Titan to pay for our time at the orphanage," Jessie explained.

"What do I have that you don't? We are likely to end up in the same place," Andy persisted.

"You have Eva," Richard spit out. Andy gulped and turned red. He was quite fond of her, but didn't think he made it that obvious.

"Yeah, you should protect her. Plus, let's be honest you are the smartest one here. If any of us could figure out how to avoid becoming a servant to the king, it would be you. I'd bet you could easily find a job once you turn eighteen and pay back your costs to the kingdom. You probably wouldn't even have to serve in the King's army," Jessie continued.

"I...I don't know what to say," Andy quietly responded.

"Don't say anything!" Jessie insisted.

"You sure?" Andy asked, "What if you are forced to join Kings Fraust's Titans? Or worse... That's not fair to you."

"Like Jessie said, do you really think we could avoid it anyways? Most farmers can only afford to pay one of us, I ain't leaving my brother," Richard argued.

"It's okay! We will have each other, that's all we have left," Jessie said, persuading Andy to listen to them.

There was a sad silence because no one wanted to say it. Their silly adventure had turned into something far greater than what they could have imagined it to be. The boys knew that living in an orphanage was horrible, and all three of them would do anything to have their parents back. Knowing this, none of them could bear the thought of separating Eva from hers too. Sadly, they all knew what had to be done.

"Maybe we should go now," whispered Richard

"What? Don't you want to wait for Eva to wake up so you can say goodbye?" asked Andy.

"You know she would try to stop us; If she knew what we were going to do. I don't want to make this harder than it has to be," Jessie explained. Again, there was silence. Andy knew that they were right, this was best. Nothing was said as they picked up this burden and put it upon themselves. It was a sad moment but they made peace with it.

The seemingly motionless moment was broken when Richard reached inside the collar of his shirt and softly pulled out some sort of necklace. The soft light of the clearing made the golden pendant sparkle. Andy could see the necklace's pendant was a golden compass. The necklace itself was a simple black string that looked as if it had been loved. It was frayed and worn, but sturdy. He slipped the necklace from around his head and held it out towards Andy.

"Here, take this, will you?" Richard asked.

Both Jessie and Andy looked at Richard, shocked.

"What are you doing? Mom gave you that!" Jessie said frantically.

"I know, I know! But don't you think they will take it from us? I bet when we turn ourselves in they will take everything from us. It is the only thing of value we have, the only thing meaningful from mom. I would rather you keep it…" he said while looking at Andy, "Instead of those rotten guards." The excitement settled down on the three boys again. Andy was honored that Richard would entrust something so special to him. They hadn't really known each other for very long, but the bond that they had formed during this adventure had become something very strong.

"If there is any way to return this to you, I will," Andy said as he allowed Richard to lower the compass into Andy's cupped hand.

Richard nodded farewell. The two brothers began to take steps backwards before they turned away and began their journey back towards the meadow. Andy stood watching, wondering if this was the last time that he would see his two friends ever again. As Richard and Jessie became outlines in the distance, and their figures disappeared into the Blackwood forest, a tear rolled down Andy's cheek. It was one of those tears that you let run its course, one you're too shaken to the core to wipe away. He looked down at his hand, still resting in his palm was Richard's golden compass. For five minutes Andy stood in silence, secretly hoping that the two boys would reappear because they had changed their minds. But his hope was in vain for they did not come back. Realizing that they were gone, he unraveled the tangled string of the compass and hung the necklace around his neck and tucked the compass under his shirt. Then he walked over to the nearest blackwood tree, leaned his back against it and slid down to his butt. The heavy moment left a lump in his throat and forced sorrow into the air. His eyes grew tired as tears swelled, but he fought them forcing them to dry. But the emotion he bore made him grow weary and he passed out in the warmth of the sun.

Chapter 6
A Plan to Get Caught

Gillian trotted along in the forest as glimpses of sun rays peeked through the Blackwood canopy spotting the forest's floor with yellow polka dots. As much as this mission was important, Gillian felt free and he was enjoying it as if it was just an adventure. He had never seen such beautiful forests and meadows, nor had he seen such species of so many different creatures and beasts before. The forbidden circle had been untouched by the intelligent species for so long that the earth and wildlife flourished freely.

Gillian was able to enjoy the scenery because it was not hard for him to follow the bears' footprints. The forest floor that time of year was mostly mulched up leaves from the autumn past and the soil there held onto moisture. The earth mushed out under the weight of the bear's pressure and left obvious tracks for Gillian to follow. So, he focused more on the beauty of the forest than he did his mission.

But suddenly, Gillian halted. To his surprise he could hear something in the distance. Faint whispers murmured and grabbed his attention. The unknown whispers frightened him and caused him to remember that the forest was home to many terrible beasts. He had no clue what could be lurking about in the forest.

Gillian side stepped swiftly until his body was hidden behind a great Blackwood. Slowly inching his head around the side of the tree Gillian surveyed the forest, trying to spot whatever it was that was heading his way. As he inched around the tree, Gillian focused his eyes deeper and deeper into the forest. Suddenly Gillian found himself eyeball to eyeball with a creature. Letting out a girlish snort, he jumped back. As his hooves hit the ground, the elbows of his wings had raised but he quickly realized that it was only a bushy tailed black squirrel.

The small creatures started going berserk; expressing a combination of squeaks, chirps, and grunts, all while it wiggled and snapped its tail almost robotically. As Gillian watched the small creature, he relaxed his wings and folded them tightly to his body. *It's kind of cute,* he thought.

Although he couldn't understand the squirrel, he began to assume the tiny thing was chewing him out.

Gillian tilted his head sideways, for that was the natural reaction a Pegasus makes when something sparks their curiosity. The squirrel began to make vicious small jolts towards Gillian while clinging onto the tree. The massive threats from the little squirrel caused Gillian to bob his head and slowly step back with each pounce the creature made.

Finally, Gillian must have stepped back far enough for the squirrel because he stopped squealing. His beady little eyes glared at Gillian. Gillian stared back afraid to blink. Each one anxiously waited for the other one to move. When suddenly the squirrel scampered down the tree and stopped at the base of the tree. The squirrel's tail twitched and then stopped and its beady eyes glared again at Gillian, as if he was testing him to see if he would attack.

After a moment the squirrel scampered closer to Gillian and started rustling up the leaves on the ground. *For a little guy, he sure made a lot of racket shuffling the leaves*, Gillian thought, as he lowered his snout to get a closer look at the squirrel. The squirrel scattered the leaves this way and that and began making a chattering noise that sounded like he was snickering at Gillian.

Soon the leaves were cleared away and he began pawing at the soil. It was when the soil had been cleared that Gillian learned why the little squirrel seemed so irritated. Gillian had been standing on a nut that the squirrel had buried. The bushy tailed critter shoved the nut into his check, squawked at Gillian and darted back up the tree and disappeared into the canopy. Gillian whinnied lightly to himself. He was scared of a little ball of fluff. *Huh, it's not so bad here. I was worried about nothing at all! Just a grumpy squirrel.*

He tried to watch the squirrel as it scampered along the branches that stretched out in every direction. It followed one all the way out until the branch became thin enough to bend under the squirrel's weight and then it would spring to the nearest branch and scamper away. Gillian almost began to follow it, but remembered he had to find the traitors, and soon. Vincent would soon be discovering that there was no hoof treatment waiting for him in Sod-Omen.

The excitement settled and Gillian was again alone in the forest. He lightly began trotting south, following the bear's tracks.

Somewhere else within the same Blackwood forest, Richard and Jessie had decided to turn themselves in. In order to do that they had to figure out where the Royal Pegasus guard was.

At first, neither one of the boys said much. Unlike Gillian, the boys hadn't noticed Maizey's tracks, instead they would just point in the direction that they felt they should head. They both knew that their best bet in finding the Pegasus would be to go back to the meadow. Obviously, the Pegasus would be coming from that direction and they would run into him somewhere along the way.

Their heavy mood didn't stay heavy for long. Although they knew their fate, they too could not believe the beauty of the untouched wilderness. Jessie's voice broke the strenuous silence.

"This is what it must have been like before the Great White Eagle went missing, when all creatures lived in harmony."

"Could you imagine if all the kingdoms were untouched like this?" Richard asked. Looking at the untamed forest, rolling waves of the forest floor and small birds and varmints darting about. "...Hey, Jessie?"

"Yeah?"

"Do you really think the Great White Eagle is real? Or do you think it is all made up?" Richard asked genuinely, wondering what to believe.

"Well, I mean yeah. I'd like to believe so. Sometimes it's really hard though."

"It is hard. Mama always told us about him, but then she died. If he is the founder of our land, then why would he let a good soul like her die?" Richard asked solemnly.

"I don't know Richy; The scrolls say that one day he will return... Maybe we can ask him then."

"Well, If he is real and he comes back, I'm gonna ask him!" Richard was confident that if he ever met the Great White Eagle he would question why so many bad things happen to so many good people. It seems that the rulers of the land, like King Fraust and the all-black Pegasus ruled unfairly and harshly. They had convinced all the land that Pegasi received black markings for noble efforts, yet the Pegasi were known for being cruel and unpredictable.

He remembered when he was just a small boy, he was with his parents attending a Village gathering, five Royal Cavalry Pegasi swooped in from above. One Pegasus was mostly white, similar to the way Gillian had first looked to the boys. The other four had been painted with many blotches of black. The smudged looking Pegasi flew in circles above the crowd of people, while the younger, mostly white Pegasus, hoovered in place. The encircling Pegasi began to shout commands to the younger Pegasus.

Richard couldn't remember what was all said, but suddenly the younger Pegasus rushed the crowd swooping down upon them, shouting "You fools, The Eagle is no more! Believe in a Ghost or bow to the King!" The crowd of people rushed around in every direction as the Pegasus used its hooves to kick over chairs and benches as it swooped down towards the center of the village.

After that day that particular Pegasus wasn't the same. He had gained his 'Noble' markings. He became more confident, maybe even arrogant. He had gained not only a marking but an attitude as well, which in turn made him meaner. Richard thought about the Pegasi. He thought about how they didn't believe in the Eagle. Then again he wasn't sure if he believed in the Great White Eagle himself. The only thing he did know was that he did not want to be like a Royal Pegasus Guard, cruel and unjust.

"Jessie, do you think that all the guards are mean? Like the ones from the villages all those years ago?"

"I think some are just confused. They have been convinced that what they are doing is right. I do believe that the ones that have a lot of black hair are truly more cruel at heart than the others, but I think some really do care about all of our well-being."

"Do you think the one we saw in the meadow is really cruel?"

"I don't know. I hope not, but by the looks of it he only had two or three markings."

"Well, I hope he is the one that does care, maybe he will hear us out. Maybe even let Andy and Eva go!"

"We will have to wait and see, but first we have to find him."

The boys wandered north through the blackwood forest searching for the Pegasus they had seen in the meadow. By this time the sun was high in the sky, indicating that it was around noon. The boys marched along until they saw a flicker of white ahead of them.

"Do you think it's the Pegasus?" asked Jessie as both boys peered around a larger Blackwood.

"Well do you know anything else with giant white wings like that?" whispered Richard

"Maybe it's the Great White Eagle," giggled Jessie, for both boys majorly doubted that.

As the boys held fast to their tree, they watched closely as a small black creature shimmed down the opposite side of the Blackwood that the winged creature was hiding behind.

It was quite comical because neither of those creatures knew the other was there. As both creatures began to creep around the trunk of the tree towards each other, the brothers had to cover their mouths to try and conceal their laughter. The brothers knew what was coming but it wasn't until the other two creatures were eyeball to eyeball that they both became frightened by the other and let out little shrieks.

As the winged creature slowly moved backwards away from the bushy tailed squirrel, they could now see that it was in fact the guard that they had seen in the meadow.

A sense of fear took over the boys. It was time to turn themselves over, but they were scared of what the outcome would be. They both pressed their backs hard against the Blackwood tree, wondering what to do. They were both frightened but were not about to admit it.

Soon, they could hear leaves rustling from footsteps heading in their direction; Their breathing became more rapid. The boys tensed up their body's and squeezed their eyes shut tight, as if it would help them disappear.

Luckily as Gillian rounded their tree, the boys shuffled around the trunk. Gillian froze at first because he could hear their shuffling, but soon disregarded it as another squirrel and continued on his mission. The boys held their breaths trying everything they could not to make another sound. Jessie peaked around the tree and could see Gillian had traveled a good distance from them before he released his breath.

"Phew," the boys gasped.

"What are we doing?" Jessie said, "We are supposed to turn ourselves in!"

"I know but when the moment came… Well, you didn't turn us in either!" Richard argued with his brother in a whisper.

"I knew you were scared. I was protecting you," Jessie said, trying to convince his little brother that he wasn't at all scared.

"Sure, you were, I bet you peed your pants," Richard smarted off. And Jessie punched him in the arm, as all loving brothers do.

"Now what?" asked Jessie.

"We could just return to Regnum." Richard said with a small smile.

"But if we did that, how would we be any better than those Pegasi from when we were younger?" asked Jessie. "We told Andy we would help, now we both know that's the right thing to do. If mama was here and knew we had even thought about letting our friends down, she would turn us in herself!"

"Your right," Richard whimpered.

"It's time to make mama proud," Jessie said.

The two discussed a plan on how to 'get caught' and had decided that if they were gonna go down, they would go down swinging.

The boys ran south but looped way out so that they could pass Gillian on his left flank. They darted from tree to tree, only moving when Gillian was looking in a different direction. Gillian seemed to be in no hurry so it was easy for the boys to loop around him far enough not to be heard and get ahead of him to set up their encounter.

The boys found a clump of trees within the forest that had been entangled with vines. These vines made it easy for Jessie to climb up the large trunks of the blackwood trees. About twenty-five feet off the ground, Jessie wedged himself in a split branch and he found that there were enough vines for him to hide his body from sight. With that he was in position.

"In position!" he shouted to Richard. Richard went on the East of the tree about fifteen feet and sat down on the ground facing west, which is the direction Gillian would be coming from once their plan was in motion.

"Ready?" asked Richard while looking up at Jessie.

"Ready!" said Jessie.

Richard looked straight ahead into the woods. Then in the most theatrical way, he grasped his knee with one hand and placed the back of his other hand across his forehead and began rocking back and forth on the forest floor.

"Ohh no! Poor meeee!" Richards shouted in the most sarcastic voice he could.

"I'm a damsel in distress! Someone save me!" he said flamboyantly.

Jessie giggled in the tree above him and Richard had a smile painted across his face. "Hellllppppp! Heelllppp!" Richard exclaimed.

Gillian, who was just out of sight, heard the cry for help in the distance. Soon he found himself leaving the bear's tracks and heading in the direction of the plea for help. To him the boy sounded like he was in trouble.

Gillian raced through the forest until he could see the boy sitting on the forest floor. He could see the boy, Richard, holding his leg and assumed Richard had a leg injury. As he closed in on Richard, Gillian slowed down and began looking in all directions. He recognized Richard as one of the four and was worried about where the others could be. Finally, he was close enough that he stopped. The tree Jessie was perched in was now behind Gillian.

"Boy are you hurt?" Gillian asked

"Does it *look* like I'm hurt?" Richard announced aggressively.

"Well, it does, but where are your friends?" Gillian asked as he again looked around into the forest.

"They left me! They all left me!" Richard said while rotating his body with his arms stretched out as if to physically explain that no one was around.

"Calm down, calm down," Gillian said, trying to figure out what to do. "What can I do to help?"

"Well," Richard said. He lifted his eyes to Jessie sitting in the tree above Gillian. Jessie was waving his hands as if to say Gillian was too far away and wanted Richard to get him to step backwards. In response, Richard jumped to his feet, which surprised Gillian who had thought he was hurt. The sudden movement from Richard caused Gillian to step backwards, lift his snout high in the air, and stretch out his wings.

Before Gillian could say anything, Jessie jumped from the tree onto Gillian's back. The apparent attack from above scared Gillian so much that his wings thrust downward and he pounced up like a scared cat. Gillian danced up and down, jumping and jolting this way and that. So much so that Jessie felt as if he was in one of the shows back home where the farm hands would all take turns jumping on the backs of bulls and hold on as long as they could until they got bucked off.

Finally, Gillian was able to toss Jessie from his back. Conveniently for Jessie, Richard broke his fall. Both boys tumbled to the ground, laughing, and giggling as they rolled to a stop.

Gillian reared up, his wings extended out and cast his shadow down on the boys. He landed his front hooves on the ground and lowered his head down until the breath from his nostrils rustled the leaves on the forest floor. If looks could kill, Gillian's stare would have pierced right through the two brothers. The elbows of Gillian's wings raised as far away from his body as he could and his wings tucked back to his torso. He looked mad, he looked big, and he looked fed up with the boys' games.

"Where are the others!" Gillian snorted.

"They're not here!" Jessie exclaimed.

"Why should I believe you? You've already lied to me once!"

"We are sorry! But hey, here we are! We decided to turn ourselves in… figured we might as well have some fun with it!" Richard shrugged.

"The other two won't be a problem!" Jessie said.

"Turn yourselves in? Why would you do that?" Gillian asked.

"Well, this was just supposed to be a silly little adventure, but obviously now we are in big trouble. Then Eva, the girl, fell and hit her head," explained Richard.

"We want to turn ourselves in and take whatever punishment falls on us, but we hope that you can let them *be?*" Jessie asked hopefully.

Gillian paused for a moment. The fact that these two boys would be willing to give themselves up for their friends was truly a noble act. He honestly just wanted this to all be over, and didn't really want anyone to get in trouble. Especially not himself. However, he couldn't just let Andy and Eva get away. *What if they continued to the Devil's*

Kettle? What if they told everyone everything that had happened? he thought. His time as a Royal Guard would be over, and worse, he would be punished.

"It's very noble of you to turn yourselves in for your friends' sake, but…" Gillian paused. "We have to find your friends. They are in danger here, and if I don't turn them in, I will receive the Alatum punishment!"

The boys had only heard of the punishment, but knew it was a horribly humiliating thing for a Pegasus to go through. Yet, there was no part of them that wanted to help the Pegasus. After all, *when has a Pegasus ever done anything for them? Except to enforce order upon them and by being royally rude!* The boys thought.

"What if we told you that they were headed back to Regnum?" Jessie asked.

"Well, I would think that is good news and we should catch up to them," Gillian said.

"You wouldn't let them go if they went back to the kingdom?" asked Richard.

"I would like to, but my loyalty to King Fraust and Malus is most important. If others found out that you all snuck past me, and journeyed into the Forbidden Circle chaos would surely break out," Gillian insisted.

"What if we promised they would never speak of this adventure to anyone?" asked Richard.

Gillian paused again. He didn't want anyone to get in trouble, he just wanted it to be over. Gillian realized that he would have to answer for his lies either way. He had two options. First, he thought that if he had stopped the four, then his punishment would be much less severe than if they chose the second option. That option would be allowing the four to go home free. However, if anyone found out about this mishap, there would be no mercy for Gillian's mistake. So, it was him or them, and although it made Gillian uncomfortable he chose to save himself.

"I have to find them! In the name of the king," Gillian announced. He felt a little sickened by his words because he knew deep down that it wasn't for the king, it was for his own sake. The boys became worried because their best-case scenario was not playing out as they had hoped.

"Where are they?" Gillian questioned.

"They went to the kettle!" blurted Richard. Jessie was surprised at the answer that Richard gave the Pegasus because he knew that Andy was going to be bringing Eva home to her parents. Richard looked at Jessie, pressed his lips and made big eyes as if to tell his brother to go with it.

"Yes! They went to the Kettle!" Jessie said, looking back towards Gillian.

"I thought you said they were going to go back home, and that you promised they would not say anything?" Gillian asked. *What game are they trying to pull on me?* He thought.

"Well, they could be going home," Richard started.

"*Or* they could be heading to the Devil's Kettle!" Jessie finished.

The boys both began smiling. They knew each other so well that they could easily play off each other's ideas, which made it easy for them to mess with Gillian.

"I don't believe you! They are headed back, and so are we!" Gillian ordered.

"Okay, If you say so," Richard said, while raising his eyebrows.

"What are you trying to pull here," Gillian questioned.

"Nothing," Jessie said.

"It's just, if they didn't go home and they actually did continue to the Kettle, and you decide to go back to Regnum looking for them. Not only will they have gotten away from you, but they would also have seen the Kettle for themselves and be able to tell all Regnum about it," explained Richard.

"Plus, Eva is an interpreter so all the creatures of all the regions will learn the truth about the Devil's Kettle," said Jessie.

Richard hit Jessie in the arm, and whispered under his breath, "Why did you tell him that?"

"An interpreter?" Gillian was shocked! "I thought Somnaitors went extinct! We were told that anyone who claimed to be one was to be brought forth in front of the king to prove that they were. But if they failed they would be put to death for lying. Very few and I mean very few creatures were left to live." Gillian explained, *Is it possible? The girl might actually be a Somniator?*

Gillian remembered how the bear was charging the teenagers and somehow Eva calmed the situation. It must have been because she could understand the bear. *Incredible! She really must be a Somniator!* Gillian's thoughts raced with excitement.

Now, he really had to find them all, for not only have they broken the law, but if the King found out about an Somniator he would most definitely want to speak with her.

"So, you say they might be going to the Kettle? But what if they really do head back to Regnum?" asked Gillian.

"Well, then they will be somewhere in Regnum for you to find after you check the Kettle," Jessie said while shrugging his shoulders, acting like that option was the best one for Gillian.

Gillian pondered all of his options. Trying to figure out which one would be the best. If he found all the teenagers then no one would be unaccounted for, and if he brought the girl to the King then he would be a hero among the cavalry for finding a Somnaitor.

"We will go to the kettle to find them, but if they are not there you boys will be in big trouble," threatened Gillian.

Both the boys nodded. They knew that Andy and Eva would be heading home, and by tricking the Pegasus into going to the Kettle, it would give their friends time to get home and hide. As a bonus both the boys would get to see the Devil's Kettle for themselves, which is what they wanted in the first place.

Chapter 7
Fire Crib

Andy felt two hands grab his shoulder and began shaking him aggressively.

"Andy, wake up! Wake up!" he could hear a voice as he was jolted into consciousness. As he opened his eyes he could see that it was Eva who was shaking him.

"What's wrong?" mumbled Andy, still half asleep.

"I had another dream!" shouted Eva. Andy could now see that Maizey and her three cubs had all plopped down on their hind ends as if they were ready to hear the dream.

Andy rubbed his eyes and leaned forward readying himself to listen to her dream. Once the clearing was quiet and all were ready to listen, Eva proceeded to explain her dream in great detail. Her excitement made her speak very quickly. In turn, Andy's tired ears had to do everything they could to keep up with her dream.

"Okay, so the last thing I remembered was falling off Maizeys back. But then there was a bright light again. But this time the Eagle was flying high in the air and in his massive talons, it held onto a grass sickle. The handheld farm tool was made with a sturdy, smooth wooden handle and was mended together with a sharp golden blade that was shaped like the moon when only a sliver of it is visible during the night. 'It is time,' the Eagle said again. 'For too long have the farmer's grains dwelled among the weeds. It is time for the garden to be weeded, to ready the fields for harvest.' He said, while gliding through the air. Soon, the Eagle came low to the ground and used the grass sickle to slice the weeds at their bases, but the good grain folded over as the sickle passed by them, and then regained its posture. There were a few stalks of grain that wilted and there were stalks of grain that had become entangled tightly with the weeds, and so when the weeds were cut down, some of the good grain was uprooted. The Eagle completed the whole field and all the weeds that had infested the field laid over. The cut weeds and uprooted grain stocks all withered away, but the remaining good stalks of grain stood tall and sturdy," Eva explained. "Then at the head of the field the Great White Eagle lodged the wooden handle of the sickle into the ground. With the golden blade of the sickle high in the air, the Great White Eagle perched himself on the blade. The sharp blade was not sharp enough to pierce the Great White Eagle's callused feet. The Great White Eagle rested overlooking the field. Then! And this is the best part!" Eva shouted. "The Great White Eagle looked right at me and said 'Eva! Keep going, the harvest is yet to come.' Can you believe it? He called me by name!"

Eva was so excited that she hadn't noticed the concerned look on Andy's face. But it wasn't that Eva's dream had confused him. What caused him concern was the exact opposite. Andy had this flood of understanding rush over him. The dream that Eva was so excited about made Andy sick to his stomach. Catching himself he adjusted his look of concern and swapped it out with a smile. He didn't want Eva to know something was wrong. He didn't want her to know what he thought the dream meant but it was too late, Eva had noticed Andy's reaction.

"What's wrong?" she asked.

"It's nothing. But that sounds like a crazy dream."

"Right? I don't know what it means!"

"Yeah, I wonder what it means, have you even weeded a garden before?"

"Well, back home, my mom always had me help with the gardening."

"Well maybe that's what it means?" Andy said although he knew that Eva's childhood had nothing to do with the dream. However, he didn't want to tell Eva what his intuition was telling him.

"If you're feeling better, we should head back now," Andy suggested.

"What? Hold on! Where did Richard and Jessie go?" she said as she stood up and swiveled about the clearing looking for the two brothers. "And the dream. Andrew! The Eagle said, 'keep going.'"

As she began asking questions Andy became nervous. If he had told her that the brothers went to turn themselves in she would not stand for it, and would want to go after them. He knew that if they did that then his friend's bravery would be in vain, because all four would most likely become captured and then she may never be able to be with her parents again. Yet, if he told her that he decided to stay with her, while the brothers continued on without them, he would be lying to her. He scratched his head as tried to decide what to tell her. Eva had grown impatient and she was now standing with her arms crossed. Most of her weight was on one leg and she tapped her foot on the ground.

"Where are Richard and Jessie?"

"They…They went on to the Kettle," Andy blurted.

"Without you? Why would they do that?" she questioned.

"Well, because I decided that I want to go back with you," he admitted.

"Well, that's too bad!"

"What?"

"The Great White Eagle called me by name, and said to keep going!" Eva announced.

"But it's just a dream!" Andy pleaded.

"It's not just a dream. At first I thought it was, but it feels way too real. Like I can feel the Great White Eagle's presence during the dream," she cried. Andy swallowed hard, for he too felt that it was much more than a dream. He remembered how familiar Eva's first dream felt, but this one felt like it was a story he had heard before. Although he had never actually heard such a story, it was like he was supposed to know what it meant.

"Well, even so, what about your parents?" he asked.

Eva paused for a moment. "When we return, they will understand. They are the ones who always told me about the adventures that his followers took. The ones written about in the scrolls. All of those stories were about the Great White Eagle! The same Eagle that is in my dreams!"

"I don't know, Eva."

"You tell me, Andrew. What do good followers of the Great White Eagle do?" Eva questioned.

"They listen to him…," Andy mumbled under his breath.

"That's right! They listen to him!" Eva said boldly.

"So, sneaking away from home and leaving your parents worried sick is something the scrolls would tell you to do?" Andy said, trying to convince her to just go home.

"No, but they do tell us to do what he says, and he told me to keep going!" she snapped back. Andy was quite convinced that she had made up her mind, but because he felt he understood her dream he was nervous. It was because he understood her dream in a way that spoke of dangers that may lay ahead. "Maybe there's a garden near the Kettle," she continued, trying to process the dream herself.

"That's not it!" Andy shouted. The aggressive blurt startled both Eva and the four bears who had been sitting and watching the two interact with each other.

"What do you mean, that's not it?" Eva questioned.

"I mean… It probably doesn't mean that."

"Andrew!" she scolded. Andy turned pale, and his hands had become clammy.

"It's a warning, Eva. A warning of what's to come!" he blurted.

Eva gasped and both of her hands lifted to her face. "Do you mean that you can understand my dreams?" she asked.

Andy then realized what her first dream had meant. 'It is time' echoed in his head. He realized that it was time for the Great White Eagle's return. The scrolls mentioned very little about how he would return but there is much saying that there is no doubt he would return.

Andy felt that all the things that were happening were simple signs that it was true. Eva had gained the ability to receive dreams and to speak all languages, and now, somehow, he seemed to be able to understand her dreams when no one else could.

"Don't you see something big is going to happen," Andy exclaimed

"Big? So what? Don't you trust the Great White Eagle?"

"Not just big Eva! But dangerous!"

"Dangerous? What are you talking about?"

"Eva! Your dream says it all!" Andy exclaimed, but Eva just gave him a strange look. "Your second dream is a warning..."

"What do you mean?"

"Don't you see, The Great White Eagle is using a farming tool to clear the field. The weeds are the evil doers of the land, and the grain stocks are the good ones. If the Eagle does return, he will cut down any evil doers of the land. In the end, the Great White Eagle will rule over the people."

"That sounds like good news to me!" Eva said, not being able to understand her own dream and comprehend the severity of what was to come.

"It would be, but when the Great White Eagle clears the field it represents some sort of great battle that will take place."

"Well, I can see how that wouldn't be good," Eva said, beginning to change her tone. "But the Great White Eagle will win, won't he?" She asked nervously.

"Of course, he will..." Andy said and then hesitated enough for Eva to notice.

"But?" she questioned, waiting for the catch.

"The Great White Eagle will win; he will defeat evil. But just like the good grain that got uprooted in your dream, many evil creatures will uproot the good."

"You mean?" Eva started and gulped.

"Yes, I mean not all good creatures will survive…" Andy said out loud what Eva was thinking. "Do you see now? We could find ourselves in grave danger."

The forest fell quiet. Eva's face went blank and grew pale. The thoughts ran wild in their heads. Without a word, Eva turned around and started walking towards Maizey's den. Then Maizey and her cubs got up and followed her.

Andy wanted to follow her but knew that she needed space. After all, so much was happening and deciding what to do next weighed heavy on both of them.

He thought about how no one had seen or heard from the Great White Eagle in years. *Why now? Is it really the Great White Eagle speaking through Eva? Or is it just a dream? But if it was only a dream, why do I feel so confident about what the dreams mean?* These thoughts danced in his head.

He had so much confidence in his understanding that he had no doubts whatsoever in what the dream meant. It was weird but he believed he was right. Andy was the type of person that always thought deeply about things, he never wanted to say something that might be proved wrong. This was no different, but it was as if there was a magical force, or voice in his head that explained it to him as Eva spoke of her dream.

Andy pondered many things and ultimately felt that whichever choice he made, he was going to let his friends down.

If I continue on, would Richard and Jessie's efforts be in vain? Yet, if I go home, what are the chances that the Pegasus actually leaves us alone? Eva… you think the Great White Eagle is actually talking to you? I mean …you can speak to the beasts, which is crazy, but I see you do it! Then…why would it be that surprising that the Great White Eagle was literally talking to you through a dream?

Andy sat back down, leaning against the great blackwood tree and pondered all these thoughts. The urge to continue on began to burn inside of him. Every time he convinced himself that it was time for them to go home, or that it would be the best option for them, something inside of him told him that was not the right choice for him to make.

Minutes turned into an hour and the wind blew steadily. Clouds began to form overhead, and a gloomy haze overcame the forest. Andy knew that a storm was on its way. As the yellow illumination of the forest faded into a cold blue, then hazy gray, the air became chilled and the wind gusts grew stronger. Andy's skin formed small bumps from the light kiss of rain drops that had now begun to fall.

By the way the clouds were forming he knew he needed to seek shelter. So, he headed for Maizey's den. The soft pitter-patter of rain accompanied the whispers of the wind, causing a rustling of leaves to dance in the forest. Just before Andy reached Maizey's den, the sky lit up with bolts of lightning. The flickers of light startled Andy, for the angry rolling gray clouds, folded and meshed together, creating depth, and causing darker grays and blacks to paint an image in the sky.

When the lightning flashed Andy was surprised to see the Great White Eagle's image imprinted in the clouds. The Eagle's talons looked to be outstretched towards Andy and its head bowed forwards, the way he would look if an eagle were to plunge towards the earth. The Eagle's wings meshed with the remainder of the sky. Then the sky would go dark again and the image would vanish. Thunder began to boom in the distance, taking turns with the lightning. The flashes of light and the powerful grumbles of the sky grew louder and more frequent by the minute. With each flash of lightning, the image grew larger and formed with more of the sky. It was as if each time the sky was illuminated the image slightly changed and was magnified. Finally, the image in the sky was consumed by the aggressive rolling of clouds and the Eagle's portrait vanished. The lightning was still striking and the thunder echoed, but now the rain roared down on Andy. The drops of water pelted him and it fell so heavily that it looked like a literal white wall of water was rushing towards him. Andy's mouth hung open, stunned by the image that had occupied the sky. Finally, the loudest crack of thunder Andy had ever heard sparked his movement and he rushed into the den soaking wet.

The den harbored Andy, Eva, and the bears from the rest of the raging storm. From head to toe, water soaked his hair and his clothes. With each step he took, his shoes let out a faint squeak from being waterlogged. The cold air was now getting to him. Unlike the Gladiator Bears, Andy and Eva did not have thick coats of fur. Eva burrowed her way into Maizeys side and the cubs piled around her. Whereas Andy, still not sure he trusted the bears, stood off to the side and watched out the cave's entrance as the falling rain pelted the ground. He tried to hide from the others how truly cold he was, yet as his soaked clothing began to chill and he began to shiver so much that his teeth chattered. Finally, he couldn't bear the cold any longer.

"Can you ask Maizey if she would be okay if I started a small fire in here to dry off and help us stay warm?" Andy asked Eva.

"Yes, that would be wonderful," Eva cheerfully responded, for she too was growing quite cold.

Eva and Maizey exchanged a few grunts. It must have taken a bit of convincing for Maizey looked a little worried. However, after a few roars and growls Eva confirmed that it was okay for them to start a fire.

"Maizey said it is okay to start a fire, but you must make sure the floor of the den does not light on fire for there are years of dried leaves, twigs, and brush for bedding in here."

Andy nodded and then quickly darted out of the cave. Surprisingly the fresh rain drops felt warm as they crashed down on him. He dashed over to the fallen Blackwood and began snapping off the dead twigs and branches from the tree. Andy knew that although it was raining, his best bet at getting wood dry enough for a fire would be to start with small, dead twigs; the twigs that were sturdy but felt like the cork plug on a bottle of ale, light and dried out. Once his arms became full of damp twigs, he rushed back into the cave.

Now that he had a mission, the cold didn't bother him as much but he knew getting himself dried off was crucial.

Andy plopped to his knees and set the bundle of twigs beside him. Next he cleared away the brush, leaves, and sticks that were layered on the floor of the den until dirt was exposed. Andy then ventured into the rain again until he found nine or ten rocks. He used them to make a ring around the patch of dirt he made.

"This will help keep the fire from spreading to the rest of the den," Andy assured Maizey. By this point, Eva found it easiest to just translate for everyone without being asked too.

Now it was time to build his fire. Using some of Maizey's bedding, Andy piled some of the dried leaves and twigs that had been in Maizey's den; these were dry as dust. He then found a small rock to use as a striker stone, and a larger rock that he would strike the stone against. Using his thumb, he pinched some of the dried leaves to the top of the rock. This way, when he struck it, the sparks would ignite the small patch of kindle and he could use that to ignite the rest of the leaves in the fire ring.

Carefully, he held his fire-starting contraption over his circle of rocks, and began striking the larger stone. Andy had done this many times before so it only took him three strikes to create enough sparks to light the small clump of kindling he was pinching. The flame burst forth and flickered. Knowing that the flame wouldn't last long, Andy let the small clump of burning leaves fall into the pile of leaves on the den's floor. The little flame fell into the heart of the leaf pile and seemed to become smothered. The light from the flame was gone but smoke began to fume out of the leaf pile. Andy leaned down onto his hands and gently began blowing at the base. As his breath weaved through the leaves, it forced oxygen into the smokey pile. Soon, the smoke grew, consuming most of the pile. It twisted and turned its way through the air and escaped out of the den's entrance. Andy continued to fuel the pile with long deep breaths until finally, a flame emerged.

"Quick! Find as many small twigs as you can," Andy said to Eva, as he began to pull small twigs out of the mess that Maizey called her bed.

Andy made a square out of four twigs, each side entrapped the flame. He then continued to build square after square upwards adding new layers to his structure.

"I call this a fire crib," Andy explained. "Because it contains the fire until the fire becomes big enough to get out!"

Soon, the small simple flame had grown and spread outwards towards the fire crib and began devouring the wall of squares. The flame grew higher and the den gradually warmed up. Andy was then able to take the damp twigs and add them to the fire. It was hot enough that the fire dried them completely, allowing them to be consumed by the flame as well. Gradually Andy added larger branches to the fire until it was a healthy fire that would dry them off in no time.

A new light had been given to the cave. As the fire crackled away they all peered about the cave.

A curious growl came from Maizey, and at first the two teenagers had thought that she was amazed by the fire. She was a bear after all, she didn't have a need for fire. However, instead, Maizey nodded towards the back wall.

"Look," Maizey roared at Eva.

Eva swiveled around, and the new source of light had illuminated the den so much that for the first time, Maizey realized that something was on the back wall.

"Are those drawings?" Eva asked, looking at some markings painted on the den's wall.

"Huh! It looks like it!" Andy said. He was intrigued by the drawings but remained by the fire trying to dry his clothing. Eva on the other hand, had stood up and brushed the clinging mulched leaves from her pants and made her way to the back wall of the den. She got to the wall and dropped to her knees, because when she stood, her shadow produced by the flame made it difficult to examine the images on the wall.

"What is it?" asked Andy, who had just started warming up.

"I don't know. But it looks like two boys here," she said while pointing to the drawing on the left side of the wall. Two stick people were drawn side by side. "And these look like two worms?" she questioned while pointing to the image of two squiggly lines to the right of the people. "This one looks like one of the boys killed the other one," she said while looking back at Andy in disgust. "Maybe it's the story of the two brothers from the scrolls?" she suggested. Andy could see why Eva would have thought that because one of the people in this drawing was standing with its arms outstretched, while the other was drawn laid down in the middle of a circle. Just like with the dreams, Andy sensed something about the drawings, but he wasn't quite sure what it had meant yet.

"What else is there?" asked Andy.

"That's it," she said while turning around and returning to the fire, as if her lack of understanding in the drawings caused her to lose interest in them.

Andy, though, stayed very interested in the images. He soon made his way to the back wall, and dragged his fingers along the outlines of the drawings. In the back of Andy's mind, the stick people etched on the wall caused him to see a vision of the two brothers. The only two brothers he really knew, Richard and Jessie. As his fingers traced the squiggly lines of the second image, he realized that they were not worms at all but were rivers. The images on the wall told a story. He senses the first was two brothers, who then followed the second image, a river. *Maybe it's about Richard and Jessie?* Andy thought as he pondered the images. *But this cave is so old and Maizey has lived here for years. Is it a prophecy about Richard and Jessie?*

He arrived at the third image, and thought about what Eva said. It did look like one boy had killed the other, so he could see why Eva thought that, but he wasn't convinced that was the case. It was clear to him that something bad had happened to one of them, but what it was remained a mystery. Andy's head was filled with thoughts and images. *What did all of this mean? I really need to get Eva home. Safe with her parents. But I can't deny that her dream means something. And the Eagle. Was it really him in the clouds before the storm?*

His head was telling him to turn back, but his heart was telling him to continue on to the Devil's Kettle.

Slowly, Andy walked back to the fire. Maizey and her cubs curled up and snored away. Eva leaned into Maizey's side, she rose and fell from the inhale and exhale of the bear's gentle sleep.

Eva patted the ground beside her, the leaves sprung beneath her palm. Andy hesitated but looked at the sleeping bear. *She hasn't hurt Eva… I should be okay.* He thought as he slowly crouched next to Eva and leaned into the bear's side.

Maizey opened one eye to see who it was, then smiled and closed her eyes again.

Andy relaxed, gazed into the crackling fire, and pondered the two choices he had before him. Return to Regnum, or listen to the Great White Eagle.

Chapter 8
Washed Away

Back in the forest, before the storm, Gillian and the brothers had been making their way towards Maizey's den. Gillian was hot on Maizey's trail, following her footprints. Gillian had been smart, instead of letting the boys in on his tracking tactic, he just told them that they needed to head south to reach the Devil's Kettle. So, in turn, they were just happy that their plan seemed to be working.

The soft patter of rain whispered as it tapped the leaves of the forest, the wind would blow and the trees shivered. Soon it began to rain harder. A cold front overtook the forest and the boys knew they needed to find shelter. But to their dismay they could see nothing in sight. There were no caves, no holes in the ground, or even a hollowed tree. Nothing that the two could crawl into for safe harbor. Richard untied his plaid shirt from around his waist and stretched his arms through the sleeves to try and stay warm, but it was in vain. Their shirts quickly grew damp and they began to shiver. Gillian began to notice just how cold the boys were, so he swiveled his head looking for anything that he and the boys could use for shelter, but he too could find nothing.

The rain drops swelled in size, thunder barked and the lighting began to flicker violently.

"Get under my wings," Gillian said as he settled down to his knees. His great big wings spread out creating a canopy. The tops of his feathers caused the rain to bead up and run off, leaving the ground beneath untouched by the falling rain.

"Why should we trust you?" spouted off Richard. Both boys stood staring at the Pegasus as water ran down their faces and their clothes could no longer take on any new water because they were already soaked through.

"Why would I harm you? If I wanted to do that, I would just leave you out here exposed to the storm. Your tiny human bodies wouldn't last ten minutes in this rain," Gillian said.

Soon the white wall of water pounded its way towards the three, and the boys no longer had a choice. They rushed towards Gillian, making it under his wings just in time. If they had waited any longer they would have been overwhelmed by the flood of down pouring water. Gillian wrapped his wings tightly, sandwiching the brothers between his wings and his body. Immediately the boys could feel the warmth of the Pegasus. The combination of Gillian's body heat and insulation of his waterproof feather's gave the brothers a sense of comfort.

Outside Gillian weathered the storm with the two boys safely under his wings. As the rain beat against Gillian's body, his ears laid pinned back and his eyes closed. He could not hear anything over the roar of the thunder, the pounding of rain, and the gusts of wind that howled around him.

"Can you believe this?" Jessie whispered.

"No! Why would he help us?" Richard questioned.

"Maybe some Royal Pegasi really do want what's best for us?"

The boys were completely shocked. They had never respected the royal cavalry. All Pegasi were the same to them. Rude and pushy, yet this one was different. Gillian was sacrificing himself to the storm to protect the brothers. He was helping them, even though they were the ones that had gotten him into so much trouble. This act of kindness from Gillian, caused a flood of great respect to flow over the boys. They still couldn't completely trust him, but it wouldn't be fair to say that trust hadn't begun to grow between the beast and the two brothers. Richard and Jessie began to wonder, *maybe this beast does really want to make sure everyone stays safe.* The boys understood that the Pegasus had a job to do. To uphold order. However, it was becoming evident that this particular Pegasus seemed to be willing to do everything he could to help them, as well as uphold his duties as a Royal Pegasus Guard.

The storm continued nonstop for at least two hours, but Jessie and Richard remained dry under the umbrella that was Gillian's large wings. Gillian really thought nothing of the storm. He was chilled but he had been conditioned to various weather climates. Being a Royal Guard of the Forbidden Circle did require him to stand guard under all-weather circumstances. Because of this, he was able to maintain enough body heat that the downpour was more of an inconvenience than it was a problem.

Finally, the heavy rain subsided and all that was left was water droplets rolling off of the leaves in the canopy above. Gillian raised his body and stretched out his wings. The boys felt a rush of cold meet their skin and could smell the scent of freshness that lingered in the post rain air. Gillian held his wings straight out to hold any water from falling off onto the boys and trotted off to the side. Once he was clear of the boys, he shook his body and his wings so that all the rainwater jumped off of him in every direction.

"Kind of looks like a big dog with wings," Jessie snickered towards Richard.

"What now?" Richard asked. He wasn't about to waste any more time. The downpour left him feeling odd. It was as if the adventure had become real all of a sudden. He realized that there was no shelter for him and his brother, and that being caught in such storms could be dangerous for them. *To think we have to rely on him?* he thought. Richard would have never admitted it, but after the storm, he had hoped that Gillian would want to turn back.

"We continue on," Gillian ordered without hesitation, causing Richard to slouch his shoulders in disappointment. Gillian trotted over to the last place he had seen the bear's paw prints.

"No, no, no!" Gillian shouted, as he paced back and forth frantically looking for the trail. To Gillian's dismay the paw prints had vanished.

"What is it?" asked Jesse.

"The tracks! The bear's tracks! They're gone!" Gillian started.

"Maizey?" Richard curiously asked.

"Yes! That… *Beast!* I was following her paw prints. But the rain washed the tracks away," Gillian said distraught. The boys looked at each other with big eyes. They had not realized that Gillian was following Maizey's trail in the first place. That new detail to their adventure meant that they were headed right towards Maizey's den. In fact, now that the boys thought about it, they were not very far away from her den at all.

Gillian was not defeated though; he had known that so far the trail had brought him straight south. So, he was determined to continue on that way, in hopes that he would find the bear.

The boys did everything they could to try and redirect Gillian. However, they knew it was important for them to be careful, because if they pressed him too harshly, he would be able to sense that they were trying to hide something.

"If we go this way, we can lead the way," Richard said.

Gillian looked at the younger brother. "What do you mean?" he asked.

"He means that when we came to turn ourselves in, we came from that direction. So, we have already seen that part of the woods and can easily navigate it," Jessie explained, trying to get Gillian to leave his intended course. Unfortunately, Gillian never slowed his pace, even with the efforts of the boys.

"That may be," Gillian said, "but we are headed to the Devil's Kettle, and the kettle is south!" he announced sternly. Gillian was disappointed that he lost the bear's trail, however his mission was to find the other two teenagers. Those teenagers had allegedly gone to the Devil's Kettle. So, with or without the bear's tracks, Gillian was headed south.

The boys didn't know what to do, but knew they needed to remain calm. If they acted at all differently, the Pegasus would know that he was close. Soon, the three of them made their way into the clearing that stood off to the side of Maizey's den. The rain had washed away the tracks and the wind brushed the forest floor so that any disturbed leaves had been displaced and looked natural. So, there was nothing to indicate that Maizey had actually been there. This left Gillian clueless that he had found the exact location of Maizey's den.

Something about the clearing gave Gillian an odd feeling and stirred his interest. So, he decided to examine it closely. His hot pursuit decreased to a soft, cautious walk as he made his way across this opening in the forest. Then he came to a stop. He lifted his head high into the air and looked around the forest, observing it carefully. He was either trying to spot any sign of the other two, or trying to decide which direction to head next. The boys could not tell which.

The brothers grew nervous, each direction Gillian looked they could see the events that happened only hours ago. The puddle was where they soaked the Blackwood leaf for Eva's headache. To the right of the clump of trees was where they followed Maizey to her den, and behind them now, was where they stood when they departed from Andy. The brothers' palms grew sweaty and their skin felt cold.

Gillian was so close to finding Andy and Eva that he might as well have been standing on them. Panic grew in their heart, because if Gillian found them, all four teenagers would be doomed. *Don't make a sound! Don't make a sound!* Jessie shouted silently in his head, as if he hoped Andy or Eva could hear his thoughts and would remain quiet and out of sight in the den because of his warning.

"Should we keep heading south?" Jessie tried to ask in a way that seemed genuine.

"Yeah, we should keep going, besides we don't wanna be out here in the dark, do we?" Richard said softly.

Dark? That thought never crossed Gillian's mind. Venturing into the forbidden circle was one thing but trying to survive the night with all these beasts crawling around would be a whole other something.

"Take it from us," Jessie said. "It's no picnic out here at night."

Oh boy… the night in this untamed land. Would we even survive? Gillian thought. *What to do…?* Gillian slowly walked over to the water hole to get a drink. Trying to decide what to do next, he lowered his head to the water. However, he noticed something strange. The water had begun to ripple. As he looked closer, the surface of the water would shiver and then settle back to a smooth surface. Then it would ripple again, and settle. Each time the water was disturbed the ripples became bigger and bigger.

As Gillian wondered what could be causing such a disturbance, Jessie and Richard had already figured it out. The boy's eyes opened wide, and they both sucked in air, like they were going to scream at the top of their lungs. But the boys found no sound, instead they just looked at each other, grabbed each other's shoulders, jumped up and down a couple times with their mouths hanging wide open and bolted. Before they knew it they were headed south straight towards the Devil's Kettle.

"Hey guys, check this out! I wonder what's causing the water to…" Gillian said, as he began to look over his shoulder for the boys. However, the boys were gone. Soon he swiveled around and began shouting for the boys. Quickly he had eyes on the boys and could see them off in the distance.

Running away? Gillian thought at first, but then he began to feel the ground start to shake. As he turned around he could see something massive barreling its way towards him.

At first Gillian froze, he couldn't find the strength to run. A large brown beast bellowed and bared its teeth as it headed straight for him.

Another Gladiator! Gillian thought these words but the only real sound that came out of his mouth was a high pitch, "Ah!"

Naturally his wings lifted for flight, but Gillian soon remembered that flying in a forest would be no use. Not taking his eyes off the bear racing towards him, Gillian folded his wings tightly to his body. Finally, he grasped the ability to turn tail and run like he had never run before.

Gillian could tell that it wasn't the same bear as before because this one made Maizey look small. This massive Gladiator Bear thrashed its way towards the clearing. It had three large scars plastered across its face. They each looked similar to Gillian's *Noble Mark*, but were real scars. Presumably from a fight the bear had found itself in sometime before.

Luckily for Gillian, the bear only crashed through the clearing far enough to scare him and the brothers off. However, once they had escaped the bear's sight, he returned to the clearing.

Chapter 9
A Change in Plans

Andy and Eva followed timidly behind Maizey as she poked her head out of her den and made her way into the clearing. The commotion from outside seconds before alarmed her and she decided to investigate.

Andy and Eva's eyes grew wide as they peered upon the second Gladiator bear. He was so much bigger than Maizey, who was already considered massive to the two tiny humans. However, they remained calm because it was clear these two bears knew each other. Calmly the two bears waddled over to each other, as they became nose to nose, they both reared up onto their hind legs. This new bear stood at least two feet taller than Maizey and his fur was a darker brown. His snout on the other hand, had faded into a lighter gray, indicating that he was older. A closer look showed that not only did he have three slashes across his face, but most of his right ear was missing as well. He had seen more than one fight in his lifetime.

The two exchanged growls for a moment and then plopped back down to all fours again. Resting on the larger bear's side, near his fore shoulder, was what looked to be a pouch that had been deer hide stitched together by thin leather straps. In addition, there was a thick leather strap that was used as a sling and kept the strap at the bear's side. *That is quite strange, a bear wearing a purse?* Andy thought. Either way, this purse, or pouch, or whatever you want to call it, allowed the bear to carry things around as he navigated the forest.

Maizey looked at the two and started communicating with Eva, then Eva translated for Andy. "This is her husband Koden. He will bring us no harm. Maizey explained to her husband that we are friends and can understand them," Eva continued as Maizey growled.

Soon, Andy felt one of the cubs dart past his leg, then another cub brushed Eva's, and finally, the last cub busted through; almost taking Andy and Eva off their feet.

All three barreled toward Koden and pounced on him. Though the three cubs stood no chance against their father, he rolled over backwards as if the cubs had taken him down. The two teenagers stood in silence as they watched the cubs play with their father. One cub flew this way, then another went that way and then they all darted circles around Koden. Koden rose to his hindlegs and let out a weird roar. To Andy, as weird as it sounds, it sounded as if it was a sarcastic roar. Similar to when someone from back home would say, *"Oh no, you got me!"* The short snorts of the cubs and their playful manner made the damp forest feel warmer than it had before.

Their playfulness settled and Koden made his way towards Andy and Eva now that he was in no hurry and seemed to waddle as he walked. His big rear end swayed back and forth. As he stood towering over the two teenagers, he looked to Eva.

"What brings you into the forbidden circle?"

"Well, um… We wanted to see the Devil's Kettle," Eva answered. Her response looked to have shocked Koden, for his eye grew wide and his body shifted backwards while his nose lifted slightly into the air.

"The Kettle? Don't you know that the legend says once you fall in you never return?"

"Well, yes of course we know the legend! We had planned to head home… You see, my parents are back at Regnum and must be worried sick," Eva explained. "But then I had a dream, where the Great White Eagle told me to keep going… frankly, I don't know what to do!"

"Well, clearly you are a Somniator. So, you must receive dreams as well?" Koden said.

"How did you know?"

"Well, for one, you're talking to a bear… and believe it or not but you are not the first Somniator that I have encountered… So far every Somniator I have met has had dreams of some sort."

"So, do my dreams really mean something? They are not just dreams, but actually messages from the Great White Eagle?" Eva asked, building confidence in her case.

"Oh yes. Somniators receiving dreams are as common as it is for them to speak all languages. Too bad you don't know a Reader."

"You mean someone who understands my dreams?"

"Yeah, like a dream reader. They are called Lectors."

"Well actually, I think Andy can understand them. But he doesn't think we should continue on, he says what lies ahead is very dangerous," She said, while turning towards Andy. This made Andy uncomfortable for now everyone's attention was on him. Eva had yet to translate anything, so he just stood there confused listening to the various growls, roars, and bellows. He felt very awkward and sometimes questioned his sanity.

"Wow! A Somniator and a Lector together! I haven't seen this since… How long has it been?" Koden asked, looking back at Maizey.

"It's been at least one hundred years. We were merely cubs," she replied. Eva was shocked, Maizey didn't look to be one hundred years old.

"Long before King Fraust. There used to be all sorts of Somniators and Lectors. That's how our fathers lived in harmony with each other. Everyone could understand each other because of the dreamers and the readers," explained Koden.

"So, that's how it was when the Great White Eagle flew in our very sky?" asked Eva.

"Well actually, according to my father," Koden started, "Somniators never came about until after the Great White Eagle vanished. While the Great White Eagle was here, he communicated with a peacekeeper who kept the peace among the land, Henry Adams was his name. Unfortunately, something happened. Henry and the Great White Eagle grew apart. After the Great White Eagle left, Henry Adams lost communication with him. Years went by and eventually Somniators began to show up to pick up Henry Adam's slack. This was now the new and only way for all creatures to communicate with each other. Like your dreams, that's how the Great White Eagle spoke to his followers. He used Somniators to share their dream, and then the Lectors could tell the rest of the creatures what they meant."

"So, I'm like a messenger?" Eva marveled.

"You could say that. But what I do know is that what you and Andy have are real gifts, you should be thankful to have. It seemed that when Malus became a significant ruler of the land, the Somniators and Lectors went extinct."

"Why do you think that is?" Eva asked.

"No one really knows, and we haven't been able to communicate with other creatures for years," Koden explained.

Eva took a moment to catch Andy up on all this information. Many questions flooded his head. "How did his father learn of these things?" Andy asked. Eva turned to Koden and repeated the question in Gladiator bear's tongue.

"When my father was younger there was still an abundant number of Somniators and Lectors keeping peace. It was over two hundred years ago that my father served with the Elves, and he served them for over sixty years." Koden explained.

"Whoa!" Eva marveled.

"In fact, Maizey's father served right alongside my father," Koden said.

"That's awesome!" Eva said.

"There was peace between all creatures for almost five hundred years, but that all changed around one hundred seventy-five years ago."

"Oh no… What happened?"

"The Somniators slowly began disappearing, and so did our peace and understanding. For forty years, small bursts of violence arose. Spurts of raids and riots flooded our planes. Only a handful of Sominators held onto the little bit of peace we had left."

"That sounds terrible…" Eva said solemnly.

"It gets worse. After those forty years, our leader, the High Elf Timmins, was killed in battle. He was the last stronghold for peace. He worked harder than anyone else to keep the peace. But with him gone, chaos spread. Creature against beast, man versus Elf, Dwarves and Centaurs, it was a brutal time with no sense of peace in sight."

"All because us Somniators disappeared?"

"Basically. High Elf Timmins was the glue that held the Beasts and the Elves together. We were the greatest force in all the land. No one stood a chance against us, and High Elf Timmins sought peace among all creatures. With our combined forces we could make sure that happened. However, he was met with a grave fate," explained Koden.

"That's too bad. Could you imagine a world where we all lived together. That would be amazing. Plus, it's so sad to think of all who died because of it... Like Maizey's father. That must have been a terrible thing to see."

"It really was. But one good thing came of it."

"There was?"

"Yes! That is how Maizey and I met."

"Really?"

"Absolutely! Maizey's father, Samson, was a very loyal comrade of my father's. When Samson was wrongfully killed, my father took my siblings and I, along with Maizey, into Terribbia where we could be safe."

"Wow, all this was 200 years ago?" Eva asked.

"Well not quite. I was born near the beginning of the Babble Wars; I still have fifty good years ahead of me!" Koden said.

"And we were just cubs at the time, not much older than my three boys here!" Maizey added in.

"Wait, so how old are you?" Eva asked

"I'm one hundred thirty-three!" Koden said proudly.

At this point, Andy had made himself comfortable upon the forest floor and had been tearing up leaves out of boredom for he had no clue what anyone was growling about. Eventually Eva took a moment to catch Andy up with all the new information she had learned from Koden.

"I wonder if we should turn ourselves into the King. That way we can communicate with all creatures! Maybe that's what the dream meant? Maybe the Eagle wants to use us to bring peace to the regions? We can weed out the issues!" Eva said, while feeling useful.

Andy's face cringed, for he knew that was not what her dream had meant. He could feel that a great battle lay ahead, and that it had something to do with the Devil's Kettle and the Great White Eagle. On top of all that, he had a funny feeling about the king. He ruled by the law... which was his law, it seemed cruel but at least he lived by it. However, the king seemed more interested in keeping order than keeping peace. *If we go to the king, would he even care to bring peace amongst the regions?*

"Ask what the Koden thinks about us turning ourselves in," Andy asked Eva.

Eva turned and looked at the two bears. "Do you think that we should turn ourselves into the King?"

The bear's looked at each other as they were trying to decide what to say. Finally, Koden spoke up. "That's an interesting question. When the Great White Eagle reigned over the land, there were no Kings, not even regions, only a Peacekeeper and all creatures roamed freely. The Eagle was the compass for all the creature's direction. He had direct communication with his chosen Peacekeeper and the Peacekeeper guided all creatures. However, when the Great White Eagle disappeared, the Peacekeepers slacked off and Malus took command over. He introduced kings, and divided the land into the regions we have today."

"You mean Malus appointed King Adams the first? And King Ezra? And King Fraust?" Eva asked. There were many other kings, but those were the ones most talked about in school.

"Yes, all the different kings of Regnum, the Speaker of the Dwarves, as well as the High Elf Rundo that ordered Samson to be murdered. He even appointed an overseer for the Centaurs. The only creatures unruled are the Beasts of Terribbia," explained Koden.

"Do you think Malus is bad?" Eva questioned.

"Well, do you think that all the leaders that Malus has appointed have been good and carried out justice?" asked Koden.

"Well, I mean there is a lot that I disagree with, but that doesn't necessarily mean that they are evil," cautiously stated Eva. She thought about the King's she learned about in school, and the more she thought about them the more she realized that they only talked about them because of what they were famous for. In most cases it was not for good things.

Eva's heart felt heavy, she wasn't sure what the right thing to do was. She missed her parents, but she felt that the Great White Eagle was commanding her to carry onward to the Devil's Kettle through her dream. *But could I really bring peace to all creatures, should I trust that the King will use my gift for good?*

She took a moment to catch Andy up again, hoping that he would have some sort of idea or direction for them. She had a comfortable trust in him and knew that he had their best interest at heart.

"I don't have a good feeling about the King…Or Malus. If the Great White Eagle wanted to cut down evil, why didn't he choose the King to receive the message? You are just… well in Royal terms a peasant," Andy said. His statement seemed to offend Eva for her mouth opened and her eyebrows slanted sharply towards her nose. "Eva, you know what I mean, we are just common folk. Why wouldn't the Great White Eagle try to reach out to someone with the power to easily change the world? Unless the ones with power are the evil ones?" questioned Andy.

"Maybe I am the only Somniator left?" Eva blurted as if proving that she was important to the mission.

"I mean, maybe… but that could prove to be dangerous for you as well. Besides who gave you the gift? The Great White Eagle! So, if he gave you the gift, couldn't he have given it to anyone he wanted?" Andy softly replied.

"I guess, that makes sense. But if the King and Malus are both bad, why would they even want to protect all creatures from the Devil's Kettle? After all the legend says, 'If you fall in you never return.' Sounds to me like the King is concerned with our safety," Eva continued.

"That is true, but I'm just not sure what the right answer is," Andy said gloomily. Unfortunately, Andy didn't provide any useful direction for Eva. She felt all the more uncertain in what direction to go.

Before she could think too heavily on her options, Koden had sat back on his rump and rotated his pouch from his side to in front of him on his chest. He then started digging around inside the pouch and seemed to be wrestling with something inside of it. Soon, a few fish fell to the forest floor. Koden's big paws made it very difficult to grab the slimy fish.

"Shall we go inside and eat? You must be very hungry?" Maizey asked before picking up one of the fish with her mouth. Koden picked up another with his mouth, one of the cubs picked up another and the last two cubs both grabbed the same one and carried it to their den together. Eva and Andy both looked at the final fish laying on the ground.

"We can't eat raw fish!" Eva said.

"No, but don't worry we can cook it over the fire," Andy explained, as he picked up the fish by its gill. The two walked back towards the den. Once inside, Andy went to work cooking the fish as best he could. The fire that he started when the rain came, still had life to it but was beginning to dwindle. While Eva sat back wondering what to do about their adventure, Andy began to prepare their fish. First he gathered a few more sticks and branches and laid them on the fire to bring life back to the suffering flame. Then Andy took the larger rock that he originally used to start the fire with and set it in the center of the flame. The plop of the rock smothered the fire, but the coals were hot enough that the fire reignited seconds later and the flames danced around the rock. Andy took the fish over to Maizey. He put out his hand palm-up towards Maizey. She looked at Andy with her head slightly cocked, then leaned forwards and sniffed Andy's hand. Andy then laughed because he wanted to see her paw, not for her to sniff his hand. He reached out and gently grabbed her paw. Maizey was unsure of what Andy wanted, but she hesitantly let him direct her paw. Once her paw was out in front of her, Andy pointed at her razor-sharp claws and then pointed at the fish. Maizey then realized that Andy was asking her to use her claws to help filet their fish. She nodded and accompanied her motions with a soft growl indicating that she understood him. Andy picked the fish up and ran his finger along its back, starting just behind the gills slightly offset from the dorsal fin and motioned back towards the tail. Then he gave it to Maizey. Using her sharp claw, she extracted the meat from the fish. Andy was quite impressed with her precision. Once both slabs of meat had been separated from the fish, Andy took the two slabs back to the fire. Maizey offered Andy the remainder of the fish but he shook his head no, politely declining the fish's carcass. For Maizey it was a delicious treat that she gobbled down quickly. As the fire died down, short flames crackled away, however the important part was the red-hot coals that remained. They had properly heated up the rock Andy placed in the heart of the fire. He laid the slabs of meat down on top of the rock, making sure that the side of the slabs with scales was face down; He didn't want the meat to stick to the rock. As the slabs of meat touched the heated stone, the meat began to sizzle.

He waited until the scales of the fish began to turn black against the rock, and for the meat of the fish to become opaque. While the fish was cooking on the hot stone, Andy asked Eva to translate to the cubs to go get him two Blackwood leaves. The three cubs scurried out of the den, and soon returned with two large leaves. Andy grabbed the leaves from the cubs and then handed one to Eva. She must have looked at him strangely, for he had to explain that she could use it as a plate.

Soon, the slabs of meat had been cooked enough, so Andy with nimble fingers, quickly reached over the fire and pinched one of the fish flanks. Lifting it from the stone he wasted no time laying it on Eva's leaf plate. Then he grabbed his. As they sat staring at their meals waiting for it to cool, Eva began to think about all the good that she could do if she was given the chance to help all the regions communicate. She could bring peace and understanding, she could show everyone that the terrible beasts of Terribbia were not so terrible at all. The Great White Eagle said to continue on in her dream, and she was confident that didn't mean to go home. She was certain now that the Great White Eagle would use her for good, as long as she followed his directions.

Andy began to eat his fish, holding onto the edges. He arched the meat upwards like a bridge and pulled meat off in small chunks with his teeth. Eva followed suit. Once they both finished their meal Eva knew she had to tell Andy what she had decided.

"We must go to the Devil's Kettle as the Eagle has instructed, but then I think we should turn ourselves into the King. If there is any chance that I could make a difference and bring peace and understanding to all the regions, we should," Eva explained. Andy turned pale and swallowed hard. He knew that her dream was important and that it seemed that the Great White Eagle had chosen them, but he had a feeling of anxiety rush over his being. He knew deep down that Eva was right about continuing on.

"I will go with you to the Devil's Kettle, but I don't think I trust the King. He might use you for good, but what good am I to the King? To him, I've only broken his law, what if he has me killed?" Andy responded. The thought of anything happening to Andy made Eva sick to her stomach. She knew that she couldn't bear the thought of him being killed because of something she made him do.

"Okay, we will go to the Devil's Kettle but after that, I will see the King on my own," Eva assured him.

Andy was hopeful that on their journey to the Devil's Kettle, he could convince her not to go and see the King. His gut was telling him that the King was not as good of a ruler as he portrayed himself to be.

"We are going to go to the Devil's Kettle," Eva explained to Maizey

"Really? I must warn you not to go! Even the beasts of Terribbia will not go there."

"We have to, the Great White Eagle told me in a dream. You believe in him don't you?"

"Well of course I do! But your journey will be dangerous. All the legends speak of a mysterious hole that is known as the Devil's Kettle. Lost souls that haunt the waters, wicked creatures that inhabit the swampy land, and of secrets that the Devil's Kettle holds."

Although these words from Maizey were alarming, Eva was determined to press on. "Even still, I believe the Eagle wants us to go."

"Well, if you insist. I will accompany you to the edge of Uada Hollow, but after that we must part ways for I do not dare venture into that haunted bog."

"Thank you Maizey, when you are ready we will go," Eva informed her friend.

Maizey and Koden exchanged a few growls and then the three cubs crawled all over Maizey. The teenagers knew that that was their way of hugging their mama goodbye. Eva nodded to Andy, expressing that she was ready to head out. Andy retrieved a large stick, in which he used to stir what was left of the fire. He stirred it until all the sticks large enough to support a flame had been busted up and the flames had been extinguished. The glowing embers crackled and sparked, as

Andy used his hands to sprinkle dirt over the fire, smoke rose and the orange glow became smothered.

"Eva, can you tell them to make sure they watch the fire. To make sure it doesn't reignite. If it does, they can put more dirt over it… Also, tell them after a day they can cover it up with more bedding!" Andy said, "Oh and tell them, thank you!" he continued.

"Of course," Eva said, while she giggled at Andy's continuous verbal train of thought.

As she relayed the message, Andy made his way out of the den into the clearing. The crisp air filled his lungs as the cold wet leaves on the ground painted his exposed big toe and edges of his shoes with cold water from the previous cloudburst.

Koden followed Andy into the clearing, lifting his nose high into the air, he took in large whiffs of air and then let the air out in forceful snorts. He began to move around the clearing in a large circle motion and lowered his nose to the ground again sniffing rapidly this way and that. Andy just stood back and watched. He could tell that Koden had smelt something, but Andy, only being human, could not smell near as well as a great Gladiator bear could. Soon, Eva had made her way beside Andy in the clearing.

"What is he doing?" she asked Andy.

"I don't know, but it looks like he smells something," Andy said.

Eva roared towards Koden.

"What are you doing?"

"When I first returned home, there were three intruders in our clearing," explained Koden.

"Intruders?" growled Eva.

"Yes, and their scent is one that I have not smelled for years. The scent of a Royal Pegasus." He roared while beginning to expose his teeth in anger.

Eva translated to Andy what Koden had said.

"The Royal Guard!" Andy shouted, "Koden said there were three intruders. What were the other two? More guards?"

Eva asked Koden Andy's questions. At this time Koden with his nose pressed to the ground, quickly swayed his head back and forth as if conveying the ground for a scent. He began walking towards Andy and soon intruded upon Andy's personal space. Koden's nose led him right to Andy and he began sniffing up Andy's leg and all around his person, until he suddenly stopped moving. Koden's snout was only inches away from Andy's chest. Koden sucked in a large sniff and then let out a bellow that Eva understood. Andy knew by the terrified face that Eva had made that something wasn't right.

"What is it?" Andy asked Eva.

Eva's hazel green eyes began to fill with fear and her soft smile faded into a frown.

"The guard has Richard and Jessie," Eva said, panicked.

"What?" Andy questioned. Although he knew that the brothers had planned to turn themselves in, he was surprised that they would have come this way. He had hoped that the guard would have taken them back and that he and Eva would be clear to return home safely. It looked now that none of the boys, neither Andy nor the brothers, were following the original set plan.

"The Royal Pegasus has them! Koden said the two other creatures in the clearing had a familiar scent to yours," Eva cried. Andy realized that Koden had smelt Richard's compass around his neck. He reached up and grabbed the compass through his shirt.

"I know that the guard has them, but why are they down here?" Andy blurted uncontrollably. Eva's eyes grew wide.

"What do you mean… You *know*?" asked Eva angrily. Andy had realized that he said too much. His jaw dropped wide, and he quickly clasped his hands over his mouth. He gazed at Eva, who had become furious.

"What have you done!" she yelled, as she smacked Andy on the arm in a distraught tantrum. Andy could now see the sparkle of her hazel green eyes begin to fade as if storm clouds were stirring up within, and he became embarrassed that he had ever lied to her in the first place. He slowly pulled out Richard's compass, and Eva's jaw dropped.

"What are you doing with Richard's compass?" she asked.

"Eva, you have to understand! We are all sorry!" Andy busted. "We never meant for you to get hurt or for any of this to happen!" Andy was distraught. All the emotions he had been feeling had bottled up. Everything began to explode before his eyes. The secret plan to protect Eva blew up and only hurt her more, there was such a burden of stress pressing down on his chest, and the decisions he felt he had to make seemed to make his head hurt. He began blubbering about how sorry he was for all of it. Sorry that he convinced her to go on the adventure, sorry that her parents would be at home worried sick about her, sorry that she was having these dreams, sorry that she had fallen off Maizey and hit her head, and sorry that he didn't tell her about their plan to get her home safely.

"Calm down! Calm down!" Eva said in a hushed voice. Andy's odd outburst was stirring up the clearing. The bears became frightened because they could tell Andy's emotions were elevated but didn't know what he was saying, and feared that he was upset with them.

"Please start from the beginning, tell me exactly what happened," Eva said gently.

Andy took a deep breath and held it in a little longer than usual and then slowly let it out. "When you hit your head," he started, "Richard, Jessie, and I all realized that this adventure was becoming more dangerous than we had ever thought it would have been. We all wanted to see the Devil's Kettle but we also knew that you missed your parents." Eva looked at the ground, remembering that she did in fact miss her parents dearly. "We would do anything to see our parents again, and we never want to see you go through what we have and are going through without our parents. We realized that we have to get you home," Andy said while looking at his feet.

Eva reached out and put her hand on Andy's shoulder. "Oh Andy, why didn't we all just turn back and go home together then?" she asked.

"We knew that the guard wasn't going to let us get away that easily. So, I volunteered to turn myself in. Like maybe he would take one of us and let the others go, if we promised him that none of us would ever speak of it again," he responded.

"Andy, why would you even think about doing that? We could have found another way," she cried out.

"What other way?" he asked looking back at Eva. "Richard and Jessie made their choice to go instead of me. Since they are almost eighteen, they would have been forced to serve the King or join his army anyways. With their mom gone, and no plans for their future, they went to give themselves up so we would have a chance." He looked down at the compass hanging around his neck. "He gave me this," He said as he wrapped his hand around the compass making a fist. "He said he would rather me have it than for the Royal guards. But our plan was that when they turned themselves in, they were to convince the Guard to go back to the Regnum. But obviously that hasn't happened… But why?" he questioned, gazing off into the forest trying to think of the reason why they would have come back south toward the Devil's Kettle.

"Do you think the Guard wouldn't take *just* them? Now he is looking for us too?" asked Eva.

"That's the only thing I can think of… But why wander aimlessly this way?" Andy pondered for a moment but then realized why. "Wait a minute! That's brilliant!"

"What is?" Eva questioned.

"Richard and Jessie knew that my half of the plan was to return back home as soon as possible. So…That's why they lead the guard south!" Andy said more joyfully.

"That is pretty smart. But now I see why you did what you did. I'm still mad. But it's pretty sweet of you to worry about me," Eva said, as her cheeks blushed. "But we can't go back now! Not after my dream."

"Eva… our journey, if we continue to the Devil's Kettle, will be dangerous. We might not survive. You understand what that means right. Dead, gone, KAPOOie!" Andy said while recalling his interpretation of Eva's dream. "Maybe we should go home after all. If the Pegasus has Richard and Jessie and their plan is to buy us more time to get away, then their sacrifice will be for nothing."

"No way!" Eva snapped back at Andy. "I appreciate that you wanted to save me, but there's no way I will let our friends go down for something we all did together! So, we are either going to save them and all try to escape, or we will all be taken captive by the Royal Pegasus TOGETHER!"

"That's exactly why we weren't going to tell you, because we knew you wouldn't stand for it," Andy said as he rolled his eyes.

"That's right, I won't stand for it! We are going to the Devil's Kettle like the Great White Eagle said to do in my dream, and we *are* going to rejoin Richard and Jessie, even if it means we all get caught!" she commanded. Suddenly to Eva, Andy's stare became blank, but for Andy images flooded his head.

The harvest from Eva's dream played out in his mind. Flashes of what they might encounter if they continued on, monsters and creatures of the night. But then, the three images drawn on the back of Maizey den came into his mind. For some reason, when he thought about them, the simple stick people began to morph and change into moving images of Richard and Jessie.

"You're right!" he blurted as he snapped back into reality. "We have to save Richard and Jessie!"

"I'm right?" Eva asked, expecting more of a fight from Andy.

"The cave drawings, they tell a story," Andy explained.

"The drawings in Maizey's den? I thought they were just random drawings done by someone a long time ago."

"No, they tell of two people that followed one of the Great Rivers to the Devil's Kettle, but only one of them returned! What if the cave drawings are like your dream? What if it is something that has yet to happen? What if it's about two brothers that go to the Devil's kettle and only one returns?" he panicked.

"You mean… Richard and Jessie?" Eva cried.

"You know what the legend says, if one of them falls in they will never come back!" Andy said with fear painted on his face.

"We can't let that happen! We have to go now!" Eva exclaimed. She translated to Maizey their urgency to get going, who in turn must have told her cubs to behave, for they all plopped on their rears while she roared at them, and they all nodded in agreement. Koden said his final goodbye to Maizey and then approached Eva. He began to wiggle and squirm until he was able to get the pouch that was slung around his body to come off. It could have wrapped around Eva five times, which is exactly what she did. She knew Koden wanted her to have it. So, she retrieved it from the ground, looped the strap around herself five times and put the pouch off to her side.

Before they knew it the three were headed south towards the Devil's Kettle.

Chapter 10
Who's Truth is Truth?

Gillian slowed his gallop into a trot, and then back to a walk. He looked over his shoulder towards the direction that the furious bear had ambushed them from. There was no sight of the bear, only two very tired looking boys running towards him trying to catch up. As the boys stumbled to Gillian's side, they both stooped over. Placing their hands on their knees, breathing so heavily they almost screeched with each breath. Jessie finally stood up straight, putting one of his hands on his hip, still trying to catch his breath.

"Do you... *inhale*...think... *inhale*... we lost him?" Jessie coughed out.

Gillian glanced over the tops of the brothers' heads into the forest, looking for any sign of movement from the bear. He could see only the mighty blackwood trees standing still, and rays of golden light peeking through the tree canvas. It was quiet once again and he could relax some.

"I think we did," Gillian said. Richard, who had still been bent over, felt exhausted. Soon he leaned his weight back onto his heels and let himself fall onto his butt, and then his body flung backwards, while his hands went out straight over his head. He came to rest with all his limbs stretched out in every direction, laying on a grassy patch.

Gillian continued to scan the forest in case he had missed anything, but he began to notice that the blackwood trees looked to be becoming more distant in relation to one another. The sea of dead leaves looked more like small bodies of water now, because there were patches of luscious green grass scattered here and there throughout the forest. Each patch had little yellow flowers that poked out just above the tips of grass. It seemed now that the whole forest had a yellow tint to it, even the great trunks of the trees seemed to glow golden yellow from the water residue that clung to their sides which reflected the sun's rays.

Finally, the boys had caught their breath. "I haven't run like that since that time we put a cow pie in Mr. Svend's mailbox," Jessie said, reminiscing with his brother. Richard chuckled at the memory as he laid on the ground. His head was submerged into the patch of grass. He just laid still and gazed high into the tree's canopy. The canopy, much like the trunks of the tree, was not as thick as before, which allowed Richard to watch the clouds float by in the blue sky. The gentle breeze caused the treetops to softly wave back and forth, and the rustling of the leaves brought peace to Richard. Out of the corner of his eyes, the tips of the grass that had engulfed his body swayed back and forth. He could see that some of the blades of grass still have droplets of water on them from the earlier downpour.

Soon Richard focused his attention on the little yellow flowers that poked up. They had unique green hexagonal stems that were rigid and crisp, which held up the head of the flower. It had a collar of green leaves that looked like three tongues sticking out with the tip of the tongues curling back to the sky. The yellow pedals of the flower reminded him of a trumpet. Its pedals were long and thin and flared out at the end. Out of the center, between the pedals, five little fuzzy green balls protruded from within the center of the trumpet shaped pedals. These fuzzy little balls extended out higher than the petals and were fixed to the flower by some sort of mini stem.

"Hey look!" Richard said. "It's a Yellow Nectorsuckle."

"Really?" Jessie shouted with excitement. As Richard was rolling to his side and extending his hand out to grab a hold of the flower, Jessie quickly reached down and snatched the flower up before Richard had a chance to grab it. As Jessie pulled on the plant, the base of the stem snapped off at ground level.

"What's a Yellow Nectorsuckle?" Gillian snorted.

"Only the sweetest flower known to mankind!" Jessie shouted. He then grabbed the hexagonal stem with one hand and then pinched the head of the flower with the other hand's fingers, and tugged until the head of the flower was extracted from the stem. The entire head of the flower was held together by a root system that fed into the hollow hexagonal stem. Now that these roots were exposed Gillian could see that the roots seemed wet. Before he knew it Jessie had stuck the roots into his mouth and sucked all the nectar out of the head of the flower.

"That's not even the best part!" Richard said, as he snatched the hexagonal stem out of Jessie's hand. "This…" - he said while holding up the stem - "This is the best part!"

Soon, Richard shoved the stem into his mouth and quickly began biting the stem shorter and shorter, filling one cheek like a chipmunk.

"You see here," he said while pointing into the hollow of the stem. He quickly swallowed the bits he had in his mouth, "the plant stores its sweet nectar in its stem!"

"It's like celery but actually tastes good!" Jessie pitched in as he plucked another flower out of the ground and began stripping the petals and leaves. Gillian was curious. He had heard of celery, but never took any interest in mankind's vegetables. He was much happier with the grasses and the alfalfa that they munched on back at Regnum. Yet, in light of their adventure, he decided he too would try a Nectorsuckle. As he plucked one of the flowers from the ground with his teeth, the boys watched the Pegasus as he tried the flower for the first time.

Gillian bit down and could feel the stem crunch under the pressure. Instantly cold nectar from within the stem busted in his mouth. As soon as the nectar touched his taste buds, Gillian's mouth exploded and the Pegasus spit everything in his mouth out.

"Ptui!" he shouted as the Nectorsuckle blurted out of his mouth. The boys rolled over laughing at his reaction. Gillian had never tasted anything so disgusting in his entire life. As he tried to use his top teeth to scrap the lingering taste from his tongue, he squinted his eyes shut and shook his head in disapproval.

"You guys like that stuff?" Gillian asked.

"Oh yes! It's very sweet, it's almost like candy for us," Richard said while munching on another one.

"Well, if that's *sweet*, then I don't like sweets," Gillian said, as he lowered his head and ripped a tuft of good old grass out of the ground and began chewing it to counter the so-called sweet taste of the Nectorsuckle.

Although Gillian had not liked the Nectorsuckle, he too found the situation to be funny. It was a good moment, as if he was among old friends and he liked that.

Eventually the excitement settled down, and all three of them found themselves laying down in the forest. The boys were filling up on the Nectorsuckles, while Gillian grazed on the grasses.

"Say, what's your name anyways?" asked Gillian. The boys were surprised. Surprised that the Pegasus even cared about them at all, and kind of surprised that the question hadn't come up at all before this point.

"I'm Jessie LeRoy, and this is my brother Richard."

"How about you?" asked Richard.

"My name is Gillian, from the Royal lineage of Manuel," Gillian said proudly.

"Manuel? Wasn't he one of the original stars?" asked Jessie.

"Yes!" Gillian whinnied with pride. "You see when Malus came to this land, one third of the stars in the sky followed him. As the stars fell to this land, many of them didn't survive the fall and were burned up as they entered the atmosphere. But six stars survived the fall, and when they impacted the earth their star vessel cracked open and the six original Pegasi came forth. Malus was their leader, and they built the foundation of the land as we know it now," Gillian said with his nose raised high and mighty in the air.

"I thought the Great White Eagle formed the land and all the mountains and rivers that flow?" asked Richard.

"No disrespect, but that is all just a wise tale. The Great White Eagle never existed; he is just a myth. Malus told us that he was the founder of the land and not to believe in any of that Eagle nonsense," Gillian said.

"But what about the scrolls? They talk about the Great White Eagle a lot, and they mention an evil power that controls the world," asked Jessie

"Yeah, we were told Malus was that Evil power," Richard said as he sat up.

"No, no, no. Malus? Evil? HA!" Gillian chuckled. He was quite confident that the boys were wrong and what he had been taught was the truth. "Let's face it… have you ever seen the Great White Eagle?"

"Well…no," Jessie said softly.

"Well Malus is here with us, and always has been. Everyone has seen him and he is very wise. In fact, Malus says the scrolls are just made-up stories. They were written by a rebel that tried to overthrow Malus years ago. Eventually Malus, being the great warrior he was, captured him and had him taken prisoner."

"I've heard about that guy, wasn't he a King's Titan?" asked Jessie.

"He used to be, until he went rogue. He was on a mission sent by King Ezra, the third king of Regnum, to fight off the rebels of that time. While on his mission, he had eaten some sort of mushroom, but the mushroom caused him to go blind for three days. He claimed that during those three days the Great White Eagle spoke to him and told him all that he wrote on the scrolls."

"That's right, he was a commander, not just a Titan. He killed many followers of the Great White Eagle during the King's Wars," said Richard, remembering his history lessons.

"But after he went blind, he changed his ways and became a follower himself," Jessie explained.

"Somehow his writings got out. No one really knows how, but while he was in prison the scrolls began to pop-up all-over Regnum," Gillian explained. "The man was a traitor to the King and to Malus and got what he deserved. He was a deranged lunatic! So obviously, anyone can see that all his stories were made up," Gillian announced.

What Gillian shared with them was confusing. The story of the man who wrote the scrolls was the same. What happened to him and what became of him told by Gillian was the same as what they had heard during the village gatherings they attended back home. Yet

116

Gillian's perspective of him was negative. This man who was praised and honored by the followers of the Great White Eagle, was thought of as a traitor and liar to the Royal Cavalry.

Which side of the story is right? Both boys wondered in their heads. They had a feeling that the Great White Eagle was real. However, any argument they had Gillian shut it down with a simple, 'Well Malus said.'

It really wasn't much of an argument, but Gillian was right about one thing. Neither one of them had ever seen the Great White Eagle before, but they had both seen the all-black Pegasus.

"How is Malus still alive, but the other six original stars are nowhere to be seen or heard from?" asked Richard.

"Well, we have been told that they all moved on to other lands, to build new kingdoms, like Malus has done here," Gillian responded. "So, all that is left of them is me and my fellow Pegasi."

"Hmm, I don't know. It all sounds good, but if the Great White Eagle is just a myth then why is Eva having dreams about him? And she can talk to animals! I think that is definite proof that she is a real Somniator," Richard stated.

"And if Somniators are really real, then there is some truth to the scrolls. Which would mean it's not *all* a lie... sooo, how do you explain that?" Jessie asked, pinching his chin with his fingers.

This question puzzled Gillian. He was told by Malus that no one had ever truly been able to receive dreams, or communicate with other beasts. The idea of Somniators was just a lie to try and create hope among the followers of the Great White Eagle, according to Malus.

Nevertheless, Gillian had no doubt that the girl was in fact communicating with the bear somehow. He thought back to the patch of blue berries, where he had first seen Eva seemingly stop the bear in its tracks. *I know I saw that girl speak to the bear. There is no other way to explain what happened. But how is that even possible? If she did, then Malus lied to me. He lied to everyone. What else has he lied to us about?* Gillian pondered Richard's question for a long while. Wondering if what he had always believed to be true was right or if the followers of the Great White Eagle were the ones who had it figured out. Richard and Jessie just stared at him, waiting for his response. It was the first time they had seemed to stump him.

"I'll be honest with you, I have only just started as a Royal Guard, I still have much to learn," Gillian finally responded. The brothers accepted his answer with disappointment. It was an easy answer to get the boys off his back about it, when in reality Gillian began to question things himself.

Silence fell on the group of three as they continued to rest in the grassy patch. Each one thought about their conversation. It seemed that the truth was unknown. The boys had grown up believing the Great White Eagle created the land, the mountains, and the rivers, yet Gillian seemed so confident that it was Malus. Deep within the brother's heart they still felt that the Great White Eagle was real. Yet Gillian's answers made logical sense. *What is the truth?* Was the question both brothers became stuck on.

As for Gillian, Jessie's question still loomed over his conscience. *Malus told me that Somniators were fairy tales made up by peasants, yet the girl is one. If he lied about that, what is stopping him from lying about other things? What if the peasants are right?* Gillian's head began to hurt. *Is this why I feel so sick about my Noble Markings? What if they are not noble at all?* He lifted his wing, and peered down at his side where his latest marking had developed and remembered the terrible lie that he had told Vincent prior to the markings appearance.

"What is that?" asked Jessie, catching sight of Gillian's mark. Gillian quickly tucked his wing back against his body, to hide the black smudge. He was embarrassed he had it. Which was another odd thing about the marking, which was supposed to bring him pride… Not shame.

"It's nothing!" he said.

"Nothing, you say?" Jessie questioned. He could tell by Gillian's snappy reaction that the marking bothered him. Jessie glanced at Richard who had already been looking in his direction. They were curious to say the least, and now that they knew it was potentially a sore subject, they began to push boundaries in search of an answer about the 'Noble Marking.'

"Are you the Pegasus from the clearing?" asked Richard. He didn't really recognize Gillian as that Pegasus, but he assumed he was.

"So, what if I am?" Gillian asked. Richard's question reminded Gillian that these boys were the root cause of all his problems. The same boys that tricked him and snuck into the forbidden circle, leading them all to where they are now. He was becoming angry again at the boys.

"Well, you didn't have that marking under your wing at that time, so it must mean something!" Richard said.

"You didn't have the big one on your face either," Jessie chimed in.

"It doesn't matter what they are!" Gillian said more aggressively.

"What's the matter? I thought you Pegasi praised those who had the most black hair?" Jessie said with a small smirk growing on his face, for him and Richard both knew they were getting on Gillian's nerves.

"We are! I mean... we do!" Gillian was beginning to become flustered.

"Well then what does it mean?" asked Jessie.

"I DON'T KNOW!" Gillian screamed at the boys. They knew now that they had pushed the young Pegasus too far. Gillian was still laying down, but now had turned his head away from the boys. He looked defeated in spirit. The boys looked at each other, giving each other wide eyed looks and pressing their lips together as if to tell the other brother that it was their fault for upsetting Gillian. Finally, Jessie spoke up.

"We are sorry Gillian; we didn't mean to upset you. We are just curious, that's all. Never really talked to a Pegasus before."

There was more to Gillian than the boys had realized. It seemed that he was not much different than they were, just a different creature with a different role in the land. In reality the mighty Pegasus was quite gentle. Maybe even just as confused about everything that was going on as they were.

Although the two brothers had ruffled Gillian's feathers, he had to admit to himself that he seemed to be growing fond of them. There was no doubt the boys had made him angry, yet they also made him wonder. The truth of the matter was Gillian was only mad because he was confused.

As he thought about the brothers, he knew deep down they were good. Their childish acts, their games, and jokes, were all just a veiled attempt to hide how they really felt. Gillian saw through the veil and could see that the boys were just as scared and confused as he was. They were in this together whether either party liked it or not.

"It's… It's fine. I really don't know what to think about the Noble Markings I have earned. We were always told that when we did good in the sight of Malus or great acts of serving the King, that we would earn our marks. We were told that we should be proud of the markings, that they meant we had great courage and valor. But when these two markings showed up, I couldn't think of anything that I had done to deserve a Noble Marking. I still cannot think of anything I may have done well for the Kingdom. In fact, I can only think of things that I have done wrong," Gillian explained.

Gillian's long face seemed longer than it did before. His head hung down, and his ears drooped. Jessie, Richard, and Gillian became quiet. The brothers thought about all the Pegasi they had seen. Slowly over time each one had earned markings. Yet, neither of the brothers could remember anything good that had come of the Pegasi's actions. They always brought terror, bred fear, and held themselves to such an arrogant place. They sensed the markings did not really mean noble, instead something much worse.

"Well… Should we continue on to the Kettle?" Gillian pressed, finally breaking the silence.

"We could, or you could just take us back," Jessie noted.

"Or maybe even let us go?" Richard said with a glimpse of hope.

"Nice try, but if the Royal Cavalry finds out about you, they will have my wings!" Gillian said as he stood up and stretched his wings out level to each side. He gazed upon his mighty wings with much pride. "Let's go." He ordered as he began walking south once again towards the Devil's Kettle.

As Gillian walked by the boys, the brothers looked at each other. Slowly they rose to their feet and began following the Pegasus. Gillian occasionally looked over his shoulder, just to see that they were still following along. Which they were, but strategically they followed close enough to keep Gillian comfortable and slow enough that they created enough space that they could talk privately.

"What do you think Jessie?"

"I think that this isn't good either way."

"What do you mean?" asked Richard.

"I mean, Gillian seems nice, he seems like he cares. Frankly, he's not at all what I thought he would be. But if it came down to us or him, what do you think he would choose?"

"Not us, that's for sure!" Richard said.

"That's right, not us. Our plan isn't working. He won't just accept us, he won't stop until he has Eva and Andy too," Jessie explained.

"So, what do you think we should do? He said if the other Pegasi found out about us, he would lose his wings. We really can't let that happen… We did break the law; it would be our fault!" said Richard.

"It's him or us, Richard!" Jessie whispered aggressively.

"What's your plan then?"

"When we get closer to the Kettle, we should try and escape."

"How will we do that?"

"Well, I think we are beginning to earn some of his trust."

"You think so?"

"I mean, yeah… To be honest he's starting to earn my trust…" Jessie said surprisingly, "If we find a quiet moment, one like we just had, maybe we can get him to rest his eyes. If we can get him to doze off, we could sneak off."

The hair on the back of their necks straightened out as their quiet conversation was interrupted.

"What are you two talking about back there?" Gillian inquired.

A few paces ahead of them, they could see Gillian had stopped and turned his body towards them. He must have heard them mumbling, and their conversation was making him nervous.

"We are talking about ice cream," Richard said nervously, blurting out the first thing that popped into his head.

"Ice cream?" asked Gillian, "What is this creamed ice you speak of."

Jessie began to chant, "You know… Ice cream…. You scream…"

"We all scream for ICE CREAM!" the boys chanted together, finishing the chant in a full-blown yell.

"Why would I scream at ice?" Gillian asked.

"No! It's a cold, sweet, creamy treat!" Richard said really getting into the fib.

"Sweet? Yuck!" he said while sticking out his tongue. "No thank you!"

Thankfully for the boys, Gillian bought the fib. He didn't like the Nectorsuckle and was sure ice cream wouldn't be any different, so he moved on and turned back toward the south.

"Phew that was close," Richard whispered.

"Yes it was, but do you understand the plan?" Jessie asked, wasting no time, and getting back to business.

"I do, but don't you remember when we were standing in the clearing outside Maizey's den. When that Bear chased us, we started running first, yet Gillian outran us! How do you expect us to get away?"

"That is true, but that's why we will not run far. Instead, we will escape from his sight, hide close by and then he will assume we ran off and go searching for us."

"Ahhh, that makes sense. Once he goes looking for us, we can head in a different direction," said Richard, finally understanding Jessie's plan.

"Exactly! Once we escape, we can hopefully get back to Regnum, find Andy and Eva, and warn them that Gillian will not stop until we are all found," Jessie said, still believing Andy was holding up his end of the plan.

"Maybe we can all go hide in Terribbia with the beasts after this is all said and done. No one would dare look for us there, and Eva can be our translator," Richard said filled with hope. A picture had been painted in their minds of how their new plan would play out. Now, it was time for them to wait for the perfect moment and until that moment came, they continued to follow Gillian through the forest.

Chapter 11
A Walk Down Memory Lane

Andy and Eva slowly trudged behind Maizey. Each new step seemed to be heavier than the step before. The gloomy thoughts of what lay ahead seemed to hover over Andy's head as he followed behind Maizey. He wondered what dangers they would face, and what mysteries they would uncover.

Things were different for Eva. Each step she took was full of life and looked refreshed as if her shoes were filled with tiny little springs.

She wore a big smile on her face, and would occasionally spin in a circle while continuing to move forward. It was as if she had waited her whole life for this adventure and now it was finally here.

This adventure, dangerous or not, was the first taste of real freedom she felt she had ever had. Growing up, her parents had been very strict. She had a very short list of things she could do, and a much longer list of things she could not do. She knew her parents meant well, but their seemingly cruel rules were the exact reason she ended up on this adventure in the first place.

She turned sixteen, seven months ago, and was tired of being treated like a child. Her parents never let her hang out with her friends and always told her that it was for her own safety, but she never understood their logic. Before long she began pushing her parent's boundaries, slowly bending their rules.

Eva had always known of Andy. After all he was only a year older than she was in school, but she never really knew him. She thought of him as one of the older cool kids. He was popular in their village and with all the other school kids. He was the fastest boy in class and all the older girls wouldn't shut up about him.

At first Eva found herself being annoyed by his boyish behavior and her parents only ever talked about him being nothing but trouble, so she never paid much attention to him. Until one day, only a few weeks after she turned sixteen that had all changed.

She remembered that her parents had wanted her home early after school that day, because it was supposed to rain. However, instead she ignored her parents and stayed out later to meet up with her friends.

Soon, dark clouds overhead forced her to head home and face her parents after disobeying their order. As she cradled her schoolbooks in her arms, the rain began to fall and she quickly picked up her pace into a sort of jog, just as all the other kids around her had done. Everyone was trying to get home quicker to avoid becoming drenched by the rain clouds. As the dirt streets began to drain of kids, it began to fill with water causing various puddles to grow here and there. Water from the sky began to fall harder, leaving Eva no choice but to aim straight for her home, even if that meant splashing through mud puddles. As she made a break for her house, she didn't notice that one of the other kids had dropped their books into the puddle she was headed for. Now sprinting towards her house, the book that had been engulfed by the puddle hid in silence as her right foot safely cleared over its position. Dreadfully, as her left leg drug forwards through the puddle, her toes caught the book causing her to fall forward flat on her face.

The impact of her body into the puddle forced all the water to splash in every direction. Moments later the low spot she found herself in began to refill. Eva felt humiliated. Her clothes were soaked and muddy. All her books and schoolwork had been scattered below the surface of the puddle. At first she was shocked and she didn't know what to do.

She hoisted herself out of the puddle and looked around. Propped up in the pool of muddy water she could see all her friends and classmates peering out their windows laughing at what had just happened to her. Of course, it was all at her expense. She felt cold, wet, and horrified. Pulling herself together, she began collecting the loose papers floating in the puddle. The rain crashed down around her and soon her tears did too. There she sat alone, in the rain, while all her friends sat and watched. As she attempted to keep her eyes dry, from both tears and rain, she noticed a pair of shoes standing before her. As she slowly looked up she could see a boy. Between the raindrops she could see a worn-out black raincoat, soaked blue jeans, and a ragged pair of shoes with a big toe hanging out a small hole. The rain roared around them, thunder echoed and lightning flashed in the sky. If she spoke, she knew she would have to yell over the rain. She peered up at the boy's face. Water droplets burst as they collided with the top of his head, and streams of rain dripped from his nose, ears, eyebrows, and chin.

The boy was Andy. He extended his arm to Eva to help her out of the puddle. Clinging to the papers and books she had found with one arm, she clasped hands with Andy with the other. He hoisted her to her feet. She was grateful he came to her rescue and tried to choke back any new tears that were making their way to her eyes. Although in vain, she quickly wiped them away.

"Are you alright?" she remembered him asking.

"Yea…Yeah," she responded in between sniffles.

"Here, take this," he said, while removing his jacket and draping it around Eva's shoulders. She remembered thanking him for the kind gesture. Eva felt warmth from the jacket, but soon she could tell it had many holes in it. Nevertheless, she was grateful for his extreme act of kindness. Eva was so flabbergasted that all her friends stayed inside and watched her in her misery, while a mere stranger came to her rescue. She just stood there and shivered from the cold. Andy quickly crouched down and began fishing out the rest of her books from the puddle. Once he gathered them all, he straightened back out and tucked them under his own arm.

"Let's get you home, shall we?" Andy asked, while lifting one arm as if to suggest she go first. The rain continued to fall, but they both just walked to Eva's house. At this point they were both as wet as they were going to get, so they were no longer in any hurry.

As they approached their destination, both of Eva's parents rushed out of the house with a large black umbrella. They ran down the path that led from their front door to the edge of the street and stopped in front of Eva. Her mom wrapped her arms around Eva while her dad held the umbrella over the three of them. Eva looked over her shoulder at Andy who was still standing exposed in the rain, and had noticed that his hair looked like the rain had glued it tightly to his head. He looked kind of funny, but she recalled thinking it was quite cute.

Eva's mom wasted no time and began applying pressure to Eva's lower back guiding her to the house. Her mother's nose flicked high into the air, and she let out a short high pitched "Hmmfpt" as if telling Andy, she didn't approve of him being around her little girl.

Andy handed Eva's books to her father, and then took a step back and put both his hands behind his back. All Andy could hear was the pitter patter of the rain crashing down around him. But he noticed Eva's father gave him a short nod as he turned around. With a swift turn, he too headed back to their house as well. Andy sensed that Eva's parents didn't like him, however he hoped to have earned some respect for helping their daughter.

Eva remembered watching Andy walk back to the orphanage from her front porch window. He kicked at the puddles as he walked through them, with his hands stuffed in his pockets and his head hung low.

The next day at school, Andy found Eva looking for his raincoat.

"Hey, Eva!" he said as she ran towards her. "Could I get my raincoat back?"

"Oh! I'm so sorry, I completely forgot. Last night I was so worried about trying to dry my schoolwork that I forgot," Eva said, rubbing her tired eyes. She spent most of the night drying the loose papers and books over the fireplace, and then the rest of the night trying to keep up on her schoolwork.

"I'll bring it tomorrow, I promise!" she said.

"I tell you what, why don't you bring it by tonight. A few friends and I are going to be hanging out at the river tonight."

"My parents would never allow it," she said, although she really wanted to go. Now that his hair was dry it was puffy and well formed.

"Come on! It will be fun," he urged her.

"Maybe… I have to get to class. If not later, I'll bring it tomorrow," she said as she turned and headed into the classroom.

That night, after debating with herself, she had decided that she would sneak out and go find Andy. That night, they had so much fun at the river that she began to sneak out every night.

Unfortunately for Eva, being out most of every night caused her to be extremely tired during the day, to the point that her parents finally caught on to what was going on. They were furious, but never once raised their voice at her. They simply expressed their disappointment in her, which was the most crippling punishment she could receive. She hated it when her parents were disappointed in her.

She began to study harder in school, and picked up more chores around the house to help regain her parents' approval, but it didn't stop her from finding ways to hang out with her newfound friend.

Instead of sneaking out, she began to make up excuses so she could get out of the house. She would make up stories about having to work on school projects after school. She even told her parents that she was helping Mrs. Griffin, the village librarian during the weekends. But instead of actually doing those things, she was hanging out with Andy and his friends.

Innocent battles with wooden swords, turned into practical pranks on Mr. Tilley, the old grump that lived at the end of the street. Those pranks turned into hikes in the forest and eventually turned into the adventure they found themselves on now.

Eva thought about her parents constantly. As she remembered back, she thought about how she wished she had been more honest with them. That she could have found a better way to be up front with them, instead of sneaking around and lying about it.

It was obvious to her now, as she walked through the forest, that she had grown apart from her parents. However, there was no doubt that she still loved them dearly and missed them terribly.

As she walked along, she would look back at Andy trudging along behind her. She remembered all his gestures. He was always sweet, always thinking of others, and always doing the best he could to help anyway he could.

She pondered all these things and wished she could run back to see her parents and tell them she was okay. However, she knew she had to keep moving forward. Something big was going to happen and for some reason the Great White Eagle wanted her to go to the Devil's Kettle. She was hopeful that one day she would see them again and could apologize for everything. To have the chance to explain everything that had happened.

Suddenly, Eva's thoughts were interrupted. Maizey had led them into an opening that was home to a body of crystal blue water. This small lake was fed by the Great Northern River, the same one that they had a great water fight with Maizey's cubs in early that morning.

As the rush of water pushed its way into the small lake, the water swirled around until it settled into a glass like surface. The edges of the lake were met by grassy slopes that harbored flowers and the occasional Blackwood tree, before it faded back into the dense forest they emerged from. As their eyes traced the edges of the water, they soon fell upon the reason for the lake. At the south end there was a huge beaver dam.

All of a sudden they heard a splash, and immediately their eyes became glued to a set of ripples that had formed in the center of the lake. Then again, across the lake nearer to the dam, another splash echoed. With eyes fixed on the water, a little brown creature poked up and its broad flat tail slapped the water. The culprit quickly disappeared below the surface. Eva pointed out over the water at the furry beavers. They could see many swimming swiftly towards their dam, and then diving under the water out of sight. Maizey let out a roar and spoke to Eva.

"The beavers are warning one another about the danger," she said.

"Danger? What danger?" Eva roared back in question.

"We are the danger," Maizey explained. Eva didn't like that answer. Her soft smile quickly turned into a frown and her eyebrows slanted firmly.

"We are no danger to them!" she growled.

"I know that, but they don't," Maizey explained in a soft manner while looking at the upset girl. "But that's neither here nor there, we are not here for them, we are here for that," Maizey said, as she turned her snort back out towards the lake. Her nose pointed all the way across the lake.

Eva squinted in that general direction trying to see what Maizey was trying to show them. Eva scanned the other side of the lake again, but this time she noticed what Maizey was talking about. Tucked along the edge of the forest, there was another mine shaft. Similar to the first one, this one had vines and grasses draping over the opening. To a passerby they would have never seen it because it blended in very well with other vines that hung from the Blackwood trees. However, because Maizey pointed it out, both Eva and Andy recognized the opening.

"Why did you bring us to a mine shaft?" Andy asked after Eva had translated everything for him.

"That is our path to the Humilis Pines," Maizey explained.

"Humilis Pines?" Eva asked.

"Yes, the Humilis Pines are the lower pine forest. Down in the Centrum's Core," Maizey began. "You see, if we had continued to head straight south the Blackwood forest turns into the Superius Pines, which is a vast forest of tall Evergreen trees. But that forest will only bring us so far. At the brink of the Centrum's Core is a massive cliff," Maizey explained. She and Koden had lived in the Forbidden Circle for years and had ventured in many different directions. She knew the land and its lay out. The mine shaft would be the easiest path for them to follow.

"So, this Centrum's Core you speak of… It's lower than here?" Eva asked.

"Oh yes, we will have to travel through the mine shaft, underground to descend to the Centum's Core ground level."

"Won't it be dark? How will we see?" Andy asked.

"One would think that, but somehow there are odd lights that glow down different tunnels which leave enough light for us to see our footing," Maizey explained.

"That's weird? Where does the glow come from?" Andy asked.

"I have never ventured to see. I don't want to get lost."

"Maybe it's a magical light!" Eva shouted in excitement. She then translated to Andy.

"Oh exciting! I wonder how long the mines are?" Andy asked, thinking it would be at most a two- or three-hour journey.

"It will take us long into the night, if not until morning light," Maizey explained. Andy didn't like that answer, he thought the tunnels would be cool but not cool enough to wander through all night.

"Just think! The Dwarves created so many mine shafts that we can travel underground for miles!" Eva exclaimed. She was beyond excited for this adventure. She didn't care how long it would take and was excited to see the magical glow. She hoped they would be able to wander a bit from the main path and discover where the lights were coming from.

"It is exciting, but we must be careful. The beavers created this lake, but because of it, many mine shaft openings have been submerged," Maizey began to explain.

"You mean there are a bunch of mine shafts underwater?" Eva asked, creeping close to the water's edge.

"Yes, many! Be careful!" Maizey scolded Eva as she wandered close to the water's edge. "The edge of the water is a massive drop off, there is no slow wading into it, it's all or nothing with this bank. Not to mention that the current of this lake is strong. Weak animals... No offense," Maizey said, talking to Eva, "Are no match against the massive pull the water has as it's rushing down into the mine shafts below us. So please don't fall in."

Andy's face lit up with excitement once Eva had translated.

The wild beasts strike again! Andy thought to himself. He had always heard how strong and scary the beasts of Terribbia were, but never really thought of them as anything other than creatures that could crush their enemies by the strength of their jaws, or slash their foes to pieces, or devour threats with ease. However, learning about the underground mines that became flooded by simple beavers, he realized that they by their own nature were able to dismantle structures built by mankind, Dwarves, or any other species alike.

"That is so cool!" Andy said, thinking about it all.

"That it is," Maizey growled back. "You will get to see many underground rivers. These mines criss-cross below ground. Many are flooded by water and you will get to see that!"

Andy knelt down by the water and gazed in trying to see past his reflection. He was trying to get a good look at any mine shafts below the surface. Eva's attention was drawn back over the water. The little head of a beaver was poked out, but it was swimming away from them.

"I really think we should talk to them; I don't want them to think I'm a threat," Eva said, wanting terribly for the beavers to like her. Soon Eva started squawking and chattering out over the water towards the beaver's dam.

The sudden burst of noises from Eva startled both Andy and Maizey. As cool as it was for Eva to speak to creatures, she still sounded insane to Andy. She must have said something of interest. The beaver stopped swimming and swiveled its head in Eva's direction. Then its head disappeared under the water and its powerful tail slapped the water.

"Eva," Maizey said with a deep sigh. "We have to keep moving. The tunnels make it much easier to travel to the floor of the Centrum Core, but it is still a long journey. We have the tunnels marked, but there are many different turns and twists. If you take the wrong tunnel, there's no knowing where you will end up, or if you will ever find your way out. We must stick together and not get distracted."

Eva turned around and looked at Maizey. The amount of disappointment in her eyes even made Andy feel bad, despite knowing that Maizey was right.

"Fine… I understand… Let's go," she grumbled, slightly rolling her eyes.

"Okay, you two must crawl onto my back and hold on as tight as you can. Those mine shafts create massive currents, and unless you're a mighty swimmer, the currents will suck you down into the water." Maizey explained sternly. The two teenagers' eyes grew wide.

"Hang on tight…" Andy repeated. "Got it!" he mumbled out loud, quite nervous about it.

They crawled up onto Maizey's back, running their hands through her thick fur. Eva clung onto her tighter than ever because she flashed back to earlier when she fell off and hit her head; she decided that she didn't really want to do that again.

"Ready?" Maizey asked, looking over her shoulder at the two perched on her back. Both Eva and Andy nodded.

Maizey aimed her nose forward, and began towards the water's edges. Soon, Maizey began to wade into the water. With all four paws now wet, she leaped forwards into the lake. She was buoyant enough that her head and back remained above the water. The crisp water climbed higher up Andy and Eva's legs, and soon it was clear up to their thighs. By this point, Maizey was now swimming.

As Maizey swam straight across the lake, the teens could feel the water moving aggressively below them. They noticed that they had to use extra effort to keep their legs glued to Maizey's sides.

In fact, the two began to get nervous because they could hear Maizey's breathing grow heavy. The current from the mines submerged below, were proving to be a challenge for Maizey especially considering all the extra weight piled on her back. Her breathing grew louder and their forward momentum began to slow. It seemed that the current was winning this battle. Panic overcame Andy, for now the water began to rise higher up his legs, almost to his waist. The current was pulling Maizey under.

"What are we to do?! We can't out swim the current, and with us on Maizey's back, neither can she!" Andy gasped, looking down at the water, which had now completely overtaken Maizey's back.

"I'll… make…it!" she snorted, taking massive breaths between each word she growled. Although Maizey said she would make it, Eva wasn't so sure. Their progress slowed to at most an underwater crawl.

Suddenly, out of the water below them, a beaver poked his head up. Maizey was concerned at what the beaver wanted but had no room in her effort to pay any attention to the furry little creature. Just as the situation seemed to have escalated to the point of no return, the beaver began to chatter loudly at Eva.

Eva's face looked shocked. As if what the beaver told her was crazy. Eva squawked back at the little creature, who was having no issue at all staying ahead of the current. They chirped and growled back and forth briefly, but before Eva could translate, their situation turned for the worst.

"Come on!" Eva shouted, with no explanation at all. Soon she slipped off Maizey's back and disappeared below the surface of the water.

"Eva!" Andy frantically shouted. He was now terrified, for not only was Maizey struggling, but Eva seemingly was lost in the water. He feared that she would be sucked down the mine shaft and be lost or worse… But to his dismay the tides began to turn in their favor. With Eva gone, Maizey began to regain control and started making headway through the water again.

"I will…Get her…" Maizey assured Andy, between breaths. The shoreline was getting closer, only seconds away, although it felt like it took minutes to get there. Andy's heart pounded in his chest; he could barely think straight. As he unloaded from Maizey's back, she pushed off the shore's edge back out into the blue and she too disappeared under the water.

He began to shout hysterically for Eva. Calling her name as if she could hear him under the crystal blue water. The deeper he gazed into the water the darker blue it grew. He could see nothing but black at the bottom. No movement, no life, and no sign of any kind that Eva was okay.

The minutes felt long and drug out. He began to pace back and forth along the shoreline. He felt helpless. He had never faced a foe such as the water or the current that hid within it. If it had been a sword, he could have helped, but against a mighty current he was helpless. Any negative thought you could imagine, he had floating around in his head. As he paced back and forth, a beady eyed little beaver stopped him in his tracks. The furry creature treaded water, leaving only his head exposed. His big round eyes poked out from behind his big black nose.

"What did you do with Eva!" Andy shouted at the beaver.

Although the beaver didn't understand him, he knew that the boy was angry. The beaver began to screech back at Andy. At this point, both had almost engaged in a screaming match. What Andy didn't know was that the beaver in the water was only a distraction. In the heat of their argument, a second beaver had made his way out of the water and circled up behind Andy. While Andy aggressively shouted at the first beaver, the second beaver quietly crept in for an attack.

Out of nowhere Andy felt something solid and flat smack him from behind. Andy was forced into the water from the beaver's strike. He flailed his arms and legs, fighting the water, doing everything he could to resist the current. Suddenly he felt his body being lifted to the water's surface. At first he thought it was Maizey, a short-lived sense of relief came to Andy. However, as soon as he surfaced and was able to get a deep breath of air, the creature that had brought him to the surface began to pull him down. The more he reached for the water's surface, the further away it became. Soon, Andy had realized that it was the beaver dragging him down. Not only that but Andy could feel the current helping the beaver. Down, down, down he went, his surroundings became darker and darker the closer he got to the bottom of the beaver-made lake.

Suddenly, to Andy's surprise the beaver let go of him, but because he was so close to one of the mine shaft openings, the current's grip was so strong now that there was no stopping his motion.

As Andy felt the last bits of air slip out from his lungs, he could see the wooden frame of the mine's opening as he passed through into the tunnel. It was so dark he couldn't see anything but felt his body tumbling in all directions. It must have been luck, but somehow he never collided with any of the mine's walls. The current was so strong that it kept him centered as he was pulled down the throat of the mine. Andy squeezed his eyes shut, fighting with everything he had to hang on to any remains of oxygen he could. He couldn't breathe, he couldn't control his movement, he couldn't do anything to stop the jaws of death from swallowing him. In that moment he was truly helpless. The only thing he could think of doing was to call out to the Great White Eagle. Through thought he called out, *Why is this happening? Save me! Get me out of this!* He cried in his heart.

Just then, Andy felt bursts of cold air beat against his soaked body. He felt different too. *Am I dead?* He thought. No longer could he feel the pull of the current, instead he was free falling as if in the mists of a waterfall. Quickly, he sucked in any air he could get. As he breathed in he would get a mixture of water and air, but it was enough to bring new life to his lungs. *SPLASH! He* felt his body plunge back into another pool of water, but his tumbling crept to a calm float. The only disturbance Andy felt now was the water from above breaking the surface tension of the pool he found himself in. As he began to float back up towards the surface, rain-like water penetrated the water's surface and Andy's mind returned to the Great White Eagle, remembering his image painted in the storm clouds.

His thoughts were interrupted by the pounding of the water above, for his head was now completely exposed and it was as if the small waterfall was his own personal storm cloud raining down viciously on him.

The crashing water echoed in the underground cavity he found himself in, but he could hear an echo other than that of the water. As he swam forward, out from under the falls, the echo became clear, it was Eva.

Chapter 12
Two of a Kind, One of Another

"You made it!" Eva exclaimed.

"Made it?" Andy angrily said, as he spit out water from his mouth. "I was pushed in by those blasted beavers!" He gazed around the cave expressing to Eva he wouldn't take any other explanation about it. He could now see that the small pool of water was at the base of the cave and was being fed by the mine shaft that was directly above the pool. (The one he had just come from). Both

Eva and Maizey had found an elevated platform to rest upon. The cave was illuminated by a strange glow. As he peered around, he noticed that the light was coming from crystals, many of which hung like little stalactites from the cave's ceiling. There were also clusters of small, dagger-like crystals protruding upwards near the pool's edges. Like a set of fine China, the crystals looked delicately beautiful.

Without those crystals the cave would have been black as night, but instead they let off a beautiful blue light that shimmered and sparkled, reflecting in every direction. The disturbed water's surface reflected the light onto the cave's walls causing round circles to dance about. *Are these the source of light Maizey mentioned before?* Andy thought to himself.

Beyond Maizey and Eva, there was another mine shaft. Possibly one that might lead to their original intended pathway. Still floating in the pool, Andy glanced to his right. At the far side of the pool, he could see water slowly creeping towards the mouth of a third mine shaft, where it swiftly vanished over the pool's edge down the mine's throat.

A familiar growl brought his attention back to Maizey. She and Eva had begun to communicate. Maizey sat on her butt, with all her fur drenched. The wet fur on her head hung heavily over her face, and she looked like a big brown mop. She was slouched, frowning, and did not look thrilled to be in the cave.

"Andy, the beavers were helping!" Eva explained. The moment had settled and she felt he was ready to listen now.

"Helping? They tried to have me killed! I haven't been paddled like that since that one time I stole that Titan's shield while he was peeing around a corner," Andy said, while chuckling to himself remembering the brutal spankings he got after pulling off that stunt. "But anyways, I deserved those. What did I deserve this one for?" he said, looking at Eva puzzled.

Just then Andy heard a loud splash behind him. It frightened him so much that he began to panic, and he scurried out of the water up onto the platform that Eva and Maizey were on.

"Berg!" Eva shouted. Just then a furry brown head emerged from the water. Followed by his beady little eyes that seemed to pierce right through Andy, then his big black nose and his beavered bucked teeth showed themselves.

"That's the one! That's the one who pushed me into the water!" Andy exclaimed. He didn't really know if that was the one who pushed him in, but at that moment he was sure it was.

"Berg would never! It was probably Dawn!" she spouted off as if she had known these beavers her whole life. Just then another beaver plunged into the pool of water and came swimming beside the first beaver. They had come into the cave through the same mine shaft Andy and the others had.

"Wait, No that's the one who pushed me in. He's the one!" Andy now insisted. He really wasn't sure which beaver had done it.

"Well, Dawn's a she. She's Berg's wife."

The beavers began squawking at the three of them, and Andy could tell that Maizey was just as confused about the situation as he was.

"Berg and Dawn want to help! They told me about this pool and that is why I jumped into the water. *And* that's why they pushed you in. I told them you would not understand them, so I guess they improvised," she explained.

Eva and the beady little creatures exchanged more noises and squeaks to one another, and Eva translated.

"These beavers are a part of a large colony that used to work for the Great White Eagle. Their colony leader was named Dux. Get this, he too was a Somniator like me. Apparently his brother was a Lector like you Andy. Anyways, through a dream, the Great White Eagle commanded Dux to elect twelve beavers to go into the Centrum Core and map it out, to discover the mysteries of the Devil's Kettle. Berg said that he and a good friend were of the twelve tasked with the mission."

"That's really great, but what does this have to do with us?" Andy asked grumpily.

"I'm getting there!" Eva scolded, "The twelve departed from the colony and used these very mines to get to the Centrum's Core. Slowly they mapped out the Centrum's Core as they were instructed. But then, they reached the Uada Hollow. Some of the beavers became frightened, and rumors of danger and death swept through the twelve scouts."

Andy and Maizey's faces grew long and distraught, for they began to let fear overtake them. It really was a funny sight, because Eva would translate for Andy and his face grew distraught, yet Maizey sat comfortably unaffected until Eva finally explained it in her language.

"Ummhmmmm, that's why I ain't going anywhere near that place!" Maizey sassed Eva.

Eva politely nodded in Maizey's direction, even though she wanted to roll her eyes at the big scaredy bear.

"Anyways," she continued to translate the beavers. "Despite their fears they pressed on, they navigated their way into the Uada Hollow and began to chart the area. But it was difficult. They too believed that it was haunted and extremely undesirable. The ground was soft, almost bouncy, and wet too. The trees were less dense and were all dead. Plus, the grass was tall, making it difficult for them to even sense which direction they were facing. But the worst part was that they began to hear voices in the distance; voices of all creatures. Some voices they could understand and other things they couldn't. One beaver even claimed to see things, people, and other beasts. Another claimed to hear chains dragging at night and screams that followed," Eva explained.

"They *believe* that it's haunted? It sounds haunted!" Andy interjected.

"It wasn't until the whole group of scouts were collected together one evening, when they all witnessed a shadowy figure floating around them in the bog. The beavers call it a Messorem. They all saw it, moving in the shadows of the night, but in the morning there was no evidence that anything had been there. After that they had no choice but to return to their colony out of fear for what lurked in the Centrums Core," Eva said casually, as if it was just a scary story she was telling around a campfire.

"So, why would we even dream of going there?" Andy questioned their sanity.

"Because the Great White Eagle said so!" she exclaimed.

The two beavers again began squawking and Eva translated.

"But anyways, when they all returned here to their colony, all but two let fear overpower their faith in the Great White Eagle's plan. They convinced the entire colony that it was not safe for them to venture to the Devil's Kettle. Only Berg and Asher, Berg's friend, were willing to go back and complete their mission, just as the Great White Eagle had told them to. It didn't matter how hard Berg or Asher begged the colony to go with them, they refused. They even threatened to kick them out of their colony. Finally, they had no choice but to give it up. That's when they settled here. They built the dam, made it their home, and began to raise families."

"I still don't get why you think this is a good idea," Andy said.

Eva paused for a moment, her confidence seemed to leave and the cave seemed to grow darker. She slowly looked at Maizey, then at the two beavers treading water, and then looked Andy right in the eyes.

"I just do," she said calmly yet sternly.

Silence fell on them all for a moment, then Andy looked at Eva. "Can't we go around?" he solemnly asked.

Eva repeated the question for the beavers, they squawked back, but by the solemn look on Eva's face and a soft shake of the head, Andy knew there was no other option but to go directly through the Uada Hollow.

The sound of splashing water was the only movement in the cave after that. It seemed like hours had passed as they all just sat there in silence. Andy pondered those words. He too felt as if they were meant to go to the Devil's Kettle, but fear still resided within him. *If the Great White Eagle chose a whole colony of beavers to carry out his mission but they failed, what makes Eva think two teenagers could?*

"What now?" Andy built up the courage to ask, finally convincing himself to follow Eva's lead. "We are trapped in this cave. Should we try and find our way through the mine shaft?" he asked, as he glanced over his shoulder and gazed down the dark tunnel.

Eva's face lit up with excitement, she knew that this was Andy's way of telling her he was still on board.

"Hold on," she said, then she turned to the beavers and chirped at them; they squawked back.

"We are not trapped at all! In fact, the beavers brought us here on purpose!" Eva explained. The beavers began to squawk again.

"Dux, their colony leader, has long since passed, but before he died, he received one last dream. That dream was translated by his brother to say that this generation of beavers would one day meet two beasts of a kind and a third beast of another kind. Those creatures would carry out their mission, discovering the mysteries of the Devil's Kettle and learning the truths about our land," Eva translated proudly.

"And they think that's us?" Andy said with a huge lump in his throat.

"Well, one, two," - she said while pointing at herself and to Andy - "And a third of a different kind," she said while pointing to Maizey.

"Will the beavers come with us?" Andy asked. Thinking to himself that they would know best how to navigate the Centrum's core. Eva translated his question for him.

"They say they no longer can; they are much too old now and have families to care for," Eva said. This was the first time that Andy had noticed that both beavers did have gray whiskers and wrinkles in the crease of their eyes.

"Can they at least give us the maps they created of the Centrum's Core? Even if they are unfinished?" Andy asked.

"They cannot. Sadly, years ago, Asher and the maps disappeared," Eva explained after translating.

"Disappeared?" Andy questioned.

"Apparently he decided to venture on his own. He took the map and went south. But was never seen or heard from again," Eva explained. Andy's skin began to crawl. Everything about this Centrum's Core sounded terrible. Suddenly Berg began to chirp and squeal. Eva paid close attention.

"He said, he remembers some. He said he remembers entering into a thick Pine forest," Eva said.

"That must be the Humilis Pines Maizey mentioned," Andy suggested.

"Yes, but then he remembers the pine trees losing their needles and it was only bare pine trees. He called this the Nevergreen Forest. After that, the ground became wet and the grass became taller all around them. That's when things became spooky. Slowly the dead pine trees became less and they found themselves in the Uada Hollow. The ground was floating, the grass tall, the fog thick, and truly solid ground was few and far between," Eva explained.

"You're kidding," Andy said, thinking going to the Uada Hollow would be insanity.

"Nope… He said that many times they have ventured to the brim of the Centrums Core and overlooked it from up here. Apparently from above it all, they could see that there are three rings to the Centrum's Core. The Humilis Pines, the Nevergreen Forest, and the Uada Hollow. Each ring is smaller than the outer."

"So, like a Bullseye?" Andy asked.

"Sounds like it!" Eva said taking the layout of the Centrum's Core very seriously.

"Well, what's the Bullseye then? Can he explain what he has seen of it?"

"No. They never made it beyond the Uada Hollow, and from up above, the fog of the Uada Hollow has always concealed the bullseye from sight. It's a mystery."

"Great…"

"A mystery we are going to solve," she added. Andy rubbed the back of his neck in discomfort. He felt that Eva had committed so violently that it didn't matter how crazy their mission seemed to get, she was all in.

"So… There's still no way you're changing your mind?" he asked, as Eva shook her head no in response. "Well… how do we get out of here?"

Eva looked at the beavers for guidance.

"Down that," she said while pointing towards the mouth of the mine in which the water from the pool drained into.

"What do you mean?" Andy asked.

"We are going down that!" Eva explained while jumping back into the pool of water.

"Are you crazy, don't you remember what the last one was like? I almost died!"

"Oh, quit being a baby," she said with a smile as jumped into the pool and swam over towards the edge where the water flowed. She then growled at Maizey and filled her in on the whole situation, and she too didn't sound thrilled about it. Begrudgingly she waddled over to the pool and splashed in, causing a huge wave to rise up and drench Andy who was still sitting up on the platform.

"Really?" he complained about the burst of water.

"Oh, stop complaining you big…" Eva began, but before she could finish her sentence, Andy finished it for her.

"Baby… Yeah, yeah, I get it," he grumbled as he too jumped into the water.

Fear lived inside of Andy at this point. Here he was in an underground pool, about to go down a dark mine shaft flooded with water in which he really didn't know where it led to. All while two beady eyed bucked tooth beavers squawked at him. As the current pulled at his body he glanced one last time at the cave, the crystals flickered in the cave, and the beavers waved to the three of them as they continued on their journey. Eva was the first to slip out of sight, down the mine shaft she went. Squealing with joy as she plunged into the dark abyss. Next was Maizey, she hoisted her large body over the lip of the pool and she too disappeared out of sight. Her deep growl echoed throughout the mine shafts. Although he knew it was her, all he could do was think of what other beasts lay waiting down that tunnel. Then Andy's mind began to panic. *Maybe the whole thing was a trap!* He thought frantically. He couldn't help but panic. He started to flail his arms. With every ounce of strength he had, he tried to swim away from the edge but it was too late. The small river tugged at Andy. In one last effort, as Andy began to slip over the edge down the tunnel, he grabbed a hold of a crystal hoping he could hang on and prevent himself from barreling down the mine shaft.

SNAP! The crystal busted and Andy found himself skidding down the mine shaft on his belly with his arms dragging above him. With his left hand he tried to grip any surface he could to try and slow himself down, but the water was a mighty force of nature and had eroded the floor of the mine shaft into a slick smooth surface. In his other hand he held tightly to the busted crystal. It still glowed a mesmerizing blue color and was useful in helping him see around himself as he plugged down the tunnel.

He could hear the joyful screeches of Eva as she plunged down the mine below him. Although he did his best to stay uncomfortable about the situation, the slippery slope overpowered his grumpy attitude. Soon, he found himself rolling over onto his butt and sitting up with his knees bent in. He could feel the water pushing him from behind. Sudden drops in the mine shaft made his heart race. Down, down, slightly up, and then down again. It was a ride of a lifetime. At one point, he had built up enough speed that when a small rise in the mine shaft's floor came about, Andy's body launched into the air and then seconds later returned into the stream of water. Occasionally a different mine shaft would intersect the one he was plummeting down and add another gush of water, jolting him this way and that.

As he splashed his way down the mines, for almost ten whole minutes all he could see was darkness, slightly illuminated by the flicker of blue light which came from the crystal he held tightly in his hand.

Just as Andy began to think the tunnel had no end, he saw a small white light lingering way up ahead. He instantly knew that it was daylight and the end of the tunnel was before him. Just a speck at first, the source of light began to grow, swelling with each second he slid towards it.

Andy couldn't help but feel disappointed that the tunnel was coming to an end, once he got over his fear, he had enjoyed it much more than he had anticipated. However, his disappointment vanished and panic took hold. Again, Andy found himself rolled over on his belly, clawing at the mine shafts floor trying to stop his motion. His sudden change in heart came after he became close enough to the mouth of the tunnel and could see what lay beyond the mine opening. To his dismay he could see trees. Not just trees in particular, but only the fat middle branches of pine trees. Not their bases, which would be at ground level. This could only mean one thing. The mouth of this mine shaft was not close to the ground, but likely high up on the side of a cliff.

SWOOSH! Andy's body rocketed out of the mine shaft into the open air. He had enough momentum that he became separated from the water which fell into the pool of water below him and he found himself a good distance from the cliff behind him. He felt as if he was flying because he was at least fifty feet in the air and moving fast.

Andy panicked. While being suspended in the air, there was nothing he could do. He tried to flap his arms like wings, hoping by some magical force he could land safely. However, this was in vain. Not only was he about to plummet but the blue crystal he had gripped in his hand was sent flying through the air and landed in the mists of the Humilis Pines. Now without the crystal he flailed his arms with no end. Down he went. Luckily his legs went first and he found himself falling upright. The sudden drop made Andy feel like his heart jumped up into his throat.

A loud scream forced its way out of Andy as he fell. Down, down, down he went, until his body crashed into the lake below. A slap echoed through the forest as Andy's body broke the surface of the water.

By the time Andy was able to find his bearings, Maizey and Eva had both made it to the shore. Floating to the water's surface, Andy felt like he had been slapped by a giant hand. Half his body felt numb with sharp tingles from the high-speed impact against the water.

Luckily nothing seemed to be broken. Slowly, he began swimming towards shore.

"Wow! That was so fast! I can't believe we are already down to the Centrum's Core!" Maizey roared. "It normally takes almost a day's journey by walking!"

"That was awesome! It was like a giant water slide! There were all sorts of twists and turns and at one point, I'm pretty sure I had some air!" Eva marveled. "Wasn't that fun?" she shouted out at Andy who was dragging himself out of the water onto the grassy shore. Andy had decided that a drastic fall of fifty feet was the straw that broke the camel's back and made none of it fun at all. The tunnel was dark and he wasn't in control of the situation. He thought he was going to die most of the time, especially when the cliff spit him out. He did everything he could not to let his emotions speak loudly. He knew Eva was quite excited about it and did not want her to feel guilty for dragging him along. Afterall, it was his choice to come this far. He put on a smile and responded positively.

"Yes, so fun," he said as he stood up, soaking wet.

Turning away quickly, for it is always hard to hold a fake smile, he turned back to look at the lake he just pulled himself out of. The crystal blue water shimmered in the low sunlight. The lake puddled up against the massive ledge of the Centrum Core's edge. The cliff towered high above him and stretched both to his left and to his right as far as he could see before it rounded around the Humilis Pine forest.

He spotted the mine shaft that spit him out. Water gushed out of it as well as many others. At various heights on the face of the Centrum's Core's massive wall other mine shafts released water from their own underground rivers. In addition to those, the Northern River poured water over the edge way up above. Apparently not all of the water was held up by the beaver dam, and the Northern River was able to carry out its natural duty of channeling water.

It was clear that the Centrum Core's edge was extremely high, not because Andy could see the top lip, but because most of the water from the Northern River had evaporated by the time it reached the lake below. Evidence of the great river was only a faint fall of mist that filled the air.

It was the mine shafts as the water that flowed through them that filled the lake and allowed the Great Northern River to continue on into the Centrum's Core.

The golden sunset painted the rocky rim various shades of golden yellow. Andy walked over to Eva and Maizey who had plopped down beside the base of a large evergreen. Andy crouched down next to them and leaned against the tree, finally settling to the ground.

In reality the day had flown by. The sun was now setting and the shadows became long. The last rays of sunlight filtered through the trees and were vanishing fast.

"I think we should rest here," Eva suggested.

"Only for a moment," Andy mumbled as his eyes fell shut and he quickly drifted off to sleep. It had been an exhausting day.

Chapter 13
A River's Tale

Meanwhile, Richard and Jessie had still been walking in the heat of the day. As they walked the ground was becoming fuller with grass and the trees had now separated even more than before. Slowly the dense Blackwood forest dissipated and only various blackwood trees in their youth remained. It was on the outskirts of the massive forest that an open plane presented itself. Off to their right a grassy meadow sloped like a valley towards them. The Blackwoods trees lined one side, and a great Pine forest the other. To their left the narrow valley they were passing through fed into a low land. Black birds perched on the cattails that protruded above the green grasses and plant life beneath them. Behind that swamp, the Blackwood forest and the Superior Pine forest merged and integrated with one another. It was a nice break in scenery for the three of them. Staring at tree trunks had gotten old. Now the sun beat down on them and the blue sky was the only thing above them. Little pink and orange flowers poked about the valley and unique rock formations resided at the head of the valley to their right.

As they crossed the valley, the Superior Pine forest grew closer. Baby pines began to grow, but were only two or three feet tall. At first they were few and far between, but gradually they became so close to one another that Richard, Jessie, and Gillian couldn't avoid having them brush against them.

They had left one forest and were now closing in on another. Clumps of evergreens grew closer and taller. Four feet, five feet, six feet tall. Soon, the only way to navigate the bushy green needled trees was by following some sort of animal trail that already existed.

As they moved along, Richard gazed up at the sky. Because the pine trees were becoming taller with each step, the skies above filled with their pointy green tips. Eventually, the evergreens crowded the skyline so much that Richard could not see the blue of the skies any longer.

Although they were on a well beaten path created by elk or deer, they had to focus intently on the trail they were following.

Bobbing and weaving around the branches their trek began to become difficult. Not only that, but they had to dodge branches Gillian threw at them. Gillian was not aware of this, but when his body pushed a branch out of the way as he walked, the branch acted like the arm of a catapult. As soon as Gillan's body cleared the branch, it would let loose and fire its needled branches in the boy's direction.

They sometimes found it easiest to crawl under the lowest branches, which helped them avoid being beaten up by the sharp prick of needles and the violent swipe from branches. Richard and Jessie had never experienced the brutal attack an evergreen tree was able to provide. The needles constantly scratched and poked them as they pressed on.

They began to feel trapped and lost, engulfed by the Evergreen forest, not being able to see five feet in front of them. The only hope they had was in the worn-out trail below their feet. If they remained on it, it would lead them on. At some point things would have to clear up.

Maybe we should turn back. Richard began to think to himself. Yet before the words could reach his lips, he reached out his hand and pulled down a branch to move it out of his way. "Oh, thank the Eagle," he mumbled. He realized that they had finally made it to the heart of the Evergreen forest.

They all stopped for a moment and brushed the needles from their clothing and rubbed the scratches that had formed on their skin. Now, all the close-knit pine trees stood behind him, and what remained in front of him was a forest of massive Evergreens. Their flakey bark covered their tall narrow trunks, as they seemed to shoot straight up forever. You could tell the Superior Pines forest was a mature forest because there were no low hanging branches. Dense pine forests like this one block out the sunlight, therefore Evergreens shed the lower branches to the forest floor. The forest floor itself was covered by dried up needles from seasons past. Their orange color reminded them of autumn, even though it was still only early spring.

Gillian pressed on. Wasting very little time. The brothers looked at each other because they were hoping for more of a rest, but followed him begrudgingly. The sun was well on its way back towards the earth. The boys couldn't help but stop and stretch their arms and legs. It had become a long day.

They all began to notice the ground was harder than it had been before. Soon Gillian's hooves began to clop. Jessie drug his toes along the ground sweeping the dead needles clear from it. It exposed that the ground had become rocks, similar to what you would expect high up in the mountains. Interestingly enough, the solid rock below their feet had not hindered the growth of the Pines. Powerful are their roots which took hold in cracks and crevices, forcing the rocks aside so that the trees could grow up big and strong.

Gradually the rocks become more uneven and more jagged making their journey a bit more difficult. Off in the distance the three could see some sort of wall entangled in the Evergreen forest. It seemed that the wall was the edge of the forest, for the dense Evergreens seemed to halt and only few evergreens dug their roots in on the shelf formed beyond the top of the wall.

In between the tree trunks, they could all see the sky beyond the mysterious wall. It was painted blue accompanied by white smears that floated peacefully above the horizon. Rays of yellow and orange seeped into the forest, leaving streams of light visible for Gillian and the brothers in the darkening forest. The wall before them seemed to be naturally formed, for there lie boulders and rocks that had broken loose and fell to the base of the fifteen-foot ledge.

As they approached the wall, they looked left and then to the right, looking for a way around the vertical wall. But they could not see its end.

"Should we try and go around? It looks steep and look at all these loose rocks," Jessie said, hoping he wouldn't have to apply much effort. Gillian swiveled his head around, and then trotted off to his left.

"Where are you going?" Richard asked. However, Gillian gave no answer.

Instead, Gillian's wings shot out to his side, raised high into the air, and thrusted down to the forest floor causing all the dead pine needles to rustle. His hooves left the ground, and in a few short bursts he had traveled from the base of the wall to on top of it with very little effort.

"I needed a bit more space for my wings," Gillian finally said, looking over his shoulder down at the boys in a prideful manner. The boys peered up at the Pegasus who folded his wings against his side.

"Wish I could do that," Jessie said, as he rolled his eyes.

With the obvious notion that they would have to climb the miniature cliff, the boys began scaling the boulders that lay at the foot of the wall. Carefully, they watched their foot placement. The rubble was loose, so keeping solid footing and balance wasn't the easiest task.

"Like this!" Richard shouted to Jessie who was watching his feet. Jessie looked up and Richard had climbed on top of a large boulder and began to jump from that one to the next. Soon the two looked like frogs hopping this way and that.

"Wow!" Gillian gasped.

"What? What is it?" Richard questioned. He had finally made it to the wall. Grabbing the first ridged ledge of the cliff, he looked up and could see Gillian staring off into the distance. From his vantage point it was a unique sight for Richard. Gillian's chest was glowing a bright yellow, and his entire figure had been outlined by the setting sun.

Excitement overtook them and they scrambled as quickly as they could up the wall. Finding an edge, crack, or ledge to grab onto and hoist themselves upward. Finally, their heads poked above the wall and the bright yellow sun falling to the west, beamed right into the forest. It took them a few moments for their eyes to adjust to the bright source of light but as they peered out they could see what Gillian had spotted. The brothers gazed upon a sea of baby evergreens. Thousands and thousands of little trees poked out of the ground. As the wind whispered a breezy song, the little trees danced back and forth, swaying endlessly. They dug their fingers into the moss that covered the earth, and began to pull themselves up.

As the boys made their ways to their feet, the short evergreens grew with them. The taller the brothers stood, the seemingly taller the evergreens grew. This intriguing illusion confused the boys, but made them step forward towards the sea of evergreens. And again, with each step they took, the trees grew taller and taller. Until the boys had encountered a massive cliff that dropped off before them.

The baby evergreens were not small after all, in fact they were massive full-grown trees. Before, at ground level, they could only see the very tips of the full-grown trees. However, now that they peered over the edge of this massive cliff they could see that the base of these trees stretched far below. It was a glorious sight and they soaked it all in. They inhaled deeply, savoring the new refreshing breeze. If you have ever smelled pine needles then you know kind of what it smelled like. Although between the Superior Pine forest behind them and the vast sea of evergreens before them, the sappy aroma of evergreen needles flooded the air with greater strength than you could imagine.

Jessie and Richard didn't know this, but this overlook was exactly as Berg, the beaver, had described to Eva when he explained what the Centrum's Core looked like from above. A perfect circle bordered the entire Centrum's Core. It was a tall rocky cliff that corralled the rest of the rings of the bullseye below. Calling it a bullseye was in fact accurate because the rings of the Centrum's Core looked exactly like an archery target. The massive rocky cliff was the outermost ring. The pine trees they mistook as baby trees, which is the Humilis Pine forest, made a thick green strip which looked like the second ring of a bullseye target. Then they could see the third ring, which looked like evergreen skeletons. Berg had described this ring to Eva and called it the Nevergreen forest. The gray corpses of dead evergreen trees stood bare. No needles or life left in them. It was after the Nevergreen forest that things became a bit more difficult. Dense fog rose up from the ground and consumed it. Jessie and Richard were unaware of what lay in this portion, but Andy and Eva would have known it was the Uada Hollow. It is not until later that the four of them would discover that before the bullseye, the Devil's Kettle itself, there was one more ring on the inside of the Uada Hollow that bordered the mysterious hole. Making the Centrum's Core a collection of five rings and a bullseye.

"Wow, what a view!" Richard exclaimed.

"No kidding! This is beautiful!" Jessie said, as the wind rustled the pine trees around him.

"I wonder if that's the Devil's Kettle over there?" Richard asked, as he pointed to the foggy center of the Centrum's Core.

"That would be my guess. Look over there!" Gillian said as he stretched out his nose straight south. He was looking over the Centrums Core to the Ledge opposite of his.

"That must be the Eagles Plateau! It's a great cliff that divides the Region of Terribbia from the Eastern Region of Borrian," Gillian said.

The boys could see that the ledge on the other side looked very similar to theirs, a rocky edge that helped contain the sea of trees below. On the north side, the side the boys stood on, the Superior Pines loomed behind them. However, in the southern region, there was some sort of meadow that resided on the brink of the Centrums Core. A forest began much further inland.

"Legend has it, the Eagle's plateau is so tall that only the Great White Eagle could reach the flat top," Jessie explained, as he marveled at the massive rock formation. They all gazed at the massive pie shaped wedge that stood so tall the clouds in the sky consumed its very tip. Back home, they could see its very top on clear days peering above the forests, but never had they been so close to it.

"It kind of looks like mama's homemade pie. You can see those rocks along its side layered and uneven just like slices of apples or peaches trying to fall out of a slice," Richard suggested. The front of the edge hung over the brim of the Centrum's Core leaving a looming shadow below it. It was a wonder of the world. How it formed was always a marvelous mystery. The narrow edge hung over the vast chasm that was the Centrums core, yet as that Plateau stretched back into Terribbia it widened, just as a piece of pie would on your plate.

Most legends or myths stretched the truth in one way or another, but to this day, no man, Dwarf, or Elf had ever been able to scale it. No Centaur, Grog or Creature had ever climbed it, and no winged beasts had ever been able to fly over it. The boys gazed at the glorious cliff, remembering what they had heard during the village gathering they attended. They were told that plateau was where the Great White Eagle rested after he had formed the land.

"Wow, wow, wow!" Richard said while sitting along the edge of the Centrum's Core, dangling his feet over the edge. He closed his eyes and soaked in the moment.

Jessie stood behind his brother and gazed at the amazing creation. The soft warm breeze kissed both Richard and Jessie's skin, and they could hear the whispers of the forest behind them. As they listened longer, they soon picked out the sound of pounding water echoing in the distance.

"Over here!" Jessie said. Richard had opened his eyes, scrambled to his feet, and chased after Jessie, who was already moving to the East along the brim of the chasm. He waved his arm as to signal Gillian to follow along, leading him to the sound of water.

Soon, they could see the rushing river. They could see it weave from within the Superior Pine forest, carving its way into the earth's crust, leaving rocky jagged banks on both sides of the river. It really had carved out its path. The fifteen-foot wall they had to climb had been eaten away by the river. Peering down at the flowing water they could see a large boulder in the center of the river straddling the ledge. This boulder forced the flow of water to divide into two streams before it poured over the Centrum Core's brim.

"Do you think this is the Northern River?" Richard asked as he was looking in Jessie's Direction.

"I do believe it is," Gillian said, as he approached the bank of the river, gazing in at the rushing flow of water.

"Wow! Just think this river flows all the way from the No Man's Land Mountains all the way down here. Crazy!" Jessie said.

Richard and Jessie sat down on the bank of the river and kicked off their shoes. They each rolled up their pants to about their knees and slowly let themselves down the bank of the river. As their feet dipped into the water, they felt a cooling sensation flood through their veins.

"Oh man! I am thirsty!" Jessie said as he reached down and scooped water with his hands and brought the refreshing treat to his lips.

"Be careful!" Gillian shouted from above them. He had to shout because the river was loud. It roared as the water swept by them and vanished over the cliff only a few feet away.

Where the boys had been crouching, the river was only inches deep, but the more they waded into the water the deeper it grew. The current seemed to gain strength with every step the boys took, but because Gillian warned them to be careful they desired to test their limits just to spite the Royal Pegasus guard.

They boys waded in deeper, and could feel that the further they tread, the smoother the rocks beneath their feet became.

"Whoa! It's getting slippery," Richard said as he looked over at his brother who was just upriver from him. Jessie could see his brother standing centered in the river. The water was now to his waist, but you could see that his legs were spread wide beneath himself bracing his body against the firm current. Richard's arms were raised from his sides with his fingertips stretched out, making himself readily available to catch himself if he were to fall. Jessie could tell his brother was a bit nervous. His face was painted with a worried look and it made Jessie giggle. The two of them were always pushing limits and it was rare that one of them would back down from a challenge.

"You scared brother?" he began to poke fun at his little brother. "It's not that…" and before Jessie could finish his sentence, his feet slipped out from underneath him, and the current overtook him. Soon, Jessie felt the fear that he had seen in his brother's face moments before. He became submerged in the waist deep water, and startled kicking and flailing his arms in every direction trying to find something; anything to grab. Only seconds had passed, but it felt as if he had been pulled under for minutes. If he opened his eyes, all he could see was the uncontrollable water swirling around him as the current pulled him towards the cliff. His arm swung through the water, and to his relief he was able to maintain a grip on something in the water. But before he was able to come up a breath, the grip he had was lost, and something came crashing down on him, pinning him to the bottom of the river. He began to panic, thinking this was the end for him. As the remaining breath in his lungs began to wither away, Jessie could feel his entire body slowing down. Not by choice, but forced by the lack of oxygen. He was losing consciousness. Slowly everything around, him began to fade into a black abyss. Jessie's arms stopped moving and he seemed to have accepted his fate.

Suddenly, just before Jessie blacked out, he felt his body being yanked out of the water. His tired limbs plopped upon a hard rock at the center of the river. As he frantically gulped up air, he began to cough aggressively. Air entering his body and water attempting to exit, clashed with one another.

"Jessie are you okay?" asked Richard with a soft frantic look on his face. As Jessie looked up to see his brother, he could see that Richard too was dripping wet with water.

"I'm okay," Jessie coughed.

"When you fell into the water, the current swept you right into me, and you took me out with you!" Richard explained. "But luckily we were thrown against this boulder before we were both swept over the edge!" He peered over the cliff's edge. The boulder they found themselves upon, was itself clinging onto the utmost edge of the cliff. Jessie cautiously gazed over the edge, feeling gravity pulling at his body. The boulder that was dividing the river, saved their lives, and now that he was so close to the brim he felt the severity of the cliff's towering height.

"You saved my life!" Jessie gasped as he grabbed onto his brother's arm.

"That was a close one!" Richard admitted.

As the adrenaline running through their veins settled, Jessie began to feel a sting coming from his knee. He looked down, and could now see that he had ripped his pant leg open and had scraped his knee on some rock while flailing his limbs in the river. A small stream of blood began to seep out of the scrape.

"Jessie!" Richard gasped with weight in his voice. Both boys felt humbled by what they had just been through. It was one of those moments when you realize that what you're doing could have serious consequences.

"It's just a scratch, don't worry about it," Jessie responded. His words were calm, but he could feel his heart pounding within. Jessie scooched closer to the flowing water, but held onto a protrusion of the boulder tightly as he lowered his other hand into the water. He used water to splash and clean his knee.

Gillian, who had witnessed the entire ordeal, snorted from above as he peered down at the boys.

"Are you done, messing around now?" Gillian asked, annoyed at their carelessness and in a hurry to get back to their mission.

"Yes I think we can safely say we are ready to move on," Richard said, looking at his brother cleaning his scrape.

Soon, Gillian stretched his wings out to his sides and flapped them, lifting himself from the ground. Gracefully he flew, until he hovered over the boys, and gently lowered himself onto the boulder they were perched on. Carefully, he knelt down so the boys could climb onto his back.

"Get on," Gillian ordered.

"That does not seem very safe," Jessie said, while looking up at Gillian.

"Now you're worried about safety?" Gillian asked.

"Haha… with all due respect, falling in the river is one thing.. But falling out of the sky is a whole other level," Richard said with a soft smile.

"Well, the way I see it, is that you only have two options. Either you find a way down the cliff, or we fly down there," Gillian said. The boys again peered over the edge of the cliff, watching the water seemingly evaporate out of sight.

"Hmmm, yeah I guess falling from the sky wouldn't be much worse than falling from this cliff," Jessie thought out loud, listening to the water crash its way over the edge.

"But do you think we could rest for a moment?" asked Richard, still shook up from the incident.

"We have to keep going, we have to find the other two!" Gillian snorted.

"I get that but we are tired!" Jessie explained.

"And besides, we have an advantage!" Richard claimed.

Gillian jolted his head backwards.

"An advantage? How could you assume such things? They must be much further ahead than us!" Gillian said with a long face.

"We have you!" Richard explained.

"That's right! You can fly us down!" Jessie chipped in.

"Exactly! They have to find a way down this cliff on their own!" Richard said with might in his voice. Still unaware of Eva's abrupt change in the original plan, Richard hoped that Andy and Eva had already made it back to Regnum.

"It would take them much longer to travel such a distance," Gillian pondered out loud. "And now that you mention it, my legs have grown quite tired…" he paused. "Maybe we should take a few minutes to rest?"

"That is a great idea!" Richard said building up Gillian as if it was his own idea.

"What a smart royal guard you are!" Jessie said sarcastically. Thankfully Gillian was so proud of himself that he didn't notice the rude tones in the brothers' voices.

"Might I suggest, maybe not taking our rest here?" Jessie asked.

Gillian snapped out of his self-gloat, and the three peered down at the roaring river from the boulder they tightly perched on.

"Yep, let's go!" Richard said excitedly, as if to express extreme importance that they get off that rock as soon as possible.

The boys were in a hurry to get to safer ground, but still moved slowly to their feet, carefully adjusting themselves to ensure that neither one of them slipped and fell again.

Using Gillian's wings, the boys hoisted themselves up onto the Pegasus' back. Gillian's mane was much longer than Jessie had expected, from the ground it looked very short. Although it was not as long as other Pegasi, it was still long enough for him to get two solid handfuls of hair. Richard sat right behind Jessie and wrapped both arms around his waist tightly.

"Ready?" Gillian asked.

"Ready!" the boys shouted simultaneously.

Gillian's wings shot straight out to the sides, lifted high into the air, and then thrust straight down, lifting all three off the ground. Gillian's wings were so powerful he didn't even have to start standing, but was able to clear the ground from his knees.

"Wow!" Richard gasped from under his breath as they began their flight.

Gillian overheard Richard's faint marvel and decided to give them a little excitement. He shot out over the tips of the Humilis Pines. As he grazed the tops of the trees with his dangling legs, the trees bent and swayed at his mercy. Gillian flapped his wings mightily and began to gain momentum. The boys were in awe at the creature's great strength and power. Before they knew it, Gillian adjusted his wings to scoop the air, and was able to maneuver a full circle where all three of them were upside down for a moment before returning to the right side up. He swayed this way and that, and swooped through the air majestically. The boys couldn't believe how graceful and beautiful the Pegasi species really was.

After a few minutes, Gillian returned to the upper ledge of the cliff and gently landed. He tucked his wings against his body and lowered himself to his knees to let the boys down.

Showered with excitement, the boys wore huge smiles on their faces and couldn't help but let out little childish giggles. Richard was so thrilled that he couldn't help but run his fingers through Gillian's mane, just between his ears and give him a good scratching. Gillian began to feel warm inside, as if a bond had grown between him and the brothers. Part of him stopped thinking of them as just fugitives of the King, but as actual friends.

Gillian settled lower to the ground and found himself resting. As the boys wandered off to the side and found a place for themselves to lay down, Gillian soaked in the last remaining rays of sun as the painted sky slipped behind the horizon. Slowly, the light faded into darkness and the night sky began to rule for the evening.

The night sky always intrigued Gillian. He never really knew why, but the way the stars danced and twinkled way above made him feel like they were a part of him somehow. He was told that his original ancestors came from the stars, but he really didn't know what that meant.

His eyes grew heavy as he pondered the origin of the land. *Who really created the beautiful forests and painted the sunsets? Was what I was told really true? Was it Malus or was it the Great White Eagle like the boys thought?*

Oh, how his life felt dismantled. Not only did he now question everything he thought was real, but he knew he was in deep trouble. It had been a whole day since he made up his fib. Vincent would have obviously figured out that he had lied to him by now. *It's only a matter of time. If he's not looking for me yet, he will be soon.* He thought. *Surely they will take my wings for this…*

Gillian was too tired to let his worrying keep him awake, soon the royal Pegasus, along with the brothers, fell fast asleep.

Chapter 14
Mysterious Red Glow

The moon lifted high into the sky that night, and nocturnal creatures began to awaken. The spiked talon owl took flight through the Superior Pines gliding silently in search of its prey, a family of possums paraded along the edge of the cliff down to the water's edge for a midnight drink, and a red bandit fox scampered over the rocky earth. These creatures are nocturnal for a reason, which is to stay hidden and out of sight, masked by the night. They did just that, the three strangers had no clue that these creatures were only feet away at times. Some stopped to investigate, but for only a moment, then they continued on their way.

Gillian was lulled by the gentle hum of the wind and rustling of the forest. For hours nothing interrupted his rest. Until all of a sudden, the yip of a wolf startled him awake.

As his eyes shot open, he had to blink a few times before he could focus on anything in the low lighting. Luckily for him, the predator's call was far across Centum's Core in the open meadow of Terribbia. He could see a pack of eight or nine wolves running about. They chased each other, darting around as if they were playing tag. They all yipped and howled. They pounced, tumbled, and raced back and forth under the pale moonlight.

By nature, the hair on Gillian's neck straightened out with fear, but after consideration, he was able to suppress his anxious mind. *They are way over there. No threat to me. Look at them play, just as I did when I was only a pony,* he thought.

Now that he was awake, he found himself feeling fairly rested. Instead of drifting back to sleep as he would have done if he was at home in his comfy stable, he stared out into the Centrum Core's and listened to the night. The silhouettes of the Humilis Pines gently swayed with the breeze. Crickets chirped and frogs croaked. Yet it all felt so still. Like it was a painting that he could stare at for hours. The pure beauty of the untouched wilderness amazed Gillian. *Wow… Just wow. How did all this really come to be? Was it Malus? Or… The Eagle?* His thoughts began to grow. *I don't think Malus would be caught dead out in the wilderness. Even when I was in training to become a Royal Guard, I had to do wilderness training and Malus would only spectate for a short bit. Then he would return to the castle before dark… But why? If he were the one to create the land, why wouldn't he enjoy his own creation? I mean how could anyone not appreciate this intricate beauty?* Gillian thought, as he gazed into the night. Which causes his mind to ponder deeper thoughts. Questions he would have never dared to wonder before. *What if Malus really is not the creator. What if the Great White Eagle is the true maker, who carved the rivers and valleys and formed the mountain tops?*

Just then, as if in reaction to his thought a faint flicker of red flashed, but quickly vanished.

"Psst, guys wake up!" Gillian loudly whispered.

"Nectorsuckle Jam is good for a...ZzZzz," Richard uttered while being fast asleep.

Gillian's attempt was in vain but he didn't care, he became focused in the direction of the faint red light, which suddenly flashed again. He could now see that it was coming from amongst the Humilis Pines below him. Soon the light flickered like a candle and vanished again. Gillian found himself on his feet, pacing along the edge of the cliff trying to get a better look at what the light was. The pines were so thick below that he could only get a slight glimpse of the light when it would flicker but was never able to distinguish what it was.

Gillian grew anxious, wondering what it was or what it could mean. He stepped closer and closer to the edge. With his hooves still planted firmly on the cliff but as close as possible to the edge, he stretched his neck out towards the light. Basically, dangling himself over the edge.

The flash of light began to become more frequent. Yet the needles blocked the true source of light. He came up with all sorts of ideas on what it could be, but just as he felt he was making progress on deciding on what it could be, a silhouette of a giant bird soared through the night sky. It was so sudden, that it scared the daylights right out of Gillian. Like a cat being scared off the dining room table, he pounced right off the side of the cliff. Luckily for Gillian he had wings, and shortly after his dive he regained his senses and hovered over the drop-off. Then the light changed consistency. Now it seemed to be flashing at a slower pace. Glowing for a longer period of time before it would vanish again.

Being airborne, he convinced himself to try and get closer to it, but the branches of the pine trees were so thick that his large body could not manage to get close enough to know what the light truly was.

Suddenly, the bird let out a terrifying screech, which spooked Gillian and forced him back to the cliff and to solid ground. As he landed, he peered around in every direction to see where the winged beast had gone.

Worried it was after him he wanted to be ready if it attacked. Gillian raised the elbows of his wings, and took a low stance ready for a fight. Confusingly enough, the winged creature was nowhere to be seen. In fact, it was as if the bird vanished into thin air.

After a few minutes on high alert, Gillian relaxed his wings and turned his attention back to the light, but there was no light. No more red flickers, no more faint glow in the night.

What! Where did it go? Gillian thought. His heart rate had settled, but he was still thoroughly worked up. Frantically he searched for the light. Gluing his eyes to where he saw it last.

Literally, over an hour's time had passed. At first, he vigorously paced back and forth, but over time he couldn't help growing overwhelmingly tired. His vigorous pace slowed to a trudge, which eventually turned into a collapse to the ground. Although his legs had had enough, he still found himself staring into the pine trees, hoping the light would reveal itself once more. Sadly, the light never returned. Gillian's blinking even became laborious. Each blink began to become more difficult, until at last he failed to open his eyes again.

The sunrise quickly came the next morning and soon Gillian was awakened by the chirping of the birds as they sang their morning songs. He could hear Richard and Jessie chatting away as they soaked in the crisp morning air and overlooked the Centrum's Core.

Gillian blinked a few times, trying to force his body awake. His mind was up and ready to go, but his body moved much slower as if it was forced into a trance from his sleep. Regaining the connection of his mind and body he jumped to his hooves and trotted over to the boys.

"Did you guys see the red light?" Gillian said, almost shouting at the boys.

Richard yawned and stretched his arms out high above his head. "What red light?" he fumbled out.

"Down there!" Gillian said, while turning around and pointing to the pines with his nose.

"I didn't see anything except for the back of my eyelids!" Jessie said with a chuckle.

"Well surely you boys heard the terrible cry of that bird thing last night!" Gillian pleaded.

"Bird thing?" asked Richard.

"Yeah it let out a terrible squeal!" Gillian spit out.

"Squeal? Maybe it was a pig with wings!" Jessie said while poking fun at Gillian. Gillian didn't find the jokes to be very funny at all.

How could they have slept through that awful noise? Was it all a dream? He pondered. *It felt way too real to be a dream.*

Just then Gillian realized that he woke up this morning in a different spot than where he had first laid down to go to sleep the night before.

"It wasn't a flying pig, that's impossible!" Gillian snorted as if to prove a point. "But I saw something last night, something big and scary. And I saw a light, a flickering red light that glowed ever so beautifully," he said. "It was just down there." Everyone's attention was directed towards the pine trees. "But it's in the trees and I can't get to it… Will you boys climb down the tree and look for it?"

"Yes! Let me just strap on my wings and fly down there," Richard smarted off.

Gillian's head dropped. Jessie could tell that Gillian was quite serious about it, that he had really seen something the night before. Something that made him excited, almost passionate.

"Of course, we will go look for it, after all we love a good adventure!" Jessie said while giving Richard a look that told him to just go along with it. Richard rolled his eyes, but respected his brother's request.

Gillian whinnied a happy bray and knelt down for the boys. One at a time the brothers crawled onto his back and grabbed on tightly.

"Here we go!" Gillian shouted, followed by whispers of, "I'm gonna find you," referring to the red glow from the night before. With no hesitation Gillian lifted the three of them into the air.

Gillian swooped over the treetops near where he saw the light, and began to hover over the tips of evergreens.

"A little closer!" Jessie ordered.

"Almost!" Richard announced, as Gillian slowly sank amongst the treetops.

"This is all the further I can do, if I try and go any further, we will all go tumbling down!" Gillian informed the boys.

"This will do!" Jessie said as he began to lean over and grab ahold of the biggest branch he could find. As he shifted his weight off of Gillian and on to the tree, the branch began to bend under his pressure. Once he got to the point of no return, he slipped off Gillian and aimed his feet to a branch lower than the one he held on to. His foot landed right where he wanted it. Firmly at the base of the branch right next to the trunk of the mighty pine tree. He shimmed down the tree a few branches to give room for his brother who was making his transition next. The tree was very top heavy now and began to lean.

Richard too leaned over and grabbed onto the prickly pine branch and shifted his weight off of Gillian and landed his feet against the trunk of the tree. Richard tried to reposition his footing by moving his foot away from the base of the branch.

SNAP! The branch gave way under his weight. Thankfully he only fell an inch for there was another branch directly below this one stopping his fall.

"Whoa! That was close! Pretty sure my heart stopped for a second," said Richard, giggling out of fear.

"Yeah, just what I would have needed, your butt in my face," Jessie said, while looking up at his brother.

"Do you guys see it yet?" Gillian shouted from above, ignoring the close call. He had lifted himself higher into the air and was peering down at the boys.

"You know we literally just got onto this shaky stick!" Jessie shouted out at Gillian while looking to find his next set of branches to climb down too.

The boys climbed their way down the tree. Their movement made the tree shake and wiggle as if it had a massive itch it was trying to scratch. Pinecones and needles shook loose and fell, bouncing and tumbling to the ground.

The boys had now vanished from Gillian's sight as they had scurried their way beneath the uppermost branches of the tree. Like the crystal, the boys were concealed by the close-knit branches of the Humilis Pine forest.

"Anything?" Gillian barked from above the treetops.

"Nothing! Are you sure this was the tree?" Richard asked.

"I'm most certain, but let me fly back to the cliff and see if I can get a better view. It was dark last night you know!" Gillian commented.

Gillian flew off towards the cliff and the boys continued to survey their tree and the surrounding forest. They could neither see the blue sky above, nor the mossy earth below, only a thicket of pine branches. It was rather uncomfortable for them both. The sticky sap of the evergreen coated their hands and fingers, and the pine needles scraped their arms and face as they weaved their way down the branches. The only benefit now was that the branches were becoming bigger and stronger, making them feel much more secure the closer they got to the Centrum Core's floor.

"Did you hear that?" Jessie forcefully whispered, looking at Richard dangling above him.

"Hear what?" Richard said looking confused.

"Listen!" commanded Jessie as he began to peer down towards the base of the tree.

At first Richard thought Jessie was crazy, but then he heard something too. It sounded like faint whispers. Yet, the longer they listened the louder the whispers became. Soon, it wasn't whispers at all, it was two humans talking below them.

"Ssshhhh!" Jessie said, as he looked up at Richard and put his pointer finger in front of his lips.

The boys froze, doing everything they could not to move or to make a sound. They had worked their way closer to the ground before they had heard the voices which provided them little gaps in the branches to peek through and see the forest floor below. Before long they could see two people walking side by side.

"It must have fallen to the ground over here somewhere," a boy's voice said.

"What did?" questioned a girl.

"I grabbed onto one of the crystals in the cave with the beavers. Right before I was forced down the water slide, and it broke off." he said. Their voices sounded very familiar. "Here it is!"

Jessie could see bits of the boy jogging over his way. Soon, he was just below them and picking something up off the ground. The branches were still thick enough that he couldn't make out what it was that he found or who the boy might be. Not too far behind him, he could see the girl making her way beside him. It was quite frustrating because Jessie could not see who she was either. Only the tops of their heads were visible.

"I think it's Andy and Eva!" Jessie whispered up at Richard. "But I'm not quite sure yet." Richard's heart filled with excitement. He honestly thought that he would never see them again.

"But wait, they were supposed to head home?!" said Richard, as his delight swiftly changed to annoyance.

"Can you put this in your pouch?" the boy asked the girl. Jessie could see them put the mysterious item into a pouch that Eva had on her side.

Although Jessie was almost certain it was Andy and Eva, he couldn't trust his judgment just yet. Not until he finally saw a Gladiator bear waddling close behind them was he finally sure.

"It's Andy and Eva!" Jessie shouted. Andy, Eva, and Maizey were all startled by the sudden burst from Jessie who was perched out of sight above them. The loud voice spooked them enough that they all took multiple steps away from the tree.

"Who's there?" asked Andy, putting himself between Eva and the threat.

"It's me! Jessie!" he said, filled with excitement. He started trying to force his way to the ground, much more clumsy than before. Prying at branches, he began to shimmy through towards the ground. Now only seven or eight feet off the ground, Jessie had decided to jump to the forest floor. Leaping from the tree he expected to feel the ground beneath his feet, but to his dismay he felt something grab onto the seat of his pants instead. Causing quite a ruckus of laughter, there Jessie was dangling from the tree for all to see. A branch from the evergreen snagged him by the pants and rendered him helpless. Jessie just hung there with his arms and legs dangling towards the earth.

As their laughter grew louder, Jessie who was mostly embarrassed began to quiet them down.

"Shhh! He will hear you."

"Who will?" Eva asked.

"The Royal Pegasus Guard." Jessie responded, still dangling from his britches.

"Yes! Gillian!" Richard said, poking his head below the level of branches he clung to.

Richard scurried down to the branch that had a hold of his brother. Using his weight to bounce on the branch, he clung to the one above him with his hands. After enough bouncing, the branch gave way and Jessie thumped to the ground. Strategically, Richard clung to the branch above him and hung from it like a monkey.

As Jessie stood to his feet, he wiped his knees and arms off. "It's so great to see you! I thought we might never see each other again." He began to ramble. Then he punched Andy in the arm. "But you were supposed to bring her home," he scolded him.

"I know but she found out our plan, and wanted to save you," responded Andy.

"Which is why you were not supposed to tell her!" Richard said from above in a condemning tone.

"I know, I know. But she *actually* yelled at me! Plus… she had a dream. One where the Great White Eagle told her to keep going," he said, which made Eva annoyed. She didn't consider it to be yelling when she firmly discussed the boys' plan with Andy.

"Great White Eagle? Hmmft," Richard scoffed. He was unsure about the whole bit. He knew what he was taught, yet what Gillian had told him before seemed to make a lot of sense.

"The Eagle? You're sure it was him?" Jessie questioned. Unlike his brother, Jessie was still on board with the whole existence of the Great White Eagle. Although Gillian had solid points, his conscience wouldn't let him give up on the Great White Eagle just yet. One of his biggest reasons for holding on to the idea of the Great White Eagle was his mama. Before she passed away, she always pointed them to the Great White Eagle. No matter how bad things got for them she always had faith in him. Needless to say, he was not ready to give up on him yet.

"What's going on down there?" Gillian shouted from above. They had all become so excited to see one another, that Richard and Jessie nearly forgot about Gillian.

"Shhhhh" Richard said to the group. "Nothing!" he responded to Gillian, as he let go with his hands and dropped to his feet on the forest floor.

"What's all that commotion?" Gillian questioned.

"The pine needles. They are sharp little buggers!" Jessie shouted, trying to make an excuse for the noise they were making.

"Did you find it?" Gillian asked again.

For a moment, Richard felt a cool rush down his neck. Knowing that finding Andy and Eva was Gillian's ultimate goal, he had forgotten that they were looking for the mysterious red glow, and thought Gillian was referring to his friends.

"Find what?" Richard asked.

"The light! What else are you looking for?" Gillian snorted in annoyance.

"Oh yes, of course!" Richard mistakenly responded. He was so relieved that Gillian wasn't asking about Andy and Eva that he accidently told him they had found the source of the red light.

"You did? That's great!" Gillian brayed.

"Oh, no, I meant no! We haven't found that," Richard said, while making big eyes at Jessie, wondering what he should really be saying.

"Oh, well let me come down there! I was able to find a lake off to the north of you. That will allow me to come down to your ground level. I'll be right down!" Gillian said.

Everyone grew a panicked look on their faces.

"Quick! We have to get out of here!" Richard said in a panic.

"What are we gonna do?" Eva cried.

Before they could even think of a plan, they could see Gillian landing far off near the edge of the lake. Only pine branches and tree trunks stood before them.

"Run!" Andy shouted as he bolted south through the forest.

Richard and Jessie felt conflicted. They had grown fond of Gillian and felt that there was a kind and caring Pegasus under all that tough guy attitude. Yet, they knew that if Gillian caught all four of them, the chances of him turning them over to the King were high.

"Richard! We have to go. You know we do," Jessie announced to his brother. Jessie knew the safest option was to run.

Eva too started in that direction but paused when she realized that Maizey was not following.

"Come on Maizey!" Eva begged.

"This is where we part ways," Maizey growled at Eva.

"What? No!" she cried.

"Eva, I will run him off, you get to safety. Complete your mission! You have given me hope in the future and faith in the Great White Eagle! I am forever grateful to have crossed paths with such a full hearted young Somniator! Go, the Eagle is waiting!" Maizey ordered.

Eva's eyes filled with tears, but she knew it was their only option. She turned to run after the boys and the forest became blurry. Tears streamed down her face as she dashed out of sight.

Maizey let out a ferocious roar and charged Gillian. Gillian was shocked to say the least, he had only expected to see Richard and

Jessie in the forest, but they were not alone. At first he fixated on the humans, but as Maizey began to barrel towards him, he couldn't avoid focusing on her. In that moment he knew Richard and Jessie had found the other two traitors, which caused Gillian's nostrils to flare in anger. He became so angry that he didn't even flinch at the furious Gladiator bear. He could see beyond the big ball of deadly fluff deeper into the forest, where Jessie and Richard were escaping him with the other two.

Finally overcoming his bout of anger, Gillian realized just how much danger he was going to be in if he didn't move out of the bear's way. He quickly back pedaled out from under the forest's needly canopy and thrust his wings down, lifting himself from the ground.

I can't believe they are running from me. To think, I was beginning to think of them as friends. Gillian festered in his head. The way Gillian felt inside was different than he had ever felt before. He was angry but it was fueled by the feeling of betrayal, which made him feel sick and almost sad.

Now that he had lifted himself into the air, the only thing he could see was Maizey as she ripped out of the forest near the lakes shore and towered to her hind legs. He had to lift himself higher because the swing of her claws came close to tearing into his legs. Gillian attempted to swoop left but she swung and countered his movement. He tried to dodge right, trying to sneak past the Gladiator to chase after the traitors, but again she blocked his attempt. Having no desire to take on Maizey in a one-on-one battle, he retreated to the sky.

Gillian became overwhelmingly angry that he could feel his blood boil within him. *I will catch those nasty little humans, even if it's the last thing I ever do.*

Little did Gillian know, the longer he festered his anger the darker his shins grew. As he soared above the Humilis Pines, barreling towards the Devil's Kettle searching for the traitors, black markings that made him look like he was wearing stockings began to take root.

"I will find you!" he shouted in a fury above the trees. It could be heard by all creatures in the area. It was so loud that the four on the run shivered at the echo of his voice.

Chapter 15
The Raven's Crow

Plowing through the forest, they ran without looking back. In strides they pushed past the point of exhaustion, and felt as if they could run forever. They kicked up the orange needles that covered the shaded forest floor, weaved around exposed roots, leaped over fallen logs, and barreled through branches that hovered in their way. It was their chance to escape the clutches of the Royal Pegasus Guard and they were not going to waste the opportunity.

Everything became a blur for the four escapees. They seemed to have run for so long, they couldn't tell if they were moving or if the trees had uprooted themselves and were running past them.

Soon, they had safely cleared the Humilis Pines and had now stepped into the mists of the Nevergreen forest. A chill filled the air as they left the green needles behind them and entered into a bare and empty wasteland. The grass was taller, the bark on the trees had been stripped away, and the only remains were smooth pale gray skeletons of dead evergreen trees. From above the four would have looked like grasshoppers. It was because the ground became more uneven, heaping up in one place and sinking lower in another; it forced them to hop instead of run. If Gillian had been close by he would have been able to see their heads bouncing above the grasses and then falling amidst them. However, luckily for the four friends, the Centrum's Core was a massively uncharted area and was easy for them to change course of directions. So, Gillian zoomed slightly East, while the four teenagers raced slightly West.

Now their pace began to slow, hopping took more effort and wore them out to a slow trudge. The grass became like spider webs and snares, tangling around their legs.

Slowly the Nevergreen forest faded and the surrounding landscape became as bare as the dead trees were themselves. The high humps of ground became scarce and the land became spongy. Each misplaced step allowed water to seep into the fabric of their shoes.

"We've got to be getting close," Richard complained from the rear.

"I don't know but this place is giving me the creeps," Eva said as she wiped sweat from her brow. Despite the growing humidity the mysterious bog was giving her the chills. The kind you get when you feel uneasy or watched.

"I wonder if this is the Uada Hollow that Maizey was talking about? It's no wonder she wanted nothing to do with this place," Andy said while leading the way through the thick grasses.

All they could see was tall cattail grasses in every direction. Occasionally they would look up, but a low lingering fog blocked out the blue sky above. It reminded them of a dreary rainy day that had gone on for too long.

As they journeyed deeper, the grass would occasionally rustle or wave, which startled them all. Unsure of whether it was a wild animal, Gillian, or a monster hiding in the thickness, they all stayed close together. At this point their fear of what lay in wait around them was what kept them moving; they pressed on.

Richard kept his eyes glued to the ground. It was obvious that the ground was being swallowed by the bog itself. Each step they took became more crucial and careful aim was needed to insure their footing. Richard took a moment to peer up and check to see that the others were still nearby, but out of the corner of his eye he caught sight of something black. The grass had waved and parted just enough, that a creepy black figure appeared deep within it. Yet, as quickly as it appeared, the grass waved and seemingly wiped the figure away and it was gone.

The hair on the back of Richard's neck straightened out and stood on end. He gulped hard and goosebumps formed all across his arms. The spooky sight stopped him in his tracks. He wished he had never looked up, because soon he realized the three others had vanished into the grass before him. Frightened of what he saw and scared to be left behind, he bolted forwards reuniting with the group, leaving whatever creepy thing he saw behind him.

While he rushed forwards to find the others, Richard realized that he had begun splashing as he went. Before the ground was solid but held onto water like a sponge, but now there was standing water.

"Wait up!" Richard shouted from behind, as he soon stumbled upon the group. Richard stopped to catch his breath and standing before him was Andy and Eva on a mound of grass that had a small needless evergreen clinging to its topside.

Jessie stood in the water with both hands on his hips waiting for his little brother.

"Would you keep up?" he scolded.

"I thought…" Richard gasped for air. "I thought I saw something."

"Saw what?" Eva asked with a quiver in her voice. She was already uncomfortable with the unknown around her, a mysterious something wasn't going to help.

"I don't know. A black figure. Something that was there one second and gone the next," Richard tried to explain.

"Brother, you're seeing things. I think you're just exhausted…" Jessie said, trying to convince himself that Richard hadn't seen anything.

"Yeah, we have been walking almost all day," Andy explained, realizing just how late it was. Richard just hung his head. He knew he saw something.

"Hey Andy?" Eva said, looking towards Andy.

"Yeah?" Andy responded, still perched on top of the mound above everyone else.

"I'm hungry… And I have to imagine it's gonna get cold tonight." Eva chattered. The sun had obviously been well on its way back towards their earth, for the warm kiss of the moist air was beginning to fade into the cold gray of dusk. It was difficult for them to truly tell what time it was since the sun was blotted out by the fog. The reality was, it didn't matter if the sun was still in the sky above, because the fog would cause it to get darker hours before the sun actually slipped away behind the horizon.

"This fog is really making it hard to see," Richard said, still thinking about the figure he saw in the bog wishing the dense fog would lift and the sun would come back allowing them to see clearly just in case the shadowy figure returned.

"Yeah man, how long are we supposed to keep going? Like I know Gillian is hunting us down and Richard's seein' things… but my tummy's grumbling," Jessie complained.

"Hey!" Richard scolded his brother. "But seriously, I might not be able to speak to bears, but I sure can understand the growl that my stomach makes," he said jokingly, causing Eva to roll her eyes at his attempt to lighten the mood.

Being elevated, Andy peered over the group. Placed his hands on his hips, he began to scan the area. His hair was damp and flat, drooping down his forehead, and his face had so much sweat beaded up from the humidity that droplets dripped from his chin. The whole group looked like they had just gotten done swimming. From their heads to their toes, they were soaked.

Darkness was setting in. The fog laced the swaying grasses that towered all around them and made them feel small and anxious. It was hard enough to see where to go next, let alone think of their next move. From his vantage point nothing looked promising. He stepped down from the mound and found a large log laying in the midst of the grass, slowly he balanced his way along the trunk to try and see the area around them. Suddenly he stopped. His abrupt stop halted the three following close behind him as well. Eva managed to stop short of Andy. But Richard, who was focused on his feet, walked right into his brother. Soon they started pushing each other as if it was a game to see who could stay on the log the longest.

"Andy, do you see anything? I'm scared," Eva expressed her concern quietly to Andy while the brothers wrestled behind her. "It's getting dark."

"I'm…. looking," he said in a strung-out manner. He spoke the words slowly as he scanned the area, looking for any sign of safety or a place they could bunker down for the night. "There!" He finally blurted. Hope filled Eva's heart as she plopped off the log following Andy's lead.

Wading through the bog, the group finally found what Andy had seen through the reeds of the swamp. Somehow a patch of solid ground emerged from the hollow. It wasn't very large, but it would be large enough for them all to lay down and sprawl out for the night without water crowding their sides. The ground was covered in thick yellow green moss.

To a tired soul, the moss was bouncy and would have been quite comfortable except for the scatter of tree roots that weaved in and out of the ground leaving hard ridged lumps all over.

There was something incredible about this tree. It was unlike any other they had ever seen before. The most astonishing thing was that this tree was still alive. Seemingly the only live tree in the entire Uada Hollow. It was similar in height to the Nevergreens, but its branches looked more like a bush with twigs and they tangled in every direction. Small round leaves grew creating a canopy for them all to sit under. Its sight felt magical to say the least. Pink flowers with golden rims blossomed at the branch's fingertips. Despite the looming fog and rustling grasses of the unknown, this tree brought them all peace; a sense of safety.

"So… about the food?" Richard asked after they had all rested for a few minutes.

"Hmm yes, okay I have a plan but I will need a few things," Andy said, tracking down a solution to their hunger in his head.

"What do you need?" Eva asked. She was quite eager to hear what he had to say. She remembered how he built the fire back at Maizey's den and cooked the fish. That was impressive enough. However, she was excited to see what he could find out in the middle of nowhere without a living thing in sight.

"Richard and Jessie, I need you to go back to the log I stood on when I first saw this higher ground. Once there you will find the stump that the log fell from. I need you to kick the stump loose from the ground, and bring it back here, then find me a sharp rock." The boys were intrigued by his request.

"On it captain!" Jessie shouted.

"Eva, I need you to find me four or five different small rocks and start collecting twigs from the Nevergreens for a fire," he commanded.

"Okay, on it," she said as she set her pouch from Maizey down on the ground and darted off onto the other side of the high ground looking for the items Andy requested.

After a few minutes Richard and Jessie came running back in excitement. Both of them held onto the base of the stump, their hands covered in black muck from digging around at its base. They looked as silly as two dogs running side by side with the same bone in their mouths. Clinging to either side of the stump they ran sideways together with giant smiles plowing down the grasses and splashing through the water. The amount of achievement in both of their eyes over the stump made Andy giggle.

"Did you find a sharp rock?" asked Andy.

"Oh snap, be right back!" Jessie said, as the boys ran off looking for one.

Andy proceeded to dig a small hole with his hands. This would be where he would put the fire. After that he ventured into the bog and began pulling cattails out of the ground, roots, and all. Finding plenty of those, he brought them back and laid them next to his fire pit.

Once Eva found her way back to Andy she unloaded her arms. Six or seven rocks tumbled to the ground. She wasted no time after that and quickly scurried off for the next order on her list, twigs.

"You couldn't find anything dryer?" Andy snapped, as Eva returned and plopped damp twigs on the ground.

"There is no such thing as dry out here!" Eva barked back. They both became wide eyed and quiet. The sudden weight of their situation got the best of them. Realizing just how stressed and scared they were had made them overreact to the situation.

"I'm sorry," Andy said, apologizing for his sharp tone.

"I know… me too. I think we are both just nervous." Eva said. With a nod from Andy, they left it at that.

CLANK! CLUNK! CLACK! The sound echoed into the air. At first it startled Andy and Eva because it was unexpected. Here it was Richard and Jessie. They could not find a naturally sharp rock, so they smashed two together and split one in half. It sounded as if it was half above water and half below. If you had ever knocked two rocks together underwater you would know what it sounded like.

"That will do!" Andy said to the brothers after he examined their sharp rock. "Now, Richard, use your jagged rock to carve out the top of the stump into a deep bowl," Andy commanded, "And Jessie, if you could go to the dead trees and use your half of the sharp rock to shave off thin layers of the tree's bark? We can try and use that as kindling for the fire!"

"On it!" The boys responded.

Andy turned to Eva, "Can you help me here?"

She nodded and he began to show her what to do with the Cattails.

"This is called a Cattail," he explained. He began to strip them of their large, long leaves so only the head of the plant, the stock, and the roots were left. The stock of the plant was green, but at the base there was a white bulb which had spaghetti-like roots growing from it. Nimbly he plucked the roots off so only the white bulb remained.

"This here is called a Rhizome," he said while pointing to the white bulb. After that he broke off the soft brown head of the plant, which looked like a big sausage and set it aside.

"The last thing we will do is break the stock of the Cattail into sections. Small enough to fit into the bowl Richard is making," Andy explained.

"Okay! I think I got it!" Eva said as she got to work preparing the remaining cattails.

Andy's next task was to create a fire. He knew that they would need it. Not that they needed it to cook the cattails, but to survive the night. The night sky was well on its way and the temperature was dropping fast. If they couldn't get a fire started to dry themselves off, they would be lucky to survive the night.

Andy motioned for the brothers to bring what they had gathered. He had them place the wooden shavings at the bottom of the pit and then took the two shards of rock that Richard and Jessie were using.

Andy filtered through the twigs Eva had brought to him, looking for the driest ones to stack strategically around the wooden shavings. He knew it had to be perfect. If not, he was afraid that he wouldn't be able to get a fire started, considering everything was so wet.

Once the pit was prepped, his next step was to hit the stones together. Hope filled their hearts for the stones produced sparks with ease. Eva was excited to watch Andy get a fire going again, just like he had back at Maizey's den. Unfortunately, their hope faded because this time it went differently. As sweat dripped off Andy's nose, the sparks he was able to produce smothered under the dampness of the air.

"Come on, come on!" Andy began to whisper aggressively to himself. He struck the rocks harder and harder and sparks danced everywhere, but nothing happened.

Richard came over with his completed bowl but his smile of achievement quickly sagged when he could see Andy's defeated look as he gazed into the quiet fire pit.

Why? Andy thought to himself. Again, he struck the rocks. Yet, nothing.

The sound of a raven's call blared in the distance. It was a spooky noise, which caused goosebumps to form instantly over their arms and the back of their necks, but their task at hand seemed more important than any danger that lingered overhead.

"Are you kidding?" Andy said with anger in his voice as he held out his hand to feel the light drizzle that had begun to fall from the sky. Now everything that was too damp to catch fire before, was only becoming more soaked. As Andy refocused on the fire pit, he noticed water beginning to pool at the pit's base. Whether it was ground water soaking up from below or there had been enough water from the light rain to fill the pit, Andy knew they were in big trouble. Soaked, cold, and hungry all of them began to shiver and wonder if this was going to be their end.

What am I to do? Andy thought in his head as if he was asking the Great White Eagle himself. *Why are you doing this?*

Just then another raven's cry echoed in the fog, but this time it seemed much closer. The three members watching quickly huddled together under the odd tree with the pink flowers. By this time their breaths could be seen in the cold crisp air.

Great, Just great! A raven… something to scavenge our bodies after we freeze to death out here. Andy thought to himself.

He focused back on the pit and began clanking rocks together again. Yet again, sparks and then nothing.

"I can get more shavings," Jessie exclaimed, trying to be helpful.

"It's useless, everything is too wet, I can't get a spark to take," Andy said softly. He felt defeated, torn, and as if he was a failure. The cold and wet night would make them sick or worse. He felt as if it was all his fault.

The rest of the group shivered in the cold with nothing but fading hope.

Andy was growing weary, over a half hour had passed and he had yet to start a fire. He could feel the weight of the others, as their eyes rested upon each strike he made. He was so hungry and tired. The gray around them was growing black as night was falling hard upon them.

If the official nighttime hadn't reached them, it was only just around the corner. He pounded and beat the rocks together. More than once had the rocks shattered into shards, forcing him to find new ones. None of it helped, no matter what he did he couldn't get a fire to start.

He began to question everything. *If we had just turned back, gone home...* he thought. *I should have listened to my gut... why did I ever let Eva convince me otherwise, we both knew it would be dangerous. Why would the Eagle bring us out here in this forsaken hollow? Just to die! Why?* Suddenly his thoughts turned into words.

"Tell me why! Oh, Great Eagle!" Andy cried. "Why are we here!" He dropped his rocks and stood up, throwing his arms into the sky. "What do you want?" he shouted into the fog. To the others it looked like Andy had lost his mind. It would have been an awkward moment except Andy only said what everyone was thinking.

Just then hundreds of ravens began to crow. So many that when they all took flight out of the hollow, the flap of their wings sounded like thunder. The boys crouched low and covered their ears for the boom of the ravens' call were deafening. To their surprise Eva did the opposite. Standing up from under the tree she walked out into the open and peered into the foggy mist.

"Don't doubt?" she questioned.

Andy looked at Eva with his head cocked sideways, the way a dog would when spoken too.

"What do you mean don't doubt?" Eva questioned into the fog.

The hair on Andy's neck stood straight, he suddenly knew exactly what 'Don't doubt' meant. It was a direct message from the Great White Eagle aimed at him. Just then the rain quit falling and a strong wind blew. The grass bowed low and the trees with the pink flowers shook violently in the wind, as if a much bigger storm was on its way. The wind blew so furiously that the water in the pit dried up, leaving no trace of a puddle.

Suddenly just like ripples on a water's surface, the fog began to ripple as a raven busted through the nearest layer. It swooped low at Andy's head, swerved in front of Richard and Jessie, made a loop around Eva, and then lifted in a circular motion until it perched itself in the pink flowered tree.

The raven used its beak to retrieve a piece of paper that it had gripped in its claw, then dropped it down into Eva's hands.

"What is it?" Richard asked, still huddled together with his brother shivering from the cold.

Eva unrolled the piece of paper and her eyes filled with joy. "It's…it's a letter from my parents," she said, as she began to cry happy tears.

"What does it say?" asked Andy.

Eva looked at Andy and wiped the tears from her eyes. She then held the paper up in front of her and cleared her throat.

"It reads,"

> 'Eva, my dear. I love you and miss you, but I know. I
> received a message from a dear friend of mine, who received
> a dream all about your journey. I know I have been hard on
> you these years, but I was only trying to protect you. You

see, the truth is I too ventured into the Forbidden circle years ago... But I lost a dear friend of mine along the way. I never wanted you to go through the same, so I did my best to prevent you from venturing out at all. I guess I was too restricting... Forgive me.

I never told you any of this because I did not want you to even consider going to the Devil's Kettle yourself. But I guess the Great White Eagle has other plans.

My dear friend told me that you, my sweet child, are a Somniator. What a gift! Cherish it and use it wisely.

During our journey, we discovered many mysteries of the Devil Kettle. We didn't know what to do, much less think so we visited the Elves shortly after, but they turned us away. They said the time had not yet come. Maybe you are what they have been waiting for?

This is such a scary journey and you will face many dangers. But be strong my dear. Trust the path the Great White Eagle has set before you.

Now, my dear. Listen to me very closely. Beware of the Uada hollow! The ground is tricky, the air is heavy, and the voices at night lie! Don't believe the lies, and don't doubt the Great White Eagles' protection. Remember to always trust in the Great White Eagle, he will provide as needed.

Your father and I love you dearly and wait eagerly for your return. Be safe my love.

Love mom and dad.

The warning at the end of the letter left the group silent. Then the raven squawked loudly, startling everyone and flew off into the foggy abyss.

Chapter 16
Cattail Chow Down

Everyone was astonished. There was not a question between the four of them that wasn't asked in their minds. *How did the water dry up so fast?* Andy wondered peering down at the waterless pit. *How did that raven find us? Was it the Great White Eagle who sent it?* Jessie pondered starting to believe in the mysterious bird more and more. Many other questions like these flow as well. Yet, no one said a word.

Eva just stared at the letter. She couldn't help but let tears roll down her cheeks. She missed her parents dearly and was joyfully relieved to hear from them. *I knew my parents would understand.* She recalled as she thought back to when Andy urged her to return to her parents. *Mom... you came here too? Why? Did the Eagle send you? Why couldn't you have told me. Maybe I would have stayed home, where it was safe and warm...* Eva questioned these and more. However, she knew that those answers wouldn't change anything now. She had to focus on surviving the night. *The ground is tricky, that's for sure... The air is heavy. That's one way to put it. But what voices? There is nothing out here except us...* Eva brushed the edge of the letter with her thumb, thinking deeply about what voices her mom could be talking about.

As she continued to stare at the words written on the paper, she subconsciously continued to rub her thumb against the paper, as one might do while pondering deep thoughts. Then just as a sponge would suck up water, the paper sucked up all her attention. It finally dawned on her that the paper was very dry.

"Andy! The fire!" she shouted.

"Eva, even with that wind, I don't think the twigs and tree shavings will be dry enough to light," Andy said, feeling defeated all over again.

"No, the letter! Use it as a kindling! Like the letter says, Don't Doubt... He will provide! And he has! Here," she chirped. She then began to rip the letter into skinny strips of papers and gave them to Andy. Filled with hope once again, he placed them at the base of his twig tower. Richard and Jessie pressed in with excitement. Everyone huddled around Andy watching closely hoping that soon they could warm up, dry off, and eat a cooked meal.

Then as if it was his first strike, Andy struck the rocks together, producing more sparks than he ever had before. Instantly the spark grabbed a hold of the strips of dry paper and began to burn. The flame grew and began to burn the rest of the letter generating great heat for such a small flame. The wooden shavings below captured the hot flakes that fell from the paper and dried out, eventually burning up themselves. That in turn dried out the tower of sticks and the flame grew tall before their eyes.

"Quick!" Andy shouted with excitement. "Find any and all firewood that you can and place it around the pit so the heat of the fire can dry them out before we use them to fuel it!"

All four of them scattered, finding twigs, sticks, and logs that could be broken and burned in the fire.

For the first time, the cold, wet, dark bog felt a little warmer. A yellow glow pushed out the shadows that were crowding in on the patch of higher ground. Heat radiated out and slowly their skin and clothing dried and they felt their shivers calm.

"Richard and Jessie, bring the stump that you carved out into a bowl over to the water, scoop up the water with your hands and fill the bowl," Andy said while he fueled the fire with more wood. After the fire had burned and the pit was full of large lumps of burning coal, Andy set the five small rocks into the fire pit. The wood snapped and crackled around the stones and soon they began to warm up.

Setting the stump down next to Andy, they watched to see what came next. Andy found two sticks, which he used to pinch the hot rocks in the heart of the fire. One by one he set the rock in the water that rested in the bowl. Like the branding of cattle, the stones sizzled as the water engulfed it. Each rock added to the bowl of water changed the water's consistency. First the water sizzled, then it began to steam, until finally there were enough hot rocks that a tiny little bubble began to form on the surface of the water. Then he would take the first rock out and place it back into the fire until it was hot again and returned it to the water. With each rock he took turns doing this until the bowl of water was at a full boil.

"Okay! Now that the water is boiling," he said while looking at Eva, "we can place the Rhizomes into the water and cook them."

"Okay, the white roots. Got it," she responded.

"Exactly, Once they have softened up then we can eat them!" Andy said. While he pulled the fifth rock back out to reheat it on the coals.

Eva did exactly that. She followed Andy's step by step instructions and helped prepare a hot meal for all four of them.

"How did you learn all of this?" Jessie asked in awe.

"Well, I have been in the orphanage for a very long time now. If there is anything I have learned from my time being stuck there is that no one cares for anyone but themselves. Well, except for Mrs. Rosewood. She's our caretaker there and she's a sweetheart. But other than that, I had to learn to do things myself."

"Ah poor Andy," Eva said, letting her feelings for Andy slip.

"Eh, it's alright, I learned that I liked to be alone away from the regular world," he responded quickly. "I didn't like school, yet I had a desire to learn. Not math or history but I desired to learn how to survive. To be, what's the word…?"

"Self-sufficient?" Eva asked.

"Yes! So, I found myself venturing out into the forests. I watched the wildlife scavenge for food and wondered if those types of plants could be food for me as well," Andy stated.

"Good point, the food they feed us is nothing but slop," Richard said, thinking about how even a cattail seemed to taste better than what they ate at the orphanage.

"Right? So anyways, I began to study plant life. I used the school's library to read about plants, as well as food sources. I eventually looked into cooking tactics," he continued.

"That's awesome. I would have never dreamed of eating a cattail, yet here we are. I bet you could easily survive out in the woods," Jessie insisted.

"Oh, I plan on it!" Andy said.

"What? What do you mean?" Eva said, with sadness in her voice.

"I plan on running away," Andy said softly.

"But why?" Eva cried.

"I will not serve the King!" Andy announced. He despised the king, thought he was cruel, evil, and greedy. "The orphanage is funded by the Kingdom, so all children, when they turn eighteen, have to pay off their debt by serving the King in one way or another."

"Oh, that's right… Do you think Richard and I will have to serve the King as well? Even though I'll be eighteen in like three months?" Jessie asked.

"I would have to guess so," Andy said.

"Rats…" Richard said, snapping his fingers.

"I plan to live off the land, and frankly, the forbidden circle seems to be the place to go. No one is allowed to come here and if I can slip through the cracks again, I will stay here for good," He said with confidence.

"Hey! That sounds like a plan! I'm in," Richard said, which made Andy feel comforted. He was glad he wouldn't be completely alone.

Richard was the youngest of the group. He was only fifteen years old, while Jessie on the other hand was much closer to facing the royal requirements than the others. He was the oldest of the four and would be turning eighteen in only three months.

Andy and Richard both had time to decide their path, but Jessie would have to act fast. He hated the King just as much as the others, but had never thought he ever had a choice. *Is it worth trying to escape? Can serving the King really be that bad?* He thought.

"I'll have to wait and see if I survive this journey first before I make my decision," Jessie said with a soft smile, trying to cushion the tense mood.

"Well anyways, let's get some rest!" Andy suggested. They all settled into their own spots and finished off the remaining cattail treats. They were by no means delicious, but when you're starving, anything tastes good.

Richard and Eva sat under the pink flowered tree and sunk into a coma-like state. Andy remained near the fire, he continued to stoke the fire to insure that it would burn through the night. Jessie accompanied him and continued to find smaller logs to feed it.

"What now?" Jessie asked Andy, they kept their voices low to avoid waking the other two.

"What do you mean?" he asked.

"Well, our plan is a bust. You guys were supposed to go home. But now we are here. And Gillian…" Jessie started.

"The Pegasus guard?" asked Andy.

"Yeah, He's the one hunting us down," Jessie said in a way that made it seem like it was no big deal.

"If he catches us, we will be doomed. So much for living off the land... Am I right?" Andy said, chuckling at the idea.

"I'm not really sure about that. He seems tough and serious on the outside, but he really seemed to start caring for us. Like during that downpour that came through just after we split, he covered us with his wings to help keep us dry. All the while he got drenched," Jessie said. "And frankly the way he talks to us, is the way you and I talk. Like he and I have been friends our whole life."

"Really?" Andy questioned. "Do you think he is on our side?"

"Well, no. I think if it was him or us, he would pick him. But wouldn't you too?" Jessie said.

"Hmm well I guess that makes sense. But do you really think he cares about you and Richard?" Andy asked

"I really do, it seemed as if he had some sort of bond forming between us. It's really kind of a cool feeling. But I also think he is trying to do his job, which is protecting the Forbidden Circle from people like us," said Jessie with a sort of guilty conscience.

"Yes, us! Common criminals haha," Andy said, not taking the conversation as seriously as Jessie.

"I just feel horrible about running away from him. He was so caring towards us."

"Yet wasn't he forcing you to try and find us? What will happen if he does? Will we be turned over to the King? Who knows what the King would do to us."

"He'd probably kill us…"

"I think you're right and I think you did the right thing. Besides, like you said, if it was him or us, he wouldn't be saving us," Andy said, trying to comfort Jessie.

"You're probably right. But still, what are we to do?" Jessie asked again.

"Well going home is not an option. Well, I mean at least for Eva and me. Her dream was clear, the Great White Eagle wanted us to keep going. Plus, there were some cave drawings. It looked like two brothers, but only one came back. I was worried it was a prophecy of you and Richard," Andy explained.

"Cave drawings? Of us?" Jessie stuttered out.

"Well, I mean I think so. But given the slightest chance that it was, we couldn't risk it. We weren't gonna let anything happen to you. She had made up her mind on that," Andy said, glancing over at Eva.

"Well thanks. But I don't think it had anything to do with us. Gillian had our back," Jessie said. Thinking about his Pegasus friend once again.

"Well either way, maybe you should turn back and go home," Andy continued as he looked back at Jessie.

"Why don't we all go home?" Jessie questioned.

"You know it's not that simple, Eva is convinced the Great White Eagle is communicating with her. Heck! I am convinced of it. I've seen storm clouds before but never with the Great White Eagle in them. I've heard animals make noises before but now Eva can talk to them? There is something strange going on, I can feel it. We have to go. We have to find the Devil's Kettle," he explained.

"Hmft," Jessie snorted. "Gotta have faith, I guess," he said, with a heavy weight on his shoulders. It did seem like all of this was possible only because of some outside source of power. He had never seen water dry up as fast as it had in the fire pit. It was like there was something extra in the wind. Plus, it would be impossible to deny how slim the chances would be that a random raven would bring a letter all the way out here without some sort of guidance. *The Eagle really might be real. There is no other way I can explain these things. Don't doubt.* Jessie thought to himself as he looked out into the waving grasses of the Uaha Hollow.

It was well into the evening now. The sun had rested from the day, the fog hovered low, and only the dim flicker of the orange flame provided a source of light. The crackling fire harmonized with the songs of the frogs croaking in the distance. The dead trees towered as black silhouettes in the distance, while the fire illuminated the tree standing guard over Eva and Richard as they slept.

Andy and Jessie remained awake. Both had heavy thoughts burning in their minds. Andy wondered what it all meant. *Why were we chosen? Why was it so important that we have to go, even though it is so dangerous? What was at the Devil's Kettle?* He had no doubt in what the dreams meant, yet he still found himself doubting the Great White Eagle at times.

Jessie on the other hand, wondered what he and his brother's purpose was. *We failed to get Andy and Eva back home… Now, we are stuck in this bog. Are Richard and I even supposed to be here? Why can Eva receive dreams and Andy read them, while neither one of us can? Hmmmm, I wonder if those cave drawings were about us…* He thought hard about all of these things. He then weighed both his options. *If I go home, what is waiting there for me? The orphanage? The King's army? All I got is my brother. If we keep going, what is there to lose? We wanted to see the Devil's Kettle, and now we are closer than ever.*

"We will continue with you," Jessie finally spit out, making his decision.

Andy had been sitting quietly with both knees bent up to his chest. He stopped fiddling with the dirt and looked up at Jessie. Smiling softly, he nodded in understanding. Andy knew the journey was going to be dangerous and didn't want to be responsible for anything that went wrong. It had to be Jessie's choice to come with, and so it was.

Silence fell on the two and slowly each one fell asleep next to the blazing fire.

Chapter 17
Messorem

Eva Huntsberg

"How could you?" a spooky voice called to Eva.

Eva shot up instantly startled by an unfamiliar voice in the night.

"Who's there?" Eva fearfully asked with a quiver in her voice.

"How could you leave your parents behind? Such a rebel you have become," the voice murmured in the darkness around her.

"Where are you! Show yourself!" Eva commanded. She was becoming extremely frightened. Suddenly, by the light of the fire she saw some sort of shadow race across the boggy floor and vanish back into the darkness. Eva frantically looked at the three boys, and began to try to wake them up. Calling out their names and even trying to shake them awake, but nothing. The three boys lay motionless, fast asleep not bothered by the shadows of the night.

"And now, you have convinced yourself that the Eagle wanted you to come here? You fool! Now look at what you've done," the voice screeched. The shadow-like being blew through their camp causing the fire to flicker violently. Eva began to cry as guilt began to overcome her confidence in what she thought was true. "Now look at you! You and your friends will surely die out here!" the voice cackled with an evil screeching laugh.

"No! It's not true!" Eva sobbed. "I never meant for this to happen; I didn't think it would be this dangerous!"

"LIES!" the voice shouted! "You knew there was danger! Andy told you so!"

"Wake up! Wake up!" she shouted while shaking Andy.

Suddenly, she could hear the sounds of chains dragging through the bog. The grass rustling at the mercy of the chain links chattering as they weaved along the Uada Hollow's floor.

"Your friends will die because you made them come here," the voice whispered. Seemingly far off. Then the chains grew louder, until suddenly a black figure came bursting out of the tall grass and onto their high ground. The image was terrifying. It wore a tattered and torn black cloak whose hood was held up by nothing. It did not have a face, only blackness sunk into the hollow of the hood. You couldn't see its feet and it looked like it hovered as it went along, yet it left hoof prints in the soft ground. The only part of it she could see was its hands.

Moon color skeletons poked out of its shredded sleeves, clinging to a thick chain.

As it burst out of the grass it passed directly over the fire. Engulfing the light, causing everything to go black. Yet, Eva could sense it was headed directly for her. She scrambled backwards and found herself with her back against the pink flowered tree.

"I'm sorry!" Eva bawled. The darkness of the night stole her sight and all that resided within herself was fear. She soon felt the cold iron chains wrapping around her arms and legs. As it tightened she slipped into unconsciousness.

Richard LeRoy

"Betrayal?" a faint voice whispered in the distance.

Richard slowly sat up at the noise he heard and rubbed his eyes until his vision became clear.

"What do you mean? Who are you?" Richard asked the mysterious voice in the grass. He glanced around and could see Eva, Jessie, and Andy all sleeping next to the blazing fire.

"Hello?" he shouted a little louder. "Who's there?"

"How could you betray Gillian?" the voice asked harshly.

"It's not like that!" Richard said, looking out into the grass in the general direction the voice came from.

"Liar! It's exactly like that." the voice snapped as its shadow brushed past Richard. This brought Richard to his feet. He could feel a sense of guilt flooding over him and recognized the figure from the afternoon before. It was the same creepy shadow he saw disappear into the bog. Richard swiveled anxiously, looking for the creature that was in his presence. The creature chose fighting words and Richard became angry. He made fists with his hands and began to shout.

"You don't know me! It's not like that, we had to leave him behind. It was him or us!"

"It was him or us. Sure, it was and you chose to save yourself. How could you?" the formless being said in the mists of the bog.

"I had to." Richard said, but this time there was shame in his voice. He began to feel like he made a mistake. He began to feel like the creature was right and he had really betrayed someone who had cared for him and became his friend.

"You let him down, and you will let the others down too," the voice shouted. *Clink, clink, clink, clink*, Richard began to hear the noise of chains clatter through the bog.

"I didn't want to hurt Gillian! I don't want to hurt anyone!" Richard began to cry. His actions of the past weighed heavy and the creature in the night knew it. The weight of these burdens brought Richard to his knees and soon the shadowed figure invaded their camp and extinguished the fire. In the mists of the darkness, the chains of the creature began to crawl around Richard's torso and shoulders. Bound up by the chains, Richard felt the weight of his wrong doings. Heavy like the chains around him, he blacked out.

Jessie LeRoy

"You're the big brother Jessie," the voice whispered.

Jessie was woken up by the mysterious voice in the shadows.

"Who's there? What are you talking about?" he responded.

Jessie looked around. He was the only one to hear the strangers voice calling in the night. Eva, Richard, and Andy were all sound asleep around the fire.

"Pssstttt," Jessie whispered to Richard. To his dismay, Richard didn't move. Jessie then reached over and nudged him, but still Richard never woke up. Jessie stood up and stretched his legs and warmed his hands over the fire.

"Look at the life you have made for Richard!" The voice broke the silence, startling Jessie.

"Who do you think you are? I take good care of my brother!" Jessie snapped back at the voice. He could sense something moving in the grass. Yet it sounded as if there was more than one circling him. Jessie rotated and turned trying to pick out where the voice was coming from.

"You call this taking good care? The orphanage would be warmer and drier, yet you brought him out here!" the voice said.

"Stop it! You don't know me! It's not like that." Jessie stomped his foot in anger.

"Look at him, shivering from the cold," the voice boomed in the shadows.

Jessie looked at his brother shaking on the ground. To Jessie's surprise everyone was still sleeping despite the major disturbance unfolding. Jessie felt shame grab ahold. He was so distraught, he frantically started piling wood on the fire to try and warm up his brother. Then out of desperation, he began to shake his brother.

"Wake up! Wake up!" he screamed, but nothing.

Suddenly the shadow figure blasted through the camp behind Jessie's back, causing Jessie to spin around in a frantic daze.

"Not only have you led your brother to his demise, but you have also betrayed Gillian," the voice boomed.

Jessie's heart sunk, and he remembered back to Gillian's face when they ran away from him. The look of defeat, sadness, and anger that brewed in his eyes.

"I…I… didn't want to, but we had too," Jessie stuttered.

"You did not have to! You made a choice and now it's yours to bear!" the voice crackled in the distance.

"What have I done?!" Jessie reflected upon his choices and fell to his knees. He began to hear the clanking of chains rattling in the bog. He sobbed into his hands and completely ignored the noises for he felt too ashamed to even care anymore. Jessie never actually saw the creature, but the fire's light vanished as it entered into their camp. His guilt piled more and more on his shoulders as he sobbed into his hands. The chains wrapped around his wrists, then his shoulders, and then his legs. Although bound by chains, the heaviest burden was his own shame. Slowly, Jessie too lost consciousness.

Andy of the Orphanage

"You've failed," the voice whispered from the bog.

Andy slowly pushed himself up and yawned. He looked around at his three friends sleeping next to the fire.

"What did you say?" Andy whispered in his friend's direction trying to figure out who whispered to him.

The voice echoed from the bog once again.

"You were their leader and you have failed them," the voice said.

"What do you mean I failed them? Who are you?" Andy ordered.

"You led them out here, their blood will be on your hands!" it snickered from within the depths of the bog.

"No, Eva wanted to keep going, I told her not to," Andy argued.

"But you began this journey well before the Great White Eagle came to Eva, this is on you," it said with a loud boom.

Andy looked down and none of the others had woken up to the noises.

"Why are they not waking up?" he asked the voice, "Wake up!" he began to shout, but none of his friends moved.

"Eva will never see her parents again," the voice cackled.

Andy didn't respond, he felt that what the voice was saying was true. That he had failed, and had brought them here only to die. *Eva will never see her parents again. And the brothers? How could I have brought them here? It was supposed to be a simple adventure and now it could be our last.* Andy felt so ashamed, so terribly sick to his stomach. He was supposed to protect them all. He had always been their leader and they trusted him. He let the brothers, Eva, and her parents down. He remembered the look of disgust that Eva's mom gave him that day long ago in the rain. He felt the disappointment again and realized that her parents were right and she should have stayed away from him.

Just then the shadowy figure dashed through their camp and back into the bog. Chills ran down Andy's spine and he began to panic. He knew he was in danger and so were his friends.

"They trusted you! YOU failed them!" the voice murmured in the distance.

"I know! I know I did!" Andy cried. "What am I to do, I'm only human. I make mistakes. I'm not the Great White Eagle!" Andy shouted most desperately.

What happened next occurred so quickly that Andy barely understood it himself. He heard his own words echo in his head, *I'm not the Great White Eagle.* As the echo grew louder, he could hear chains dragging towards him. Soon, the shadowed creature emerged itself from the grasses and wrapped the chains around him, nothing he did physically could stop the chains from squeezing him tighter and tighter. The horrifying creature's cloak brushed over the fire extinguishing it into smoke and darkness. *Is this the end?* Andy thought to himself as the chains squeezed the breath from his chest. Just then he remembered what the letter from Eva's mom read. He began to shout with excitement.

"The letter! The letter!" Andy began to shout. "I'm not the Great White Eagle!" he said. Then somehow the chain's grip began to loosen. "Don't trust me, Trust the Great White Eagle! Don't doubt!" he shouted again, even louder than before. Again, the chains loosened more. "I have made mistakes and I can't change them, but the Great White Eagle has chosen us for some reason. I am not worthy but I must trust in the Great White Eagle! Don't doubt!" he screamed and the chains that were constricting him busted into tiny shards of nothingness and he was free.

Instantly Andy found himself awake, standing in the middle of their camp looking down at the fire.

"Was that all a dream?" he said out loud. But his thought was shattered by the clanking of chains and the cackles of not one but multiple creatures of the night. Finally, he snapped out of his daze and caught a glimpse of Eva being dragged out of their camp wrapped in the chains. Richard and Jessie were nowhere to be found either. It was as if the things he saw were a dream, yet now it was reality. Some unconscious state that only he had awakened from.

Before Andy could chase after Eva to free her from the creature, a huge gust of wind barreled through their camp causing the fire to be wiped out. This time he knew it was real, not a dream. The darkness was blinding, the air was chilled. He put his hands out in front of him and slowly started stepping forwards, waving his arms trying to find his bearings. When suddenly his crystal began to glow. Although concealed by Eva's bag, It glowed so brightly that it overpowered the bag and lit up their entire camp brighter than the fire had before.

Andy wasted no time and grabbed the crystal. With a new source of light, he took off into the tall grasses looking for the others. As he ran through the bog, the shadows around him shifted and danced as the light he held in his hand illuminated the way. He vigorously looked around in every direction trying to spot any sign of his friends or the creatures that took them.

The bog filled with chaos. The voices never stopped, Andy shouted out for his friends, the creatures cackled and laughed, and everything seemed to be moving.

Eva was unconscious, but the wet ground shocked her body awake. Unfortunately, now, it was too late. The reality was that she was being drug through the Uada Hollow, water splashing her face, reeds wiping her legs and arms, and her body was being tossed this way and that from the uneven ground beneath her.

The more she resisted the tighter the chains became. At this point she could barely breathe. With every ounce of energy, she pushed out a cry for help.

Andy recognized Eva's voice. Immediately he changed his directions to pursue her. He followed the cries through the dark illuminating the shadows with his crystal. This was life or death. Not like before when they would try to avoid the low spots of standing water, this time Andy stomped through the water and tall grass taking any short cut he could, despite the rough terrain.

Eva wiggled and squirmed any way she could trying to slow down the assailant's pace. Fighting with every ounce of strength she had left, but her strength began to slowly fade.

Oh no. Not another one. She thought to herself as she heard twigs snapping to her left. Then, her eyes grew wide, for in the darkness a bright glow flooded her way. Her heart began to race because she recognized the beautiful glow of the crystal. Just like the glow that was in the cave below the beaver's pond.

Clinging to the crystal, Andy came tumbling out of a thick patch of brush. The branches and twigs caused Andy to lose his footing and he tripped and tumbled into the spongy grass covered bog. Again, Andy's grip failed him and the crystal launched forward towards Eva.

As the crystal tumbled to a stop, its light seemed to glow brighter. The creature dropped the chains binding Eva to cover its face and let out the most terrifying screech you could imagine. As the chain collapsed to the ground it shattered into millions of tiny pieces. Defenseless now, the shadowy creature retreated by bolting down a hole in the ground, disappearing under the bog.

"Are you okay?" Andy gasped as he helped Eva to her feet. As Eva stood to her feet she fell right into Andy and gave him the biggest hug she had ever given anyone.

"Do I look okay?" she said in a very soft manner. Andy couldn't tell if Eva was crying but knew she was terrified. Her voice was faint and quivered, he held her as tightly as he could. Until he heard one of the brothers yelling from somewhere to their right.

"Help!" Eva and Andy heard in the distance.

"We have to find the others!" Andy barked as he let go of Eva and grabbed the crystal off the ground and began running in the direction of the cry for help.

As Andy jumped over a log, he divided the grass in front of him with his leading arm. There was Jessie on the ground wrapped in chains just as Eva was, but somehow Jessie was able to get one of his arms loose and managed to grab a stick. The creature towered over Jessie with his arms raised above his head and his tattered cloak dangling in the wind. It cackled and mocked Jessie who looked like he was going to be its prey. Jessie swung his stick but the creature just dodged it with ease. With its boney fingers it slashed at Jessie leaving shallow red gashes on Jessie's chest.

Andy never stopped running, but when he got close enough he took his crystal and chucked it. The creature lifted its arms to strike Jessie, which exposed its chest. With luck, the crystal tumbled through the air and lodged itself deep into the chest of the shadowy creature. This time the sound this shadow creature made was so loud that it pierced Andy's ears and he had to drop to his knees and cover them. Just like the chains shattering, the creature combusted into nothingness. The crystal had destroyed the being and then simply plopped on the ground. The crystal had saved both Eva and Jessie.

"Where is Richard?" Jessie shouted as he picked himself up off the ground.

"Over here, quick!" Eva shouted from the other side of their camp, deep into the bog.

Jessie grabbed the crystal and chased after Andy who was already on his way over. When Jessie arrived he could see Eva and Andy pulling on the end of a chain that was burrowed into the ground.

"What is it?" Jessies asked.

"Richard is wrapped in this chain, and the creature is pulling him down!" Eva cried.

Jessie didn't hesitate at all, he dropped to his knees allowing the crystal to fall down beside him and he grabbed onto the chain. They all pulled as hard as they could, but this tug of war was going nowhere. Jessie began to panic and became so angry; he grabbed the crystal and began to beat the chain. After only two strikes the chain shattered. Jessie then reached his free hand down into the hole and was met by ice cold water. He plunged his arm in deeper until he felt his brother's arm. Grabbing a hold of his brother, he yanked until the others could see Richard's arm above the bog. Andy grabbed onto his arm, while Jessie reached back into the water and found Richard's other arm. Now they were gaining ground. Without the chain the shadowy creature lost its leverage. Soon Richard's whole body was above the bog. Eva and Andy now had Richard by the shoulders and were dragging him away from the hole, when suddenly the horrific creature busted out of the hole clawing for Richard. Jessie, as if he had planned for it, used the crystal to beat the attacker over the head causing it to literally melt back into the water.

Jessie plopped forcefully back onto his butt, and thankfully as Eva and Andy pulled Richard off to the side, he coughed up water and could breathe again. They all sat in shock for a moment as the crystal's glow faded into a faint flicker. Now only their heavy breathing moved in the bog and all was quiet.

"What…was…that…?" Jessie asked, holding tightly onto the crystal.

"I think those were the Messorems that the beavers told us about," Eva said softly, while looking at Andy and holding on to Richard who was still in shock.

"Messorems?" Jessie asked.

"Some of the beavers had come here. They believed that the Uada hollow was haunted by these shadow-creature things. They called them Messorems," Andy explained.

"How did… How did you break free?" Richard asked very softly. He knew he tried with all his might to break free when he came back into reality, but nothing he did could stop the Messorem from dragging him below the bog.

"It was horrible. I couldn't break free either. I thought it was the end for me," Eva said heavily.

"It was like the Messorem knew exactly what I was thinking. All the shame and guilt I held within my own thoughts. It literally convinced me that I…I" Jessie started.

"That I deserved to be tied up in chains for what I had done…" Richard finished Jessie's thought.

"Me too, the Messorem was right," Eva said.

"No!" Andy barked. "The Messorems were not right!"

"You don't know what I've done or said. Even before this trip. The Messorem just exposed to me what I really deserved," Jessie said angrily towards Andy.

"That is exactly what they want you to think! Don't you see?" Andy said. By this point Andy had made his way to his feet and began to find hope within himself. Little did they all realize but as Andy continued to speak, the crystal began to glow brighter and brighter once again. "We are here for a reason, even if we don't understand why. Not one of us is worthy," Andy said.

"Well, that's really inspiring," Richard said sarcastically.

"But that's just it! He chose us, despite the fact that we have all failed. The letter said don't doubt. But we focused on ourselves. Instead, we should have trusted in the Great White Eagle. When I realized that, the chains loosened up and I became free from my own guilt!" Andy said excitedly.

"The letter, yes. But how did my parents know?" Eva question. Not really looking for an answer from her friends.

"I don't know. But once my chains were gone I woke up. To reality," Andy said.

"So, it was all a dream?" Richard asked. He was basically unconscious for the whole thing.

"No, it was definitely real! I remember passing out because the chains were so tight, and waking up once I felt the cold swamp water splashing against my body as it dragged me through the bog," Jessie explained.

"I'm really not sure," Andy started, "but once I realized it was not about what I had done, but what the Great White Eagle was going to do through me, I came to my senses. As if somehow the Messorem could get into my mind and create some sort of fake reality, to trick me into thinking I deserved to be captured by it."

"So maybe, once it has taken over your mind with your own guilt, we allow it to chain us up mentally making us incapable of fighting back physically. So, while still unconscious, they are able to literally tie us up with chains?" Eva said while trying to piece everything together.

"That kind of makes sense," Richard said. "They must have some sort of power where they can be in both our minds and here physically."

The Great White Eagle seemed to be more real to Richard than ever. He still hadn't seen or talked to the Great White Eagle himself, yet somehow he felt his presence. Despite the insane evening they had, he felt like the Great White Eagle was there somehow. Protecting them and guiding them.

"Do you think more will come?" asked Eva.

"I don't know, but I do know that this crystal is our only defense." Jessie said while holding on to it tightly.

"And remember that it's not about us, it's about the Great White Eagle. Don't doubt!" Andy said, reminding the group of how he got free in the first place. "Let's see if we can find camp, maybe get the fire started again."

Andy let Jessie hold onto the crystal, because he knew that it gave him comfort against the darkness around them. As they looked around the bog for their camp, they noticed something strange. A low orange glow flickered in the distance.

"This way!" Andy pointed towards the light. Jessie took the lead, while Andy and Eva followed closely behind. As Richard began to follow, again he noticed something strange in the bog. Yet, this time it wasn't something frightening. He noticed a glow behind him. As he paused to look, he noticed that from the hole he was pulled out of when he was saved from the Messorem, a faint flicker of yellow light shone. Something about it made him want to grab it. He got closer to the hole and began to peer into the dark water. Way below the surface he could see that the light was coming from something at the bottom of the bog. He began to reach into the water when he heard Andy yell in the distance.

The sudden shout startled Richard and he pulled himself back from the water and the light went out. Without the comforting light, fear overtook him again and he felt alone. Quickly he turned around and ran back towards the others. Following the orange light, he found the others and their camp. To his surprise the fire was burning as if it had never been put out in the first place.

Gillian a Royal Pegasus

Gillian's experience with the Uada Hollow was much different than the others. He soared high above the bog never actually swooping down into the dense fog that floated above the grass. He feared what lurked within it. The fog concealed any movement from below and only the tips of dead trees were exposed. There was no way he was going to risk his life by venturing into the foggy abyss. He hoped that the fog would clear, or at least part, so he could get a good aerial view.

However, this didn't happen. He began to feel as if the whole hunt was pointless. The wind above the hollow blew steadily and the grass rustled aggressively below. Between the wind and grass, Gillian couldn't hear anything. Even if he had come close to finding the traitors he wouldn't have known. The harsh environment of the bog rendered all of Gillian's senses useless.

Gillian almost gave up. He decided to get a broader view of the bog and decide what to do from there. He lifted himself higher into the sky. As he flapped his mighty wings, it was as if he began to zoom out of the picture. Eventually from this new height, he could clearly see the rings of the Centrum's Core, and the fog was no different. It hoovered like a ring of smoke over the Uada Hollow. Gillian remembered seeing it from the cliff, from that vantage point, the fog concealed the bullseye of the Centrum's Core, however, from directly above he could see that the bullseye was clear from fog.

The bullseye was a large hole in the ground, with a spiraling pathway that led down and out of sight. Then a small grassy ring boarded the mysterious hole. It was a meadow of sorts. It was after that that the fog began. Gillian had a whole picture of the Centrum's Core now. The cliff, the Humilis Pines, the Nevergreens, the Uada

Hollow swallowed by fog, the small meadow ring, and finally, the Devil's Kettle.

In addition to the rings of the Centrum's Core, Gillian could see the four great rivers pouring over the cliff of the Centrum's Core in each region. The forest hid most of their path, but at the brim of the Nevergreen Forest and the Uada Hollow, he could see each river in their respective regions flood into the hollow. This explained the bogs' source of water. The spooky place had become so soaked with water that the plant life somehow became buoyant and had to float over the abundant flow of water. This is why the four teenagers found themselves standing in water, and luckily for them, they never fell through into the deep water that hid below.

Gillian also noticed that only one river fed into the mysterious hole, that was the bullseye of the Centrum's Core. It was as if all four Great Rivers fed the Uada Hollow, but only one (The Great Northern River) drained into the Devil's Kettle.

After soaking in the view, Gillian went back to work. He searched for hours, looking for any openings in the fog, or the sound of the teenagers walking or talking. This task was made difficult because the mystery of what lies beneath terrified him, and he refused to set his hooves on the ground. Occasionally he mustered up the courage to swoop low, but as his hooves stirred up the fog, he freaked out and lifted himself back into the air.

His wings grew tired and his search felt hopeless. It was becoming obvious that he would not be able to spot them while they were in the bog. Gillian realized his only choice was to go beyond the bog and wait for them to come to him, just like he had done in the meadow of the Forbidden Circle.

So, he headed south, straight for the Devil's Kettle. Gillian's mind began to flood with thoughts. Thoughts about the traitors, thoughts about Malus and the King, and thoughts about everything he had ever been told or believed.

What am I even doing? Is finding the traitors even worth it anymore? Are they really any worse than I am? I can't even say I recognize myself anymore. My so-called Nobel Markings make me sick. They don't come from glory. What Malus told me they stand for are lies and lies are exactly how I ended up with them in the first place. Vincent is going to be so mad when he finds out. And Malus… Oh brother, talk about furious! But what do I care? He has done nothing but lie to me. All these things made Gillian's rage return. He had worked himself up as he flew to the meadow that harbored the Devil's Kettle.

I can't believe Jessie and Richard ran from me… I honestly trusted them. Yet somewhere inside of him he began to even question that. *They only ran because they were trying to protect their friends from me… I can't believe it. The only reason I ever became a Royal Pegasus guard was so I could protect all creatures. But now, I'm the one hunting them down. Have I really fallen this far? I have failed to do the one thing I set out to do.*

Gillian's thoughts were heavy. If he had been in the Hollow with the four while the Messorems had attacked. There would have been no way he could have fended them off with his mere thoughts. He was just as shame filled and guilty as they were. Even more so, he was unsure about the Great White Eagle and had very little faith in him to begin with. He would have been the perfect victim for the Messorems.

He finally made it to the meadow and settled into the waving grass pondering all his thoughts and questions as he waited for the others to show themselves.

Chapter 18
Apples

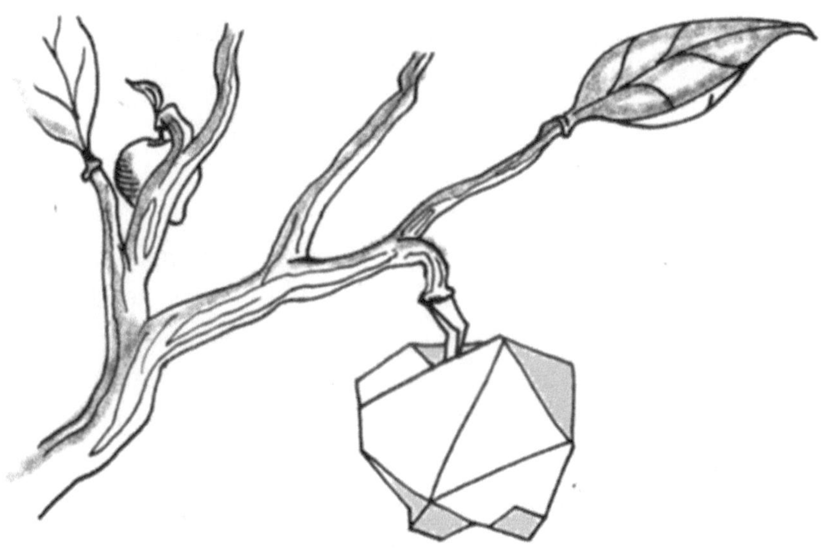

The morning brought a whole new light to the Uada Hollow. The dense fog had lifted and for the first time in almost a day they could see the blue sky overhead. They must have slept in quite late, for there was no sign of a sunrise and the sun was almost at its highest point in the sky.

Birds chirped, frogs croaked, and the water babbled in the distance. The grim hollow had passed away and was replaced by something entirely different. Although the landscape hadn't changed, the atmosphere felt like a sigh of relief. They had made it through the night and survived an attack from the Messorems.

There was something magical about it, as if the bog had been healed of a deadly disease. It was bright and vibrant everywhere, in fact overnight the pink flowers on the mysterious tree all disappeared and were replaced by plump red apples. The tree itself almost seemed to glow.

"Apples!" Eva shouted in delight.

Eva stood on her tippy toes and reached up into the tree and plucked off a fat apple. She bit into it and it was the tastiest apple she had ever had.

"Oh, wow this is so good!" she said while taking another bite.

The others scrambled to their feet and each reached up and pulled down their own apple. Richard took a bite, but stopped because he noticed that the apples on the top of the tree were much larger than the one he first grabbed. Unwilling to settle for second best, he dropped his apple and shimmed up the tree wedging himself between two sturdy branches high above the ground. They all ate to their fill. Apple after apple then gobbled down. The sweet juice was glorious to their taste buds. Plus, it was the most normal thing that any of them had eaten since before their journey began.

Richard never moved from his perch. He just leaned back against the slanted branch and soaked in the joys of the mysterious apple tree while the others lay contently underneath it.

"Well," Andy started with a sigh, "I think we must keep moving. I can sense that we are very close to the Devil's Kettle."

"I feel that too," Jessie said with some excitement boiling in his blood.

"I can't wait to see the Kettle. To see if the legends are really real," Richard giggled from up in the tree.

"Now the mystery is bigger than ever. With the mission from the Great White Eagle and all," Andy chirped in.

"Yeah, the Eagle…" Richard repeated. His mind began to wander back to the night before. All that had happened and the weird sense that somehow the presence of the Great White Eagle was there with them.

"But just remember, the main legend says whoever falls in will never return, so everyone stay away from the Devil's Kettle! We can still look from afar," Eva said, trying to remind everyone of how dangerous the legends say the Devil's Kettle really is.

"We will be fine!" Jessie said with confidence. Jessie remembered back to the night before, when he had decided to continue on to the Devil's Kettle. They were so close, turning back now would be a shame. They had come so far and seen so much, to end their journey now would be a crime.

Richard was still dazed in the tree. Remembering how the water surrounded him under the bog, and how real and haunting the Messorem was. He got chills thinking about them. As he stared into the mess of branches he could see the rays of sun peeking through. The red apples seemed to glisten golden yellow on the sides that the sun touched. The golden light flickered off the apples and reminded him of the glow that he had seen in the depths of the bog the night before. He still wondered what the light was and where it came from. The more he thought about it, the more he realized that the glow was very similar to Andy's crystal.

The color was the same. It glowed and flickered just the same. *Was what I saw at the bottom of the bog another crystal? Where did it come from? Did a Messorem leave it behind?* As he thought about this, the golden glow of the apple tree seemed to fade. As if the tree was frowning at his thought. But as he processed the options he began to think deeper. *But if it is a crystal-like Andy's, it wouldn't have been from a Messorem. It seemed to terrify them. Was it from the Great White Eagle?*

Richard thought, just then the golden glow of the apples returned to its full blazing light.

This time Richard noticed something different amongst the branches. He could see a strange looking apple. It looked perfect, but wasn't at all like the others. The natural apples were red, with only the side to the sun baked yellow with color. Yet this one had no red on it at all, but yellow in its entirety as if the sun penetrated it completely.

Richard slowly moved himself towards the apple, using branches to carry himself up the tree. As he got closer, his brown face was lit up by the soft yellow glow of the crystal, it was the most beautiful thing he had ever seen. He reached out his hand and plucked the crystal off of the tree.

It was heavy, but heavy in a good way. Like how you would want your gold to be. The glow was mesmerizing and all he could do was stare into the crystal and wonder about all the mysteries it held within it.

"Guys look!" Eva said while pointing up to Richard. She was the first to notice that he had found something.

"Is that a crystal?" Andy asked. He was shocked to see another one. Richard seemingly found this one out in the middle of nowhere. It's like it somehow just showed up. Then again so did all the other apples in the tree. Something strange was going on here.

"It is! A crystal apple," Richard said from up in the tree. He never looked at the others, but just stared into the crystal. Andy bent over and picked up his crystal that Jessie held onto the night before. *What are you?* Andy asked the crystal in his head.

Soon, Jessie scrambled up the tree. He was so excited about the crystal that he wanted to find his own. He shook all the branches, plucked a hundred apples looking for his own crystal. Even Eva walked around below the apple tree. She too was looking for her own crystal. However, to their dismay, they found nothing.

Eventually Richard climbed down from the tree, and stood next to Andy. Eva soon gave up on her search and gloomily came to Andy's side. Not Jessie. He continued to search. After about ten minutes Richard spoke up.

"Maybe you should give it up."

"Why isn't there more?" Jessie said. Richard sensed that Jessie was jealous of his finding.

"Here you can have this one," Richard said while holding out the crystal apple to his brother.

"No, it wouldn't be the same," Jessie snorted as he finally gave up and scuffled down the tree. "Just forget it," he continued as he wiped away some of the bark that clung to him while he was up in the tree.

"Well, hey we can all use it! Now we have two crystals to protect ourselves!" Eva said cheerfully. Although slightly disappointed that she did not have a crystal either, she was just happy that they had more protection against the Messorems.

"Jessie, don't sweat it, I know where we can find you one, after we get back from the Devil's Kettle! There were hundreds in the underground cave where I found this one!" Andy said while trying to cheer Jessie up.

"Yeah, well okay. We should get a move on," Jessie said, trying to put the whole situation behind them.

"Good idea," Andy responded. "This way to the Devil's Kettle!"

The four of them began that day's journey to the Devil's Kettle. As they passed by the apple tree one last time, they each grabbed another apple for later. Andy and Richard both clung to their crystals, Jessie found a walking stick to help navigate the bog, and Eva followed behind with nothing but excitement and wonder in her mind.

At first the terrain was as expected, wet and soggy, but then the ground seemed to harden. As they trudged along the patches of dry ground became more frequent. The spongy ground began to firm until it was solid. Each step the grasses seemed to shorten around them and trees began to tower. Until finally they emerged from the grasses that waved above their heads.

Behind them they left the Uada hollow. The nightmare of the night before lay in the past along with the memory of the Messorems. They were so thankful to see living trees.

From where they stood beautiful Oak trees shaded the outskirts of a flowery meadow. It was a major improvement from the skeletons that loomed above them in the spooky bog. As they rested under the mighty oaks, whose branches twisted and turned above, they gazed out into the open meadow. They had finally made it to the heart of the Centrum's Core. It was so much more beautiful than they could have imagined it. From the cliffs of the Centrum's Core, the fog concealed this gem. It had rolling hills lifted and dropped. Patches of trees here and there and an abundant field of flowers. The wildflowers battled the green grass for space and filled their eyes with colors. Blue, pink, red, yellow, and so many more painted the plain before them. The meadow was alive. Birds chirped up in the trees as the grass danced below. Buzzing filled the air as bees hopped from flower to flower and hummingbirds flapped their wings.

"Wow..." Eva gasped. The meadow was so peaceful that it warmed their hearts. It brought them joy unlike anything they had ever felt before.

As they waded into the meadow, the warmth of the sun kissed their skin.

Eva let the grasses brush across her hands as she skipped through the meadow, twirling with the breeze. She closed her eyes and took in the fresh air.

Andy soaked in the sun and gazed in every direction. Seeing the bountiful abundance of flowers, he decided to pluck a few and made a beautiful bouquet of different colors, which he then delivered to Eva.

Her cheeks became rosy red and she accepted them without hesitation.

Jessie wrestled with Richard. After pinning his little brother to the ground, Jessie moved on to climbing a boulder. Richard on the other hand had found the ground to be quite comfy. He remained on the ground and rolled back and forth in the flowers like a dog itching its back. It was soft and comfortable like a bed after a long hard day. Once he came to a rest he found shade below the flower's elevated stalks.

As Jessie climbed to the top of a boulder, he gazed out at the sea of color, seeing to his left the Northern river and its final destination. He watched as the water rushed towards a patch of trees in the center of the meadow. At his elevated height, he could now see the water came to a cliff and fell over yet another ledge.

It was the actual bullseye of the Centrum's Core. The hole that the water poured into looked to be very shallow across and to have some sort of spiraling trail that would allow them to venture to the bottom.

If they all hadn't been in such a trance, the center of the Centrum's Core would have piqued more of their interest. However, their journey had been so long and exhausting that they had almost forgotten the real reason they were there.

After a short rest, they began to run and play. The boys wrestled and Eva gazed upon the meadow, imagining she was just a little girl again playing make believe. Soon she made her way to the east and found the Northern River. She looked north, and could see the river wiggle back and forth a bit, and then widen out right before it disappeared into the Uada Hollow. She shivered at the thought of the haunted bog. Shaking it off she glanced to the south. She too saw the patch of trees that towered over the end of the Northern River. She moseyed along the river where it disappeared over the edge. Her eyes widened as she peered down. The water gushed over the edge and fell all the way down to a lake. The water of the lake swirled in a large circle as it eventually was funneled into a black hole.

"The Devil's Kettle!" she shrieked with excitement.

She closed her eyes and soaked in the noise. The babbling river and the rustling of grass filled her ears, while the sweet smell of flowers filled the air. The warm breeze brushed against her body and the grasses below her tickled her legs. She thought to herself that this is what Caelum must be like. She was of course referring to the afterlife in the sky that the scrolls talk about.

"Hey! Over here!" Andy shouted.

Eva opened her eyes and looked back to the west where the boys had been wrestling. She could see Andy waving at her trying to get her to come to them. With no time to waste, she noticed that beyond Andy, Jessie and Richard were running towards something.

Eva began to run towards the boys. As she made her way to the west, she rounded the cliff that overlooked the Centrum's Core, then straightened out towards Andy. She began to rise over one of the rolling hills and could see a weird patch of thin trees. Within the trees were some sort of rubble structure. As she got closer the boys had already made their way inside. Andy plopped his elbows down on a windowsill and set his chin in his hands and peered out at Eva.

"Hey, how do you like my house?" Andy said with a giggle. Eva obviously knew it wasn't his house, and that no one had lived there for years. All the windows were broken, the roof was gone, and all the wooden furniture inside had either fallen apart or was ready too.

"Why yes, I love it!" she said back.

"Well let me give you a tour!" Andy said, while standing up straight again. "Hmmm," he said while looking around for the door. (He found his way into the house of rubble through a hole in the stone wall.) "Right around here, my lady," he said, pointing to the other side of the rubble house.

Eva circled the house and found what must have been the front door. A small tree was growing in the center of the doorway. She could see that the top of the door frame was arched and had square stones wedged together to form its shape. However, the door itself was gone. As she squeezed by the tree, she found Andy waiting on the other side, with his hand out. She placed her hand into his and he proceeded to give her a tour of the house.

"As you can see," he began, "this is the house's entrance, and this bench right here is where I put on my shoes in the morning." The bench had the legs broken off of one side and so it was slanted to the ground. Yet, Andy proceeded to sit on it anyways, holding most of his weight up with his own legs.

"Ahh very nice!" Eva giggles back.

"If you would follow me," Andy said as he jumped to his feet and led Eva through a second doorway. "This looks like it's my dining room.. As well as my kitchen?" he said, almost asking Eva what she thought. There looked to be a table with some of the roof laying on it, as well as three broken chairs in various places in the small dining room. And in the far corner, Jessie had been inspecting what looked to be some sort of stove. There was a pile of split wood for burning next to it, and a cast iron pan sitting on top of the black iron stove. There was no chimney left on the stove but otherwise everything was still intact.

"This is where I make my wild peachew soup!" Andy said, making his way to the stove, and fiddling with the iron pan.

"Oh yummy, that sounds delicious," Eva said, playing along.

"I will have to make you a real meal when we get back to Regnum, instead of all this scavenging," Andy said while smiling at Eva.

"I would love that," she said softly, looking down at her feet.

"Eechem" Jessie coughed in the corner. He was feeling awkward. He could tell Andy and Eva were flirting, and was forced to witness the whole thing. As most teenage boys would agree, he thought it was gross.

"Umm…yeah," Andy began after becoming a bit embarrassed. "I wonder what's over here?" he said, redirecting everyone's attention.

"This room is a bedroom!" Richard responded from within a different room. His voice was muffled. Andy and Eva peered in, and there Richard was sprawled out face down on the bed. He must have peeled the bed sheets off the bed first. Some of the roof was under the blankets piled on the floor, leaving the bed clear of debris and clear for Richard to flop onto. There was one window which was surprisingly still intact; the glass panes remained. Curtains still hung bordering the window but they were ripped and tattered. Next to the bed there was a nightstand with its drawer pulled out. The drawer was resting on the floor at the legs of the nightstand. The room was completed with a large chest at the foot of the bed, but that too had been opened and nothing was inside.

Before Andy could investigate the room any longer, Jessie pushed his way past Andy and Eva into the room. As if trying to fly, he jumped, sprawling out his arms and legs and belly flopped right on top of his brother. The force from his body caused the bed's frame to break all four of its legs and the bed crashed to the floor. But the boys were not concerned with that at all but instead proceeded to begin wrestling again.

Andy was giggling at the brothers and said to Eva, "It looks like someone ransacked the place!"

However, to his concern, Eva hadn't responded. Quickly he turned to see Eva, but she had entered the other room. This one was just to the left of the doorway he was standing in. He followed her in and could see that it was an identical room to the other. Except this room was still neat and tidy. The bed was still made, the chest was unopened, and the nightstand was intact. It was also the only room in the whole house in which the roof was still together and above their heads.

Eva was gazing out the window as Andy entered the room. Andy began to snoop about the room. He opened the chest at the foot of the bed and it was filled with extra blankets. Soon he was interrupted.

"You can see the waterfall from here," she said quietly. "I was over there when you called me over. The Devil's Kettle is at the base of that waterfall."

Andy walked over to see the view. As he gazed out the window, he could see the grassy meadow sloping up towards the Northern River. From this angle, they could see the water rushing over the edge. It curved sharply down and disappeared into the large hole-like cavern.

Part of Andy was dreading the Devil's Kettle. He was worried that more dangers lie ahead and he didn't mind postponing their arrival if it meant they could avoid the dangers for a time longer. So instead of thinking about the Devil's Kettle, he focused his attention on the rest of the room. Soon he drifted over next to the nightstand and sat down on the bed. His hands ran over the sheets. He had forgotten how much he had missed a warm bed.

"The legends all say there is a Corkscrew Canyon. I never understood what it looked like until I saw it with my own eyes. There is literally a trail that spirals all the way down to the bottom. Just like the tool used to pull the cork out of a bottle of ale," Eva said, still wondering what secrets she would discover or what the Great White Eagle would uncover for her when they arrived.

Andy gave a short "Umhm," while he wiped the dust off of the nightstand with his hand. He wiped the dust off on his pant leg and then decided to open the drawer to see what was inside.

Inside was what seemed to be the most disorganized part of the entire room. There were writing quills, a spilt jar of dried-up ink, and loose papers. He shuffled the papers around and underneath was a big book. As he pulled it out of the drawer, the loose papers lifted out and drifted to the floor. He scooched himself further into the bed and gazed upon the book. The leather cover of the book felt heavy in his hands. It was one of the most beautiful books he had ever seen. It had many layers of leather that created a complex image of a Great Eagle, which was held together by a golden stitch.

Andy realized that he was looking down at the back of the book. The cover was quite odd. You could not see any of the pages because a leather flap stretched all the way from the back of the book, wrapped around the pages of the book and overlapped the front. A lock was in place which kept the pages sealed shut within its binding.

"Wow," Andy gasped. Which caught Eva's ear causing her to turn to see what it was about.

"What is it?" she questioned.

"It's a book! And it's old!" Andy said with his eyes fixed on the beautiful stitching of the book.

"May I?" Eva asked with her hand stretched out towards the book.

"Yes of course!" Andy said while handing it up to her.

Her fingers traced the engravings on the flap that wrapped around the front. It wasn't any writing she had ever seen before, but soon she began to sound out the letters and began to produce the words. To Andy it all sounds foreign. Which is exactly what it was. It was another language. However, it was clear Eva could not only speak all other languages but she could read them too. Very slowly she began to sound out the odd letters and she began to babble funny sounding words.

"It says, Book of Truth. But I'm not sure which language it's from," Eva announced after first hearing her own words out loud, and then being able to translate them.

"Book of truth? What do you think that means?" Andy asked.

"I don't know, you're the Lector! I can only read it." Eva smarted off.

To him it meant nothing and he had no sense of what it could mean. It wasn't like Eva's dreams, those he understood as if they spoke to him directly. Unfortunately, the book title left him lost without comprehension.

"Do you think we can get it open?" he asked.

She handed him back the book and he tried to pry it open. There was no luck. It was bound tight, and no pages could be seen. The flap was stiff and formed perfectly around the pages making it impossible for them to even get a peek inside. It was as if it was sealed with magic or something else besides just a regular old key. Yet their only hope of opening it and discovering the pages would be to find the key.

Soon they both began to tear apart the room looking for the key. They took out the drawer, opened the chest again and pulled out the blankets. They looked under the bed and in between the sheets but nothing. They found no key of any sort.

Richard and Jessie had taken a break from beating each other up and had overhead the commotion in the other room.

"Whoa! Were you guys jealous with our room's set up and had to reorganize this one?" Jessie asked. Both boys stood in the doorway with red faces from their intense wrestling match.

"We found this book," Andy started holding up the book, "but it has a lock on it, with no key," he said with the look of annoyance and disappointment squished together.

The two brothers looked at each other and then back at the book.

"Eh, reading sucks anyways," Richard said while shrugging his shoulders.

"Guess the lock saved us from having to read it," Jessie said, elbowing his brother in the gut.

"You got that right!" Richard said as he and Jessie turned and went back to their championship wrestling match.

Eva rolled her eyes at the brothers. She knew they never cared for school. Except this wasn't school, it was something completely different. *How could they care so little about something this mysterious?* She thought. Despite the brothers' rejection, Andy shrugged his shoulders and the two went back to looking for the key, but after a few more minutes they gave up.

"I don't think the key is here," Andy said in defeat.

"I don't either but maybe we should bring it with us?" Eva expressed.

"And what would that accomplish? If we can't open it, why would anyone else?"

"Hmmm… I bet the Elves would know what to do with it. They are very wise when it comes to the scrolls and I have a feeling they can help us," Eva suggested.

"Huh…do you really think they will help us? I heard they are kind of a bunch of know-it-alls, and if you're not an elf or like them in their ways, you are no good to them?" Andy asked.

"That may be but they do know their stuff and they are some of the biggest followers of the Great White Eagle. I think we should start there," Eva commanded.

Andy pondered the possibilities but knew that if he couldn't stop her from going to the Devil's kettle in the first place, he was not going to be able to stop her from going to the Elves either. So, he left it at that.

Eva soon found herself picking up the mess they had made while looking for the key. She reassembled the nightstand, put all the papers and writing quills back in the drawer. Folded the blankets and closed the chest. Lastly, she began making the bed. She felt as if they disrupted someone's home. Obviously no one had lived there for a very long time but still something inside told her it was the right thing to do.

Andy on the other hand, left the bedroom and went into the dining room. He pondered what was in the book. *Are the secrets in this book the secrets we were supposed to discover?* Yet with everything that has happened he felt more confused than ever. *What were the crystals? What was this book? And what sort of secrets did the Devil's Kettle hide? I know it will be dangerous but will it be any worse than the attack from the Messorems?*

"Hey when are we going to the Devil's Kettle?" Richard asked, poking his head through the doorway.

"First light. It's already going to get dark soon, I think it would be best to get some good rest and make sure we explore it with plenty of hours of daylight," Andy explained.

Richard shrugged and proceeded to tackle his brother. The next few hours were quite a different pace for them all. They all stayed in their separate rooms and just rested. Each giving the others space.

Richard and Jessie had completed their wrestling match, in which both of them claimed victory. Eventually their bickering came to an end and the two of them just talked. After a while, the sun dropped behind the horizon. Everyone still remained quiet and were settling down for bed. Richard and Jessie passed out on the bed in the first room.

Eva sat in the intact end room. With the bed made, she stared out the window with the book in her hand. Her fingers rubbed back and forth along the edge of the soft leather and she thought of all that had happened so far. She thought of her parents and how she longed to see them again. She was grateful for a bed and was looking forward to a good night's sleep before the long day ahead.

Andy cleared off the roof pieces from the dining room table, snagged a couple blankets out of the chest in Eva's room and made a bed out of the top of the table. With no roof he laid on his back and gazed up at the stars.

The day really had gone by quickly. They hadn't actually traveled far, but they had slept in that morning and were able to explore the peaceful meadow, which burned up many of the afternoon daylight hours. Andy knew that tomorrow would bring them to the Devil's Kettle. He was nervous, like you would get the night before a big test or a competition. He couldn't stop the morning from coming, but just appreciated the break in their journey.

As he star-gazed he found many constellations that roamed the sky. He found the White Bear Paw, the Elve's Scepter, and even the Dwarf's Diamond.

"When I overlooked the Corkscrew Canyon, I could see the Devil's Kettle. It's kind of scary... Are you nervous too?" Eva whispered from the bedroom doorway. She startled Andy, but he was just happy to know that he wasn't the only anxious one.

"I'd be lying if I said I wasn't."

"Well, either way, we will go together. Whatever happens we will be there for each other... won't we?"

"There is no doubt in my mind!"

"Good... Well," she paused, "I hope you sleep well. I'll see you in the morning."

"Goodnight Eva," he said as he glanced one last time at Eva before she closed the door to the bedroom. Andy looked back up at the sky and watched as a shooting star streaked across the sky. Soon the stars all seemed to blur together as his eyes grew heavy and he drifted off to sleep.

The night was quiet and all was dark. Except for the soft glow of Richard and Andy's crystals which they each subconsciously held in their hands.

Chapter 19
Ghosts in the Graveyard

"**A**ndy! Andy! Wake up," A shaky whisper came from Jessie. Andy opened his eyes from his body being shaken awake.

"What is it?" Andy groaned, still half asleep.

"They're back!" Jessie panicked.

"Who's back?" Andy questioned. Except no explanation was needed, as the word left his mouth he heard chains dragging outside the house of rubble. The chattering of iron links echoed in the night. Andy shot straight up and jumped to his feet.

"Wait… I'm awake?" Andy asked Jessie, punching him in the arm to see if Jessie was real. The last encounter they had the Messorems attacked their self-consciousness.

"Umm… Ow?" Jessie said, feeling the thump from Andy's fist. "Something is different this time, we are not asleep. But quick! Come see," Jessie said, as he ran back into the room he had gone to sleep in hours before. There Jessie knelt down beside Richard who was peering out the window. They both remained low to the ground, with only their eyeballs exposed to the outside.

"Look at all of them," Richard gasped in disbelief at the swarm of Messorems.

"What are they doing?" Andy asked. The chains spooked Eva awake and in no time she found herself huddled with the others peering out the window at the strange scene.

"I don't know but it looks like they are chasing something," Jessie started

"Or someone," gulped Richard.

"What do you mean someone?" asked Eva anxiously.

"Well, they were after us before. Maybe someone else is here too? Maybe it's Gillian?" Andy thought out loud.

That thought never crossed the brothers' minds. They felt their heart sink again for the friend they left behind. *If it came for us, why wouldn't it come for him?* They thought.

"I think there must be others out here," Richard started.

"And not just Gillian either. There are others," Jessie continued.

"What others?" Eva asked. Just then a terrible scream came from outside. The four felt like their hearts jumped out of their chests. They turned white as ghosts as they realized what they had seen.

The night sky was full of clouds. It would have been dark and grim but there was a constant flashing of lightning that allowed them to see the chaos clearly.

Their eyes focused on the scream they heard moments ago. To their disbelief, there was a Messorem with chains in its grips dragging an Elf towards the Corkscrew Canyon. The Elf was kicking and screaming, trying to fight off the creature, but it couldn't. The Elf looked to be dressed in all white. Cleaner than any linen they had ever seen before.

Just then another Messorem appeared, this one too had chains wrapped around a creature. A plump Dwarf. It was weird looking for a Dwarf. It had a white beard and was actually clean, which is unlike any dwarf they had ever seen. Normally they were always covered in a black chalky soot. The dwarf said nothing. Just followed the Messorem by chain as if it had given up any hope of escaping.

The longer they watched, the more creatures were held captive and dragged towards the Devil's Kettle. Some fought with every ounce they had, while others just followed along. Elves, Dwarves, Centaurs, Humans, Beasts and even Pegasi were chained up and hauled towards the Devil's Kettle. It was odd, each one of them seemed to be dressed in white. No matter what they normally would look like.

"We have to help them!" Eva said quietly under the murmur of thunder crackling outside.

"No way!" Andy said as he pulled her down.

"We have two crystals now! We can save them all," she argued.

"Save them all? Do you see how many Messorems there are? It would be suicide for us, even with two crystals!" Jessie vetoed her desire to save the creatures.

"This is messed up. Like really messed up," Richard said softly, breaking up their argument. "Why are almost all of the creatures that have been captured old. And what are the chances that no one has been even allowed to come here for years, and now all of a sudden us four and all of these creatures are here at the same time? Something is not right. Or else we have been lied to," he expressed his thoughts to the group. The group was kind of shocked. It was one of the first helpful insights Richard had. Normally he was always trying to make a joke, or change the subject. Yet, his words now spoke wisdom that made everyone realize what was really happening.

"They're ghosts!" Andy gasped. With wide eyes they each looked at one another and then looked back out at the creatures.

"It could be possible," Eva said. "The scrolls suggest that we all have souls that will one day be lifted up to Caelum," she said, remembering the promise of the Great White Eagles nest in the sky.

"Yeah but these poor creatures don't look like they are going to Caelum," Richard said rudely.

Just then the lightning flashed a blinding white, thunder angrily boomed shaking the ground. Out of nowhere a Messorem appeared directly in front of their window. The creature's black cloak consumed the entire window's picture and its pale skeleton fingers screeched along what was left of the window's glass, like nails on a chalkboard. The cloak's hood seemed to be held up by nothing. The creature had no face, no eyes, or teeth, yet its breath fogged up the windowpanes. The four of them sank in fear but dared not to move.

To their relief the Messorem passed on. Leaving the four unharmed. They all looked at each other confused as to why it left them when the night before, the Messorems goal seemed to be to kill them.

"Maybe it didn't see us?" Jessie shrugged.

"Or maybe they are not here for us anymore. Maybe those creatures are ghosts, which must mean they have all passed on," Andy suggested.

"But why are they being dragged to the Devil's Kettle?" Eva asked.

"Maybe… the Devil's Kettle is the entrance to.. you know.. NOT Caelum!" Andy suggested.

Eva looked at him with wide eyes. Realizing that the Devil's Kettle could possibly be the entrance to Perfidus. She had heard dreadful stories about Perfidus. The stories in the scrolls say that the Great White Eagle never visits there and that all creatures that ended up there would not enjoy it at all. That it would be more like torture than anything good. She had just started studying the scrolls herself and knew that there was a promise that all who wanted to go to Caelum would eventually be allowed to go. However, she hadn't figured out how to get there yet. Thinking about all the poor creatures being drug towards the Devil's Kettle.

Just then Richard said the most peculiar thing anyone could have imagined. "Mama?" he whispered with a voice that expressed confusion and concern.

"Richard, you know mama is gone. She died," Jessie said trying to seem tough although her death was still recent and tore him up inside. All of a sudden Jessie's face went stone cold. He had started to piece everything together. *Wait… If these white creatures are really ghosts. What if…* He started to think, and realized why his brother said 'Mama.'

"Where?" Jessie asked his brother.

"There," Richard said while pointing to a Messorem tugging at an older lady. She walked behind it, just as the dwarf did, no screaming, no fighting, no resistance at all. Only a look of sadness on her face. Soon, they vanished out of sight as they slipped down the sloping pathway of the Corkscrew Canyon.

"Mama!" Jessie shouted.

"Mama!" Richard echoed. Louder and louder the brothers called out to their lost mother. Andy wanted to tell them to quiet down, but a lump had formed in his throat. He understood the pain they were feeling and couldn't find the strength to tell them to quiet down.

"Jessie... Richard.. We have to be quiet," Andy said, trying to hold back tears. Andy was learning that being a leader was quite difficult at times. He had to say things that needed to be said for the safety of the group, yet he knew it would hurt them.

His weak attempt was in vain. Before he could say another word. Jessie and Richard both sprang up, grabbed the crystal apple, and barreled out of the house into the night.

"Come back!" Andy shouted. Unfortunately, the boys paid no attention. They just kept running and crying out for their mother.

"We have to follow them; we can't become separated again!" Eva insisted. She grabbed the Book of Truth and headed outside. Andy was right behind her with his glowing crystal. They both followed Richard and Jessie who had already made it to the start of the Corkscrew Canyon. The grassy ground beneath them sloped towards the massive hole. As they themselves reached the canyon they paused for a moment. Messorems swerved around them dragging the ghosts with them. The spiral trail that winded down to the Devil's Kettle was filled with hundreds of Messorems and the ghosts of many creatures. Here they could see the waterfall head on and its water fell all the way into a lake at the bottom of the canyon. The Messorems were swarming over the water, plunging in and out of the Devil's Kettle; entering in with creatures, but coming out alone. It was a chaotic and terrifying sight.

"There!" Andy said, pointing down to the third loop in the spiral. Eva squinted trying to see. Only when the lightning lit up the sky, could she see clearly, which was quite frequent for there was a nasty electrical storm waging war overhead. In and amongst the horde of Messorems she could see Richard and Jessie barreling their way down the sloped pathway.

Quickly Andy and Eva began to descend down the pathway. The pathway was carved out of the cliff, and as they ran the top of the cliff began growing tall alongside them. Around the canyon they ran, spiraling around the edge downward. The path even led them behind the waterfall by carving itself deeper into the cliff. If it hadn't been such a horrific night, it would have been an incredible discovery.

The wind began to pick up, and the flashing of lightning was still going strong. There was a storm coming. The type you could tell was going to be wicked just by the moist and sticky atmosphere. Their descent was extremely difficult but they had to press on. The path was not smooth. As far as they knew they had been the only physical creatures to touch it in years. The Messorems and ghostly figures left no trace at all. There was fallen rocks and rubble, boulders and grass, and trees growing in every direction. It was cumbersome, but Andy's crystal helped light the way.

Each loop they made brought them closer to the Devil's Kettle and the heavy black hole became larger as they neared it. Just like the water swirling around the hole in the lake, they swirled down the cliff towards the water. It was all happening so fast that they couldn't even process the dangers that were around them.

Richard and Jessie were in an intense pursuit. Their legs were bumped and bruised, cut and scratched but they were so desperate that it didn't phase them. The Messorem that had their mother was getting away.

The Messorem must have known that they were getting close because it began to move faster. Before they knew it, the brothers had reached the shores of the lake that fed the Devil's Kettle. There they could see hundreds of Messorems gliding across the waters in and out of the black hole and for a moment the brothers lost sight of their mother. The rushing water seemed to be louder than anything they had ever heard. Amplified by the screams and cries of the creatures. Messorems swooped in at their heads, brushed by their sides but never laid a hand on them. It was the most horrific thing any of them had ever seen. The moment was so chaotic that it is hard to even explain unless you had been there yourself.

Andy and Eva finally caught up to the brothers who were standing at the edge of the lake peering at the Devil's Kettle looking desperately for their mother. The wind caused waves to rise and fall making it that much more difficult to spot anything.

"Do you see her?" Jessie asked.

"No, I don't!" his brother panicked.

They both looked vigorously, while thunder boomed.

"There!" Richard shouted pointing out to the lake. Soon, he kicked off his shoes, dropped his crystal on the shoreline and dove into the lake.

"Richard, no!" Jessie shouted. He wanted to save his mother too, but not like this.

Jessie's instinct was to follow his brother, without even thinking he jumped into the water after him. Andy soon felt he too must follow them, but as he kicked off his shoes, Eva grabbed his arm.

"Don't!" she cried. "Don't go, there's too many! The waves. The Devil's Kettle! The Messorems!" she sobbed with tears streaming down her face. Andy looked into her eyes and knew she was right.

"Come back, Jessie!" he shouted. "Richard, come back!"

Waves towered over Jessie's head, submerging him in the water. The water muffled the noises. He flopped himself above the water getting a breath of air just in time before another wave splashed down on top of him.

He had no choice but to swim below the surface of the water as far as he could, only coming up for a breath. He swam a short distance and found himself weary and lost in the heart of the Devil's Lake. Trying to collect his bearings, he began to tread the water. Everything was so loud that it was deafening.

Frantically he looked for his brother. He had to continually wipe his face while trying to stay above the waves. Waves would rise, then fall and allow him to finally spot his brother across the surface of the water.

He began to swim, kicking his legs and scooping with his arms. "Richard!" He shouted. Beyond his brother he watched as the ghost of his mother was sucked into the Devil's Kettle and he knew his brother was headed straight for it as well. He swam harder than he had ever swam before. His muscles burned; his joints ached but he pushed through it all. He was going to save his brother, just like his brother had saved him days before in the river.

"Richard!" Jessie shouted again, managing to squeeze out his name between gulps of water.

Richard's heart sank. Now that his mother had been lost to the Devil's Kettle all his motivation perished. It was now that his mind became clear and he realized just how much trouble he had caused himself. He spun around in the water and looked his brother in the eye.

In reality time never slowed, but this next moment seemed to slow down to a crawl for everyone, especially Jessie. In the mists of the chaos, the waves seemed to slow down, the thunder grumbled instead of boomed, and the rain began to fall in slow motion. Messorems still swarmed around but they too were under the restraint of the moment.

"Mama said, 'Find the Great White Eagle!'" Richard shouted. As one flash of lightning lit up the sky, Richard was there, but then the night sky went dark. Seconds later a second flash of lightning illuminated the water and Richard was gone. He slipped into the depths of the Devil's Kettle.

Jessie's heart sank. His face went pale and he stopped breathing. His brother had just fallen into the Devil's Kettle. Tears poured out of his eyes and in a moment, the world rebooted into full speed around him.

"No, no, no!" he shouted. "Richard!" he cried.

He would have stayed floating there forever if the current would have let him. Except the current pulled at his body, dragging him closer to the Devil's Kettle. He, for a moment, didn't care. For a second he wanted to fall in, to be with his brother. The pain he felt inside is something that can't be described. Thankfully for him, his instinct didn't let that happen. He began to swim, trying to fight the current and get himself back to shore. His mind began to panic because the current was too strong.

Slowly he drifted closer and closer to the black hole. He could hear the water pouring over its edge. He kicked and kicked but it was in vain, his legs felt the brim of the kettle. He braced his feet against a rocky lip. He tried to hold himself away from it but his footing slipped. He slipped over the brim. The incident at the brim of the Centrum's Core when he fell into the river flashed in his mind. This time he truly thought it was the end for him. He closed his eyes and felt his body drop.

Shortly after this he felt the air in his lungs jolt out of his body. Something from above had grabbed ahold of him forcing his fall to stop.

As he opened his eyes. The black void that was the Devil's Kettle was slowly falling away from him. He soon realized that he was now being lifted. He could hear the sound of wings flapping as he was jolted higher into the air. Now not only was water falling into the black hole, but the horde of Messorems began to flood into the abyss. Unlike before many of them were empty handed. For a moment Jessie thought that the Great White Eagle came to rescue him, for he could see great white feathers each time the creature flapped its wings and the Messorem seemed to fear the being.

However, when he looked up, it wasn't the Great White Eagle, but instead a dear friend. Gillian had saved Jessie. In a fleeting moment Jessie's heart was filled with hope, but it was only a moment before he remembered the death of his brother and the hope was lost.

Andy and Eva watched in dismay from the shoreline. As Gillian lifted Jessie high into the air, all of the Messorems which seemed unorganized and scattered before were now funneling into the Devil's Kettle. It was as if they were running from something. Soon, the crystal in Andy's hand began to flicker brightly, as well as Richard's crystal apple which rested on the shoreline.

Are the crystals scaring the Messorems? Andy thought to himself. Suddenly the clouds began to roll and the lightning illuminated different layers of gray and black. It all looked so familiar to Andy. *It's happening again.* Andy had realized that the Messorems were not running from the crystals but from the image of what was rolling in from the sky. The Great White Eagle was painted once again in the clouds. As the clouds grew closer the Great White Eagle's image became clearer. Gillian's eyes grew wide and the image frightened him so much his jaw dropped in disbelief. Sending Jessie into a dead drop. Thankfully, Gillian was quick enough to swoop in a loop getting under Jessie catching him on his back before he plunged into the water. As Gillian raced to the shoreline his eyes became fixed on the image in the sky.

One by one the Messorem scrambled into the Devil's Kettle as if they were being chased by the clouds. As the last Messorem disappeared into the black hole, the Great White Eagle's image consumed the sky.

Then before anyone could fathom what was occurring, a sudden boom of thunder echoed as a flash of lightning bolted across the sky and everything went dark. The image in the sky was gone, the wind halted, and the sky wept.

Chapter 20
In the Mourning

"Quick, over here!" Andy shouted over the crashing rain. He had made his way from the rocky shores of the lake and found a cave sunk into the rigid edge of the Corkscrew Canyon. It wasn't very deep, but it was large enough that they would all fit.

Eva and Gillian ran for the cave, getting themselves out of the rain. Jessie was in no hurry. He felt as if he lost everything. Which frankly, he had. Slowly he shuffled to the cave with his head hung low. His entire person drooped in sadness. He walked so slowly that his hair, which seemed to reject water, had become soaked in the rain. He never looked up, never made eye contact with any of them, instead he just stared at the ground.

Once in the cave, Gillian opened his wings to the humans as he had done before for Richard and Jessie, but Andy and Eva were the only ones to accept his offer. Jessie just sat at the edge of the cave shivering at the cold. He stared at the Devil's Kettle still consuming the lake's water.

Eva and Andy snuggled into the large Pegasus feeling the warmth that his body gave off and listened to the rain falling and the thunder echoing outside the cave. They just sat in silence, in shock of what had happened. *I can't believe Gillian saved Jessie. I can't believe Gillian is protecting us from the storm.* He thought flabbergasted.

"Jessie… please come warm up," Eva begged. She knew his heart was ripped to shreds but didn't want him to catch pneumonia.

He didn't say anything. He didn't even turn to look. The group remained quiet after that.

The rain settled into a little pitter patter on the leaves of the surrounding trees. Slowly the sun began to rise. The glum gray of the thunderstorm had now blossomed into an array of colors. Pinks, purples, reds, and oranges painted the post storm sky.

Gillian lifted his wings and let Andy and Eva out from under. The air was moist and cold, but the rising sun of the new day brought with it warmth that filled the air.

"What just happened…?" Gillian finally asked. He had been positioned on the wrong side of the Meadow. All the fog hovering over the Uada Hollow caused him to lose his sense of direction. So, when the humans finally broke through they entered the meadow out of his sight and slipped by. It wasn't until he was awoken by the sounds of chains that night that he was introduced to the Messorems. He was going to retreat from the terrifying creatures but as he lifted himself into the air he saw Richard and Jessie running towards the Devil's

Kettle. "What were those… those things?" Gillian asked after no one responded to his first question.

"They are called Messorems," Andy said.

"What are they?" Gillian asked.

"Well, we really don't know. The beavers told us that they haunted the Uada Hollows, but it seems that while we were there they had this ability to tap into our sub-consciousness and convince us that our faults are the cause of other people's suffering. But in reality the creatures were luring us into a self-pitied bondage of the mind that rendered our physical selves unable to fight back, while they tied us up here in reality. But then we put our faith in the Great White Eagle and realized it's not about what we've done but that we need to trust in him," Eva rambled at the Pegasus.

"Say what now?" Gillian asked as he lifted his head back in confusion. She must have been in so much shock from the events that she was overloaded and just began to spill out everything she was thinking.

"What she means is we don't know. They tried to kill us, and seem to call that massive black hole over there, their home," Andy said, trying to make it basic for the Pegasus.

"Ahhh, Yeah. That's exactly what I thought," Gillian said even though he had no earthly clue at all. "And umm.. What was that in the clouds?" he asked shakily. The image terrified him. He had seen regular eagles before, but nothing to that extreme. He felt as if the literal Great White Eagle was present in those angry storm clouds.

"I believe it was an image of the Great White Eagle…" Andy said.

"Do you… ummm… think it was actually him?" Gillian questioned. Up until now he had completely disregarded anyone's theories on the Great White Eagle, for he blindly followed Malus. However, things had changed. Now, everything he thought he knew he wasn't so sure about. No longer was he confident in his Nobel

Markings, or in Malus, or the history of the land of which he had been taught.

"I can't say…but I sure felt like he was somehow. But I think it was a message. Or a sign that he was present somehow," Andy said. This made Jessie scoff because he thought that if the Great White Eagle had really been there he wouldn't have let Richard fall into the Devil's Kettle.

Gillian's mind was boggled. He was told the Devil's Kettle was a myth. He was told the voices in the Uada Hollow were just stories, but now he had seen with his very eyes the source of the voices. The Messorems and the lost souls. Nothing he was told before lined up with what he had witnessed. The legends were real, it was all real. Gillian had been lied to his whole life, about everything.

Utter gloom fell upon him and the death of Richard festered in his heart. *If only I had listened to Jessie and Richard. They were right about the Great White Eagle. If I had only just opened my eyes to him none of this would have happened. But instead, I was so focused on obeying Malus that I forced the brothers down here in search of these two…* Gillian thought as he glanced over at Andy and Eva. *If only I had taken them home, Richard would still be here.*

"If the legends are true, we are not safe. We must return to Regnum at once!" Gillian ordered. He may have lived an oblivious life, but one thing was still bred into his nature. Gillian cared; he still had a mission to complete. Maybe not the same mission he started with exactly but it was of a similar nature. To protect all creatures. They needed to get out of there for their own safety.

"What will happen to us?" Eva asked, remembering that he was trying to catch them for the King.

"I do not know, but we must return," Gillian said.

"Will you turn us in? Into the King?" Andy asked. Gillian paused for a moment and considered his options.

"I have been lied to, my whole life… those clouds with the Great White Eagle… and the Messorems, and the Devil's Kettle… it was all real. The legends are true. I… I don't know," Gillian started before pausing again.

"The Great White Eagle picked us," Eva started as if to try and persuade Gillian's choice. Andy looked at Eva with an expression that said proceed with dire caution. Andy was unsure that they could really trust him. Eva on the other hand was sure they could, so she proceeded to tell him all that happened. About her dreams, Andy's interpretations, and their run in with the Messorems. She even told Gillian about the Book of Truth and their discovery of the mysterious crystals.

"So that was the glow I saw the night on the cliff. Right before we found you. It was your crystal?" Gillian asked.

"I'd bet so! I lost it in the Pine trees that evening!" Andy said.

"And in your dream, the Great White Eagle said, 'It is time?' Time for what?" Gillian asked.

"Honestly, we don't really know," Andy admitted.

"Huh… Do you think it's something big? What do your scrolls say?" Gillian questioned. However, both Andy and Eva hadn't done much digging in that department. "What will you do? If I bring you back?"

"Well, I think our only option is to go to the Elves. They know the scrolls and are extremely loyal followers of the Great White Eagle," Eva said.

"Hmm. Okay… I will do my best to sneak you back, but we must never speak of this to anyone," Gillian ordered.

"Absolutely! We don't need anyone else to know about this either."

"Then we have a deal," Gillian snorted a more serious snort. "Very well, we must be on our way." Gillian stood tall and then shook his wings. The rain drops that had beaded up shook off of his feathers to the ground. "Hop on," Gillian said as he knelt down for them to hop on. Both Eva and Andy looked at the Pegasus and froze. They didn't give the trek home much thought. So, when Gillian ordered them to climb on his back they both had not been expecting that.

Jessie wiped his eyes with his sleeve and stood up. For the first time since Richard fell into the Devil's Kettle he broke his silence. "It's time to go," he said as he crawled up onto Gillian's back. He extended his hand out to Eva. She paused for a moment but grabbed his hand and he hoisted her up on Gillian's back.

"You're not going to drop us are you?" Andy asked Gillian.

"Of course not!" Gillian snorted aggressively. Soon all three humans were promptly mounted on Gillian's back, and Gillian lifted them all into the air and they were on their way.

Hovering up and out of the Corkscrew Canyon, Gillian flew level with the sun as they zoomed over the Uada Hollow. The fog had reappeared but was less spooky from above. The sun was bold and looked like it consumed the whole sky. The fog was less gray now that the sun had burned its light into cloudy layers and left the top side of the fog a mesmerizing gold color.

The morning seemed to be blissful as much as it could be considering all that had happened. The warmth of the sun beat on their skin, and the breeze of the morning air dried off their clothing.

Gillian lifted them higher as the Humilis Pine Forest presented itself and he cleared them just enough that their tips bowed and waved from the wind from beneath his wings. For Jessie this was a painful ride, that words cannot describe. However, for Eva and Andy this experience was almost unbelievable. Never had they thought they would fly, but here they were.

Eva was sitting behind Jessie and could sense some of his pain. Soon, she found herself wrapping her arms around Jessie and squeezing him tightly. She wasn't sure what to say, but found two simple words. "I'm sorry," she whispered in his ear.

Jessie bowed his head and tears streamed down his face. He never made a sound or said anything to Eva but for the first time since he lost his brother he felt comforted.

"If only we could fly," Andy gasped as he gazed out at the land below them.

"Yeah, that would be cool," Jessie said softly, looking over his shoulders and giving Andy a soft smile. Andy smiled back and nodded. He was grateful that Jessie was talking again.

It seemed like Jessie's spirits were being lifted as they themselves lifted higher into the air. Soon, Gillian brought them up the Centrum's Core's cliff and began on the home stretch over the Superior Pines Forest and then over the Blackwood Forest.

"Hey Jessie, that's where I found my crystal!" Andy said while pointing to the beaver's dam. Jessie looked but didn't say anything. He could see a few beavers swimming around at the surface of the water. Then he looked down at his brother's crystal, balancing on Gillian's back between his own legs.

"We are gonna take a quick break up at this meadow, the grass is calling my name. Can't you hear it?" Gillian said. Andy rolled his eyes, Eva giggled, and Jessie couldn't help but smile.

Then humorously, Gillian started speaking in a girly whisper. "Oh Gillian, Gillian! It's us! The grass. Come eat us!" Everyone, including Jessie began to chuckle at his childish comedy. "See?" Gillian asked with a big grin on his face as he swooped down to the meadow.

"Oh yes, now I hear them," Eva said with a giggle.

The meadow was familiar. It took a moment but once their feet were on the ground they recognized that this is where they met Maizey and her cubs. They ran across the meadow towards the Northern river and found the blueberry patch. They crawled under the bushes into the heart of the patch and began devouring the blue fruit.

Gillian took a moment to fill himself up on the grasses and eventually made his way over the river for a cool refreshing drink.

"Did you hear that?" Andy asked from in the mists of the bushes.

"Hear what?" Jessie asked, nibbling on blueberries.

"Listen!" he responded. Soon the three of them began to listen intently.

Gillian wasn't near the others but he heard something coming his way as well and was on high alert. They realized that something was shouting, from far off in the distance. As they watched closely they soon saw something high in the sky heading their way.

Gillian knew that whatever it was had seen him and was headed straight for him. So instead of trying to hide, he lifted himself into the air to address the stranger head on. The three humans on the other hand had the advantage of the bush and remained out of sight.

Just then the shouting became audible and Gillian felt a cold rush of panic stream down his back.

"Gillian!" the voice angrily shouted. "You traitor!"

The rush of panic was because he finally realized who the creature was. It was Vincent. He had finally found Gillian and was coming at him in a ball of fury.

"Get down and stay out of sight," Gillian ordered the three teenagers hiding in the blueberry bush.

Tactically, Gillian flew towards the north. It was successful in redirecting Vincent's missile of anger away from the teenagers.

"Vincent! It's not what you think!" Gillian shouted trying to defuse the situation.

"You're dead!" Vincent snorted as he lowered his head which was covered by a shimmering silver helmet with golden accents. Gillian knew Vincent was going to attack by the way he lowered his head.

Vincent was in his battle gear. A helmet that protected his head, with a flat pointed piece that ran down the top of his nose, leaving his nostrils and mouth exposed. His ears poked out of two holes in the helmet and there were metal flares protruding behind his eyes to limit distraction from the rear. Gold laced the edges of the helmet and an image of Malus was carved into the forehead piece. He also had his ankle cufflinks which were laced in gold and had sharp daggers covering the front of the hooves. His breastplate and torso shields were intact covering a majority of his body, and he had his wing blades on, which were sharp blades and lined the forward ridge of his wings to rip into the enemy when flying through the air. Gillian knew his life was in danger and that if he couldn't make Vincent understand that this was not going to end well.

"Vincent, let me explain!" Gillian cried. Unfortunately, it was too late. With his lowered head, Vincent plowed directly into Gillian. The strike had been a warning that Vincent meant business. It struck Gillian with so much force that he tumbled out of the sky. He collided with the ground causing dirt to scatter from his impact. It hurt terribly but he knew he had to act quickly. He jumped to his feet and began to try and reason with Vincent once again.

"I know I lied to you but let me explain," Gillian begged.

"Oh, don't worry, I've already explained it to Malus, and when I get back I will have to explain how you died a coward!" Vincent shouted threatening to end Gillian right then and there.

He flew right at Gillian but this time he did not lead with his head. With this attack he was out for blood. He lowered his wings as he glided towards Gillian exposing the blades fixed to his wings. Gillian dropped to his knees in just enough time to dodge the slashing of Vincent's wings. He was almost in the clear, except for the last blade on the tip of Vincent's wing, slashed Gillian's rear hip just above his tail. It stung like a bee.

Vincent swooped up into the air and hovered over Gillian.

"Why have you lied and committed treason against the King?" Vincent demanded an answer.

"When I was guarding the clearing, four humans tricked me and passed through into the forbidden circle," Gillian gasped.

"So, not only have you lied but you've failed as a guard? They will have your wings for this! That is, if you survive me!"

"I was afraid of anyone finding out, I lied to you because I thought I could catch them before anyone knew I was gone!" Gillian pleaded. "Please, Vincent!"

Vincent didn't accept his answer. He swooped down in front of Gillian. Gillian thought he had maybe talked some sense into Vincent, but he was wrong. Vincent attacked again. He reared up on his hind legs and struck at Gillian with his front hooves.

Gillian back peddled, bobbing left and weaving to the right making Vincent miss each strike, until finally one of Vincent's strikes landed a blow on Gillian's front shoulder leaving a gruesome gash across his chest. The blow to his chest caused Gillian to retaliate. Spinning around, he kicked out both his hindlegs connecting a powerful strike directly into Vincent's chest plate.

The kick stunned Vincent for a second and created distance between them. Gillian realized that their battle had been naturally gravitating towards the blueberry bush. Putting the three teenagers in danger.

"Vincent! Please stop!" Gillian cried.

"Did you find the humans?" Vincent asked. The question caught Gillian off guard and his pause made it quite obvious that he had. "Where are they! Why are you protecting the traitors!" Vincent shouted.

"You don't understand! We have been lied to! The legends, our markings, and our existence is..." Gillian started before Vincent interrupted.

"Lies?"

"Yes! Lies! The Devil's Kettle is real and the Great White Eagle is real!" Gillian said, almost shocking in himself, because for the first time in his life he had admitted that he believed the Great White Eagle was real.

"So, you've learned the truth?" Vincent said, lifting himself into the air.

"Wait, you knew all along?" Gillian stuttered.

"Why yes of course, there comes a time in every Pegasus' life that he discovers the truth. He must pick a side. I've chosen mine, have you chosen yours?" Vincent asked.

Gillian was shocked. He almost lost his breath.

"How could you choose Malus when all he has done is lie to us?" Gillian blurted.

"We are royalty! Look at us, dressed in gold and held higher than any other creature in this land. Malus has done that for us, the luxuries and the world is ours! The Eagle would rather see us perish. Just like our ancestors… So, what's it going to be?" Vincent shouted from the air. Gillian gave no response because his mind was flooded with thoughts.

"Where are the traitorous humans?" Vincent barked.

"You will bring no harm to them!" Gillian finally blurted out.

"You've made your choice then…Don't worry, I promise I will make sure everyone knows you put up a good fight when I tell them of your death!" Vincent snorted.

Vincent began plummeting towards Gillian, but this time Gillian had decided to fight back. Running along the ground Gillian extended his wings straight out to his sides. Both deadlocked onto the other, Vincent in the sky and Gillian on the ground, they barreled towards one another.

Vincent's goal was to strike Gillian from above and slice him with his wings but Gillian had a counter that Vincent didn't see coming.

As Vincent began his attack, Gillian intentionally fell onto his side, which sent him sliding underneath Vincent's low attack. One of Gillian's wings dragged behind him keeping him stable as he slid, while his right wing shot ahead of him parallel to the ground. (If he was standing up it would look like his left wing was extended straight up and his right would be tucked straight down to the ground next to his body.)

As he slid, Vincent's body glided over him, as the razors on his wings passed by, Gillian lifted his right wing hard and fast, bringing it up to the backside of Vincent's wing. Gillian was able to hook his wing into the fixed point of Vincent's shoulder and redirect his flight. Avoiding any harm Gillian successfully countered Vincent's attack and forced the attacking Pegasus into a crash landing.

Vincent's body smashed into the ground so hard sod was peeled up and dirt flung everywhere. His momentum carried him across the ground until the bush that the teenagers were hiding in brought his body to a stop.

Using his left-wing Gillian pushed upon the ground and forced himself to his feet. It was one of the coolest moves you would have ever seen a Pegasus perform, and under the pressure, Gillian executed it perfectly.

"Run!" Gillian shouted to the humans hiding in the bush. He felt that no longer could he keep them hidden from Vincent. Gillian had no expectations to defeat Vincent. He was unarmed while Vincent had all his battle gear on. Gillian landed a lucky shot, but if Vincent got up Gillian wasn't sure he would last much longer against the armored Pegasus. This was the teenager's only window to escape.

The three burst out of the bush and headed north, back the way they came at the beginning of this journey. Along the river they dashed, across the meadow, until they reached the thick jungle that was the Forbidden Forest.

Vincent was slow to get up. The take down was hard on him and his own razors left him with cuts and bruises.

Vincent's eyes darted towards the teenagers, there was no way he was going to let them get away. Gillian was running out of ideas and did the only thing he could think of doing. Which was to move himself between Vincent and the teenagers.

"How brave… betraying your own kind for peasants," Vincent snorted in annoyance. "I'm done playing games. I will cut you down if I have too. Besides, the King is waiting in the clearing. Even if you manage to escape, those little friends of yours are headed straight for the King and his army," Vincent admitted.

Gillian's mind spun. He was exhausted and knew he was bound to lose this battle. His life hung in the balance. The teenagers were headed straight for a trap and Gillian could do nothing to stop it. He took a moment to glance towards the tree lines, but Vincent capitalized on the distraction and charged Gillian one last time.

Gillian was out of ideas. He had no counter to this attack and knew if he moved Vincent would use the opportunity to seize the others.

Gillian closed his eyes and waited for the inevitable. He could hear Vincent's armor clank with each step. His blades almost jingled as they clinked together. Gillian could feel the ground beneath his feet tremble, but he stood tall. The only thing that crossed his mind was these words. *Remember me.* Those two words he had directed towards the Great White Eagle himself.

Then, as if an answer to his thoughts, Gillian heard the sharp cry of a falcon as if it burst forth from the Blackwood Forest. As he opened his eyes he peered past Vincent and could see Koden barreling from the woods with the falcon flying swiftly above him.

The echo of Koden's roar was so furious that the three teenagers, who were well into the depths of the Forbidden Forest halted in their tracks for just a moment to question what was happening behind them.

On foot, a Gladiator is much faster than a Pegasus. Easily Koden caught up to Vincent and was able to take him down from behind. Sparing Gillian from a tragic fate. Yet, brought that fate onto Vincent.

His body armor was no match for the Gladiators razor sharp claws, which ripped through it like butter. It was a good thing that the teenagers had escaped into the thick forest for the details of this scene are far too graphic to explain.

In a moment the fight was over with. Left standing was Gillian and Koden. Neither one trusted the other, but knew under these circumstances that they were on the same side. Koden nodded to Gillian who lifted himself off the ground and began his flight back to the clearing. Hoping he could beat Andy, Eva, and Jessie there and try to explain everything to the King.

The falcon had perched in a tree during the fight, but had now launched itself into the air and causally flown away.

Koden scanned the meadow one last time. The peaceful meadow who's grasses danced in the wind was left in carnage. Instead of flowers and an ocean of green waves, the grass was matted down, uprooted, and stained red.

Koden never felt good about killing, in fact he wished he never had to. However, he knew if Vincent would not have been stopped, it would have been Gillian or maybe even the humans instead. Koden hung his head low and headed home to Maizey and his cubs, leaving the meadow motionless once again.

Chapter 21
The Clearing

"The book!" Eva shouted as they climbed the overgrown pathways of the Forbidden Forest.

"Leave it!" Andy shouted as he began pushing at Eva. The three continued to run uphill towards the clearing. They could barely breathe anymore. They all huffed and puffed but never slowed their pace, weaving through vines, climbing over rocks, and dodging branches.

Finally, Eva stopped running, she couldn't do it anymore. She was not just physically tired, but she felt as if she couldn't take it anymore emotionally. With the journey, Richard's death, and now another Royal Pegasus out for blood. She felt as if she wanted to curl into a ball and hide.

She felt defeated. During the battle between Vincent and Gillian she left the Book of Truth somewhere in the blueberry bush. She felt as if the whole journey had been an utter waste, and one that cost more than it was worth.

"Without the book, this journey was pointless. The Great White Eagle sent us to discover the mysteries of the Devil's Kettle. Then I left one of the biggest mysteries behind," Eva cried.

"Don't say that" Andy said between breaths. He and Jessie stopped ahead of her and we're bent over with their hands on their knees trying to catch their breath.

"We have nothing to show for it, and Richard..." she started and then began to sob.

"Eva, Richard..." - Jessie started, and then paused to wipe a tear from his face - "Richard would not want us to give up. Once we are safe, we will come back and get the book, we still have the crystals and know that the Great White Eagle is real. We are not done, we must find the Great White Eagle, Richard said so."

Eva wiped her face and began to huff in the air trying to stop her sobbing.

"Yeah, we must keep going, for Richard," Andy said, standing upright and putting a hand on Jessie's shoulder. "To the Elves?" he said knowing that's who Eva wanted to talk with.

She couldn't get any words out but she nodded in agreement still with tears in her eyes.

"Let's go, the clearing is just up ahead," Jessie said.

With all of the chaos going on, neither Andy nor Eva noticed the change in Jessie. He had much more drive to continue on the journey than he had ever before. Now he seemed determined to find the Great White Eagle, just like his brother had told him to just before disappearing into the Devil's Kettle.

So, they pressed on. Their pace had slowed to a walk but they were steady. They had their crystals and many questions to be answered, but hope resided within them all. Climbing the hill to the clearing, they felt excitement burning in their hearts. They were almost home. Almost to safety.

About the Author

The writer, **For His Glory**, comes from a small town in the Midwest. He began working at fifteen years old, and since then has started his own small business. His most prized accomplishment is that he got married to the girl of his dreams.

His favorite hobby growing up was Taekwondo. He earned his black belt at the early age of eight years old, and has continued to teach the art alongside his father and wife. Recently earning the Rank of 4th Dan. (Master instructor Status.)

Although he had many accomplishments, life gave him many setbacks. Many times, he found himself failing to be the strong Christian man he aimed to be. However, his writing became a way to remind himself that all he did should be done for God's Glory.

He hopes that his stories can be entertaining but also that it may inspire those who read it, to dig into their own faith no matter what failures or setbacks life throws their way.